The Pig Pen

ALSO BY EMMY ELLIS

DETECTIVE ANNA JAMES
Book 1: THE PIG PEN

DETECTIVE TRACY COLLIER
Book 1: GUTTED
Book 2: CRUSHED
Book 3: SKINNED
Book 4: GRABBED
Book 5: SUNK
Book 6: CRACKED

DI BETHANY SMITH
Book 1: THE COLD CALL KILLER
Book 2: THE CREEPY-CRAWLY KILLER
Book 3: THE SCREWDRIVER KILLER
Book 4: THE SCORCHED SKIN KILLER
Book 5: THE STREET PARTY KILLER
Book 6: THE CANDY CANE KILLER
Book 6.5: THE SECRET SANTA KILLER
Book 7: THE MEAT HOOK KILLER
Book 8: THE BLADE KILLER
Book 9: THE SLEDGEHAMMER KILLER

DETECTIVE CAROL WREN MYSTERIES
Book 1: SPITE YOUR FACE
Book 2: HOLD YOUR BREATH
Book 3: GUILT BURNS HOLES
Book 4: BEST SERVED COLD
Book 5: BLOOD RUNS DEEP

DETECTIVE ANNA JAMES

THE PIG
PEN

EMMY ELLIS

Joffe Books, London
www.joffebooks.com

First published in Great Britain in 2024

© Emmy Ellis 2024

Cover art by Dee Dee Books Covers

ISBN: 978-1-83526-566-6

PROLOGUE

Angry that her husband had left her here all day to go and buy a tractor, *not* the car she wanted, Evelyn calmed herself by preparing to plant some seeds behind the farmhouse. She didn't have many of her own things here, having moved in three years ago without a penny to her name, so this little patch would belong only to her. It wasn't like Vernon bought her flowers, was it? So she'd grow her own.

She dug at the earth. Her shoulders ached from using the shovel, but after an hour she had a good-sized plot. Sprinkling seeds into a furrow she'd created, she thought of all the things she could do to make Vernon give her what she wanted. So far, her whining and cajoling had failed. She hadn't come into this marriage to be treated like the hired help, nor had she expected to get pregnant so soon. Having a baby a year after their wedding had annoyed her, but Vernon must have tampered with the condoms to keep her from walking out of his life when his promises hadn't been granted.

Her boy, Matthew, was sleeping in the kitchen on the old, battered sofa Vernon refused to get rid of. She glanced back at him through the open door, wanting to smack him awake because she hated him so much. He'd tied her here — Vernon didn't want her working until Matthew went to school — and she felt stuck, so achingly stuck that she took it out on the child every day. Little pinches here and there, out of Vernon's sight, giving him food he hated so she could watch him retch. Matthew couldn't speak, he had yet to utter one word even though he was two, so her secret was safe for now.

She rammed the shovel into the ground to create another furrow, pretending it was her son's head. God, how she wished it was, his brain exposed, blood seeping into the mud. The metal tip struck something, and she let the shovel go, crouching to use her hands to move the earth away. A skull stared back at her, worms writhing in the eye sockets, a black beetle scurrying away. The teeth formed a terrible grin, and her brain caught up with the sight, properly registering what lay beneath the ground. She screeched and sprang backwards, landing on her bum, her heart thumping.

"Oh my God!"

For some reason she looked around, expecting to see someone watching, but that was silly. Hawthorn Farm didn't have any close neighbours; the property was shielded by tall, thick trees along the country road. Still, she sensed eyes on her and, ridiculously, the fanciful thought that the dead person she'd uncovered had come to pay her a visit entered her head.

A shiver racked her body. Quickly composing herself, she kneeled in front of the hole and scraped more mud away, revealing collarbones and a necklace, the pendant a dark-blue stone with diamonds around the outside. She undid the clasp and slipped the prize into her apron pocket. She'd clean it, take it down the pawnshop, get some money for it. She was owed this for putting up with Vernon and the child.

She didn't have to think for long to find an answer as to who the skull belonged to. Her mother had told her all about it: this must be Wilma. Evelyn could use this against Vernon for the rest of his life. Blackmail. She'd keep his secret so long as he obeyed her. She wanted things, trinkets and pretty clothes, and it angered her that he must have bought the

2

necklace for Wilma. Why hadn't he bought Evelyn anything like that? Wasn't she special enough?

She covered the bones over, leaving the planting for tomorrow as those remains needed to be moved. Evelyn didn't want that woman beneath her beautiful flowers when they sprouted.

Indoors, she cleaned herself up, hastily washed the necklace and put a still-sleeping Matthew into his pushchair, draping his coat over him like a blanket. If she hurried, she'd make the next bus into Marlford city. She walked down the farm track, the spring air cooling her cheeks — her face was flushed with the rage swirling inside her, not to mention the excitement at having Vernon at her mercy. She'd been waiting for something like this, and now she had it.

If he didn't buy what she wanted, well, he'd pay the price a different way.

In Southgate, Marlford's town, she entered a back-alley pawnshop, one of the lesser-known ones, and handed the necklace to Stan behind the counter. He studied it, looked up at her, and raised his eyebrows.

"Years ago, I was asked to keep an eye out for this," he said.

Her stomach rolled over. "Really?"

"It's to do with Wilma, that woman who went missing."

Evelyn waved a hand to brush that off. "I found it in the house. I want to sell it." She smiled.

Stan didn't. "I'll have to phone the police."

Evelyn had known Stan for a long time. He drank with her father in the Plough. While he was older than her by many years, more than Vernon, he'd fancied her for ages, and always pinched her bottom if she walked past him.

She gave him her best smouldering expression. "Do you have to? We could split the money." She glanced at her son. "And he's asleep, so we could, you know, have some fun out the back to seal the secret." If it meant getting her hands on some money, she didn't care who she slept with. She'd married Vernon, after all.

Stan's grin spread wide. "I suppose I could fence this in Liverpool when I'm next up there seeing the grandkids." He jerked his head. "Sex first, money after."

"No, the other way round. How much will it be?"

He lifted a loupe to his eye to check the diamond and middle stone for their worth, then lowered it and grinned even harder. "More than either of us expected, I imagine."

"I assumed Vernon bought it for her." It made sense. He had money coming out of his ears, not that anyone would know it. Bloody skinflint.

"No, her mother, Francine, gave her this on her wedding day. Francine got it off some rich bird she used to work for when she left her job, it was in the papers and everything." He whispered the value. "Still want to part with half?"

She hadn't expected it to be worth so much. Half was still more than she'd bargained for. "Yes."

"I haven't got that much in the safe, so I'd have to nip to the bank."

"Off you go, then."

Evelyn perched on an antique stool while he was gone, totting up in her head what she could buy with all that money. A new coat, dresses, and fancy shoes. A handbag or two. Make-up. A nice engagement ring, seeing as Vernon hadn't bothered getting her one.

Stan returned, locked the door and handed her the cash. She stuffed it in her bag and followed him into the office out the back, heedless that Matthew might wake and be afraid to find himself in a strange place. Anyway, he'd likely be out for a while yet. She'd put a tot of whisky in his drink before his nap.

She did what was required of her, pretending it wasn't Stan on top of her on the floor, then left the shop.

Matthew snored softly as she entered Selfridges. Never in her wildest dreams had she thought she would shop there. People gave her funny looks, as if she didn't belong, the lowly farmer's wife, but she ignored them. From now on she'd be

4

dressed to the nines; Vernon would buy her anything and everything for years to come.

Life was looking up at last. She was finally getting her due.

CHAPTER ONE

"I did warn you to wind your neck in, but you wouldn't listen." He supposed Nigel *would* have done that eventually if he wasn't dead. Or if he had a neck.

Matthew Brignell laughed, the sound ringing out in his father's unused steel barn. How often did he get to say things to people without them answering back, as though he didn't matter? A warm glow burned inside him at how good it felt — the silence, no rebuttal. This man, this arsehole, had spoken his last not five minutes ago.

"You'd better untie me or I'll punch your lights out," Nigel had said. "You can't *do* this!"

"I'll do what the hell I like, *mate*, just like you did."

Except they weren't mates anymore. Hadn't been for a long time. They'd done most things together up until the point Nigel had poked a certain part of his anatomy in Matthew's wife, Carys. Touching what he shouldn't. Probably *laughing* at him.

How cruel of them. He'd never have forgiven them in a million years.

He shook away the images of what else they'd got up to behind his back and lifted Nigel's head off the steel butcher's table. It weighed more than he'd imagined, that head. His gloved hands burrowed into the long black hair, he took it over to the stake he'd secured to the concrete floor. Brought the head down onto the spike at the top in a sharp downwards swoop.

He stepped back to study it. To inspect his *feelings*. Nothing but "good riddance" remained, thank God. No upset; he'd drowned in that prior to the murder, in private. No sympathy; that had disappeared the moment he'd discovered what Nigel had done to him. And certainly no remorse.

Nigel's nose, now skewed, had once been perfect. His eyes, too, a striking blue, although the face was so swollen they weren't visible. His lips, puffy and split from Matthew's boot striking them, no longer had that Cupid's bow the ladies went mad over. He'd been a good-looking bastard, he'd give him that. Had all the women after him. Never needed to poach anyone else's missus. He'd walked into pubs on his own and left with some bird on his arm every time. Off to his posh little house and his bed, only for his conquests to be discarded the next morning as if they were rubbish.

So why had he homed in on Carys? She'd belonged to Matthew, yet his so-called friend had snatched her away regardless. What was the draw — because she'd been off limits? *Because* she'd been Matthew's? Nigel had spotted her first, and he'd got arsey that she'd latched on to Matthew instead. A kick to his ego. So he'd bided his time, then won her round with his charm. Or was it like Nigel had said, and Carys had been the one to get him drunk and seduce him?

Blood dripped in thick, steady droplets from beneath the head, one every ten seconds or so. Most of it had oozed out of the body when it had lain on the table, waterfalling over the edges and meandering towards the drain set in an incline at the centre of the floor. Down into the pipe, the sewer, washed away. He imagined rats sniffing the air, scenting the red stuff, eager for a meal. It would have been a fitting end for him, the *real* rat.

Matthew had already cut the body into pieces. He'd dispose of them later, and, once the pigs had eaten their fill, he'd feel happier. While Dad was away, his son would play. But first he had a head to deliver, and he'd better get a move on.

Gloves, balaclava, and his black outfit on, he unlatched the grips that held the stake in place and hefted it out. Carried it to the Transit and placed it inside on more plastic. He'd lined the whole back of the van with it, plus the barn, just in case. You never knew whether the police would be sent here, to Hawthorn Farm.

He drove into Marlford, going past the hospital on North Road, admiring the big houses along the way, grimacing at the hotel where his wedding reception had been held. He'd promised to pledge his life to Carys that day. Shame it had all gone wrong.

A quick turn at the roundabout and into Haldon Way, and he continued over the annoying speed bumps, then took a right, following the snaking road round to the bigger houses. Carys lived there — and he had once.

Bishop's Lock on Eastgate was such a quiet area, a pocket of respectability surrounded by the rest of the skanky housing estate. He had to be careful of being noisy. A lot of snooping people would think nothing of coming to the window and reporting him to the authorities. Some things were frowned upon here. No caravans or motorhomes on driveways, among other things.

Like a head on a stake in the front garden.

He snorted with laughter, parked behind his ex-neighbour's BMW, and got out. Stared at the house he'd loved. Memories flooded his mind, of hosting dinners, having friends to stay. Barbecues, parties. All gone. Not that he cared. He'd hated every single one, preferring a quiet night in with a book, although, come the end, he hadn't been home much.

He marched up to the For Sale sign and wrenched it from the ground. Popped it in the back of the van and took the stake out. Carefully dropped it in the hole with Nigel's face pointing towards the house.

Carys would see it as soon as she opened the bedroom curtains.

He slid Nigel's driver's licence into the bastard's mouth and nodded to himself. He wanted no doubt in anyone's mind as to who the head belonged to. He quietly closed the van's back door, got in and drove away, checking everything off in his mind one last time. The false number plate he'd stolen one night from an Audi. The decals he'd stuck on the sides of the van. His face and hands being covered. Now for the journey back to the farm, one that avoided any speed cameras, one where he'd dart down country lanes, taking a convoluted route to confuse the police should the Transit be sighted.

No one was about on his travels; everyone was likely in bed. All the rural houses stood in darkness. He arrived at the farm and drove into the steel barn. Pigs had once been slaughtered here, many years ago, hence the drain in the floor. Dad had sold their cuts of meat directly from Hawthorn or on market stalls. Things had changed, though. Different ways of doing things. All that health-and-safety lark. And age had crept up on his father. With Matthew unable to permanently take up the reins — he had no desire to work the farm every day, never had — Dad had sought help elsewhere to lighten his load, and now sent the pigs to the abattoir.

Matthew got out of the van. At the drain, he inspected whether any blood had got past the plastic to stain the concrete floor, and was pleased to see it hadn't. He'd cut a small square hole for the grate to sit in, and the claret had dribbled straight into the pipe.

He made a cup of tea at the old filing cabinet in the corner, having bought the kettle and a cup from a charity shop so he could dump them after all of . . . *this* was finished. He couldn't risk blood getting on his dad's.

He had six more days before Dad got back from Calais. Plenty of time. Sipping, he eyed the blood-smeared plastic sheet on the table, recalling how he'd chopped Nigel up and enjoyed doing it. Every bit of heartache he'd experienced had been channelled into those arcs of the axe, his tears falling, his sobs hurting his throat. Still, no more crying, eh? Not for that fucker. Not for anyone.

He finished his tea, took a black bag off the roll, folded it and slid it into his pocket for later. He collected the sacks of body parts one by one, loaded them into the van and, headlights off, drove over to the pig barn. Snorting and snuffles greeted him as he carried parcel after parcel inside and dumped them in the pen. Door closed, he switched his slimline torch on. Used his Stanley knife to cut the bags below the knots in the top. He turned each one over and let the contents drop to the floor.

The pigs swarmed.

New Chester Whites had arrived this morning, and he'd put two of them in this pen, the others in a small shed next door, ready for the other nights Matthew would be killing. Newbies always unsettled the rest of them. He'd bought them based on what he'd discovered years ago, how the animals behaved when strangers were introduced. He sat on a nearby stool and waited for Nigel to be eaten, clothes an' all, glad he hadn't brought his phone to browse social media to stave off boredom. He'd always switched it off at night, so if the police looked into him they wouldn't question his habits. As far as they would be able to tell, his mobile had last been on at ten p.m. in his flat.

Time seemed to pass slowly, but at last the pigs had stripped the flesh, eaten the bones. Matthew strolled out into the night, sucking in the fresh, crisp autumn air.

He had a lot of cleaning in his future.

Best get on with it, then.

"Everyone's going to be speculating now, you watch," Lenny said.

"Hmm, gossiping and whatnot. And we're all going to be clocking who isn't at work at the moment and speculating if it's them."

"Difficult to do when so many are on shifts. I never know who's on and who isn't half the time."

"Me neither. I—" She stopped at the ringing of her phone and answered it. "Anna James."

"Morning!" Karen, one of the front desk sergeants. "How are you today?"

Anna closed her eyes for a moment to steel herself for what she was about to hear. "Steeped in paperwork. Is that about to change?"

"You could say that. Uniforms were called out to a house in Bishop's Lock earlier. You'll never guess what. There's a head on a wooden spike in the front garden."

Anna's mouth dropped open. "Pardon?"

"A new one on me, I must say. I was only watching a film with that in it last night. Bloody coincidences give me the willies."

Anna had seen some sights in her time, but never that. "Is the pathologist there already?"

"On his way."

"Any identification on the deceased?"

"The woman who reported it, a Carys Brignell, seems to think it's her boyfriend. No one's been to inform his next of kin yet because his face is pretty banged up, by all accounts. There's a driver's licence sticking out of his mouth, but the officers haven't gone near enough to see it clearly."

"Okay, we'll head over there now."

"Bad choice of word, dear."

"Shit, I didn't think."

Karen laughed. "Hmm. Have a good day!"

"Sarky bugger. You too." Anna ended the call and stared at Lenny. "Well, we *did* say we were bored earlier . . ."

"Christ. What are we dealing with?"

Anna told him.

He shook his head. "Let's get going, then."

She took a quick sip of her coffee, already mourning the fact that she couldn't drink it all, and left the office behind him. "We're off on a shout. A head on a spike."

"You what?" Warren tugged his brown beard.

Anna smiled. "You heard me. All I've got for you at the minute is a Carys Brignell at Bishop's Lock. Poke into her, see what comes up. I'll let you know as soon as I can who we're dealing with. Bye for now."

She left them to it and checked in with Karen downstairs as to the house number, then led the way out of the station. In her car, she waited for Lenny to park his backside in the passenger seat, then set off.

"So," Lenny said, "today went off with a bang. A pervy colleague and someone missing the rest of their body."

"I'm sure you won't let it put you off your lunch."

He tutted. "Nope."

"Stomach of steel, you've got." She navigated a left turn. "I meant to ask you: how did the date go last night?"

Lenny stretched his legs out. "I'm thinking of using another app. This one's full of weirdos. I don't know why these people contact me when it's obvious we've got nothing in common. Mind you, I forgot to read her profile, so it's my own fault. I saw her picture and went with it."

"That'll teach you to gawp at the cover without opening the book. What happened?"

"She spent the first half an hour talking about her ex."

"Ah."

"And then she came out with a question I never want to be asked again."

"Which was?"

"Whether I liked grasshoppers."

Anna blurted out a choked laugh. "What?"

14

"I know. She blasted out all these facts about them. I'm thinking she said it to put me off her. You know, she realised I wasn't her type so thought she'd better nip it in the bud, get me to make my excuses and walk out. It's better than the fake emergency phone call, though."

"Is that a thing?"

"Yeah, people do outrageous shit to cut the date short, including getting their mates to ring them."

Anna frowned. "Why didn't she just say she didn't like you?"

"Not everyone is as forward as you."

"Clearly, otherwise you'd have buggered off inside the first ten minutes."

Lenny rubbed his temples. "I didn't want to be rude."

"Sometimes you're too nice, and that leads to being taken advantage of."

"Yeah, well . . ."

Anna veered into Bishop's Lock and followed the road round, past the smaller houses and on to the larger ones. "These must cost a fortune."

"They do. My mate's mum lives in one farther on. She paid half a million for hers."

"Blimey."

Anna tooted her horn to get some people out of the way. They milled about on the road, nosing. She pulled up behind a patrol car and assessed the scene. Two uniformed officers stood by the spike at the edge of the driveway, another in the front doorway with a blonde, skinny woman who Anna assumed was Carys. Thankfully, two cordons had been put up, effectively blocking off the slice of road directly outside number thirty. Neighbours on the other side spoke among themselves or stared at the sight before them.

"Where's SOCO and a tent when you need them?" Anna grumbled and got out.

Lenny joined her and, at the back of the car, they put their protectives on, leaving the booties off. She led the way over to the cordon and signed the log, then put booties on and dipped beneath the tape. A car sat in Carys's driveway, a dark-red Mokka, a pink blanket on the parcel shelf with a cerise teddy on top. Still a child at heart?

"Can you all go home, please?" Anna called out to the gathering crowd, and held up her ID. "I think you've seen enough, don't you?" She glanced at the bend in the road. SOCO had arrived. "Come on, chop-chop. Off you go."

People dispersed reluctantly. She'd never understand why some folks liked to hang around when something bad had happened. Were their lives lacking in excitement *that* much? One man refused to budge, his arms folded over his wrinkled white T-shirt, black boxer shorts showing beneath the hem.

"And you, please, sir." She gestured for him to go.

"No, that's my mate." He pointed to the head. "I'd like to know what's going on."

A commotion at the front door of number thirty drew Anna's eye. In a magenta trouser suit and high heels, and with a face full of make-up, Carys came barrelling up the path next to the driveway, eyes flashing.

"Mate?" she shouted. "*Mate?* You hardly know him! Go on, fuck off out of here."

Anna winced. Residents of Bishop's Lock weren't the type to bawl anyone out in public, let alone swear, so this might be interesting.

"We worked together," the man said.

"Since when?" Carys asked.

"Years ago, not that I should have to explain myself to *you.*"

Anna stepped closer to him. "Best if you go home, sir. We'll be along to speak to you shortly. Give us an hour or two. Unless you'll be at work?"

"I don't work on Fridays." He strutted off, throwing a dirty look Carys's way.

Carys reluctantly returned to her house, the PC going inside with her and closing the door to. Anna took a deep breath and eyed Lenny.

"Sodding hell," he said. "She's a fiery one."

"Grief takes us in different ways." Anna turned at the sound of doors slamming.

The grey-haired lead SOCO, Steven Timpson, jumped out of the van and approached another that had arrived. Behind that, the pathologist's car drew to a stop, a distinctive blue sporty effort. Herman Kuiper got out, his long brown hair in his usual top bun, his face tanned from a recent holiday in Marbella. He'd moved from Holland eight years ago to do a two-year stint in the UK and had never gone back.

"Bet he didn't miss the dead while he was away," Lenny said.

"Nope. Would you?" Anna asked.

She was desperate for a holiday but had never got around to booking one. The summer had vanished, although the sun still hung about, but she supposed she could go to the Canaries, where it was hot in autumn. Tenerife sounded good. Something to think about.

While the new arrivals got on with putting up a tent, she smiled at Herman approaching. "Whoo, don't *you* look well rested."

"I had the time of my life. Those adult-only holidays are a godsend."

"I bet. No kids around to spoil the quiet. Or dead bodies."

"Hmm. I hear I only have a head today."

"You do. There's a driver's licence in his mouth."

"I'll check that once the tent's up."

Lenny glanced at the house. "Shall we go and speak to Carys first, then take a closer gander at that head?"

Anna nodded. "May as well. Let's see if she's calmed down, shall we?"

CHAPTER THREE

Anna sat in Carys's lounge on a grey, crushed-velvet corner sofa, too many pink fluffy cushions behind her back for her liking. She was a no-frills kind of girl, and this room was full of them. Blingy ornaments, a lot of crystal this and that. She preferred her minimalistic home, thanks. Less to dust and polish.

Lenny stood by the door, the PC at the window. Shadows danced on the laminate floor from where SOCO were erecting the tent. Anna worried about this negatively affecting Carys, who had a good view of what was going on outside.

"So you don't have to see what's happening, shall we go into the kitchen?" she suggested. "I can make you a cuppa then."

Carys, perched as far away from Anna as she could get, hugged herself and rose. She stalked out as though Anna's proposal had annoyed her, heels clacking. Sighing, Anna raised her eyebrows at Lenny and found her way to the kitchen. Carys sat at a gleaming white island on a bar stool, drumming her silver-painted nails on a copy of *Marlford Views*, a free monthly magazine distributed by the local newspaper office.

Anna went to the full coffee carafe on the side.

"Cups are in the cupboard above," Carys said, monotone.

"Thanks."

A weird quiet encompassed the spacious room, broken only by Lenny's footsteps, then the scrape of a bar stool as he took a seat opposite Carys. Anna poured the drinks, finding only sweetener and cream, not a milk carton or sugar pot in sight. She left one cup on the side for the PC, jerking her head at him where he stood in the hallway. He nipped in to collect it and returned to his former position, his attention reverting to the partially open front door. Anna carried three cups to the island and placed them on the magazine as there didn't appear to be any coasters.

She leaned her backside against one of the nearby cupboards. "As I said in the other room, I'm sorry you had to wake up to that this morning. Unfortunately, we have to ask questions now, and some of them may seem pointless to you, but we need to build up a picture of your boyfriend. I assume you tried to phone him."

"Yes, it went straight to voicemail. I tried his work, too. He normally starts at six, and the woman on reception said he isn't there."

"What did he do?"

"He was a solicitor in that big building down Southgate. The one with loads of businesses in it."

"The Gear Hub?"

"Yes, that's it."

"What's his name?"

"Nigel Fogg."

Anna noted the woman's curt tone. She'd spat the name out as though it burned her tongue. Why be so angry at her boyfriend when the poor sod was dead? "And how was your relationship?"

No answer.

It didn't seem as though Carys wanted to be cooperative. *Tough.* "Did he live with you?"

"He stayed over sometimes, but he's got a house in Jade Court, number seven."

Lenny thumbed a message on his phone, likely contacting someone in the team to get cracking on that name and address. Anna wondered about Nigel's parents and didn't relish going to see them without proper identification. She'd have to word it so they understood the head might not be their son's.

She held in a sigh. "I apologise for being blunt, but are you sure the head is his?"

Carys nodded, dry-eyed. Anna had encountered people who didn't cry before, and it always unnerved her. It didn't seem natural.

"That's his hair, and there's the mole on his chin," Carys said. "There will be a tattoo behind his right ear. It's a Celtic cross."

"Thanks, that's very helpful. Do you know of anyone who'd want to harm him?"

Carys belted out an acidic laugh, her perfect veneers on display. "You could say that."

"Could you elaborate?"

"My ex-husband."

"And he is . . . ?"

"Matthew Brignell. Fourteen Spruce Way."

Is it me, or is she reeling this stuff off as if she's practised it? "Why do you think he'd want to do something to Nigel?"

Carys sniffed, perhaps in disdain. "They were mates. Nigel was his best man at our wedding."

Oh. Right . . . "I see. Did you start dating Nigel after your divorce?"

"No, we had an affair while I was still married." Carys smiled as though recalling the memory.

"How long ago did you divorce?"

"Two years."

While it wasn't unheard of for people to hold a grudge that long before they lost the plot, in Anna's experience these things tended to happen soon after the hurtful event, the anger too much to contain.

"How did Matthew take it when he found out about the affair?"

"He went all quiet. Didn't say anything."

"Was that a typical response?"

"Yes. He doesn't get riled up about anything much. That was part of the problem. He was so . . . I don't know, so *calm* all the time. Boring. He moved out straight away, went to stay with his dad at the farm, then I heard he got a flat a month later."

"So why do you think he'd have had something to do with this?"

Carys shrugged. "He's the only one I could think of. Nigel's a nice bloke, everyone likes him, so the only one with beef would be Matt."

"Have you had any contact with Matthew recently? Has Nigel?"

"No. Matt didn't take any of his stuff when he moved out apart from his clothes. We spoke through solicitors. He stopped talking to me, cut me off."

Can't say I blame him. "If the affair didn't seem to be a shock to him, would you say your marriage had been going downhill and he already suspected what you were doing?"

"He was hardly at home. Either at work or that bloody farm. His dad's getting on, can't handle it all. His wife's dead. He clicked his fingers, and Matthew went running. And no, I doubt he suspected about me and Nigel. We were careful."

"Which farm is this?"

"Hawthorn, a few miles up North Road. The one with an honesty basket out the front with eggs for sale. His dad's got loads of stinky chickens."

Anna had collected some eggs from there only last week on her way home from work. "So was he aware you were upset about hardly seeing him?"

"Yes, I told him often enough, but he did nothing about it. Muttered something about me changing, so being in my company wasn't on his to-do list anymore. Maybe he didn't want to be with me either, so that's why it didn't really bother him. He was crying when he caught us, though. Too fucking late for tears at that point."

She's still angry about it. "Do you know whether Nigel and Matthew had a discussion at all after everything came out?"

"Nigel never said, and he would've."

"Where does Matthew work?"

"Golding's Accountants."

Anna nodded. "Okay, I'll ask again. What was the state of your relationship with Nigel?"

Carys glared at her. "What do you mean, state?"

"Did you get along?"

"Of *course* we bloody did! I wouldn't have been with him otherwise."

Yet you were with Matthew, even though you didn't get along. "Everything was fine, then?"

"Yes."

Anna braced herself for the next question. Some people answered it without query, others barked at her for accusing them of the crime. "Where were you yesterday?"

Carys frowned. "At work, where I'm supposed to be now. Why?"

"And after that?"

"I went for drinks down the Kite. No way would I go to the Saturn up the road. It's full of oldies."

"What time did you leave?"

"I got a taxi at eleven. Got here about ten past."

"Was anyone in the street at that time?"

"Not that I saw."

"Did you go straight to bed?"

Carys narrowed her eyes. "Why do you need to know?"

Anna smiled in the hope it would soften the woman's attitude. "I'm trying to establish a timeline."

"Fine. Yes, I went straight up. Didn't wake until half seven this morning. I opened the curtains and saw . . . saw *that*. This is going to mess things up. My house is for sale — the sign's gone, by the way, so whoever put the other pole out there must have taken it. No one's going to want to buy this place now."

You'd be surprised. There's plenty of sick ghouls out there. "Any reason for moving?"

"People round here are too nosy. They get on my wick. I want somewhere secluded so I can get on with my life without being watched. Something like the farmhouse at Hawthorn. No neighbours."

"Why don't you wanted to be watched?"

Carys gritted her teeth and didn't answer.

What does she get up to that she doesn't want people to see?

Anna sipped some of her drink, and it prompted her to query something she'd spotted earlier. "Did you set the coffee machine on a timer before bed?"

Carys's severely plucked eyebrows bunched. "Eh?"

"I'd imagine seeing your boyfriend's head would be traumatic, yet your coffee carafe was full."

"I put it on while waiting for the police. I had to do *something* to take my mind off it."

"And you got dressed and did your hair and make-up, too?"

Carys's cheeks flushed. "I didn't want anyone to see me in my pyjamas with last night's slap on."

Seeing Carys was about to blow up on her, Anna said, "Again, I'm establishing a timeline." *As well as pointing out that I've noticed these things, how your morning drink and appearance means more to you than your boyfriend copping it.* "How often did Nigel stay over?"

"A couple of times a week."

"Did he get along with the neighbours? Any disputes there?"

"I already *told* you, he was nice. No one had a problem with him around here."

Anna appreciated that her brand of questioning probably rubbed people up the wrong way, but there seemed more to

Carys's snappiness than being affronted by her interviewing method. "Do you need to take a break?"

Carys lifted her coffee and sipped it as an answer. She stared through the glass in the back door, her false eyelashes flapping. Was she trying not to cry? Putting on a tough-girl act, only to break down after they'd left?

Anna glanced at Lenny, who gave her a look that said he'd picked up on Carys's behaviour, too. It was so easy to cast aspersions, but, as the woman had cheated on Matthew, staying with him instead of ending it, who was to say she hadn't done the same with Nigel? Matthew was supposedly calm, Nigel "nice". Did she choose decent men, get bored, then look elsewhere, catching a new one in her net before moving on? Had *she* bumped Nigel off to make space for the next conquest?

Anna waited until she'd finished her coffee, then dived in again. "How many relationships did you have before Matthew?"

Carys snapped her head round to face her, eyes wide. "I don't see that it's any of your business."

It wouldn't be if you didn't have a severed head in your garden. "I wouldn't ask if it wasn't important. Could a former lover have had a problem with Nigel?"

Carys's shoulders relaxed, and her expression flattened out. "Oh God, now you come to mention it, there is *one* fella . . ."

Anna perked up. "What about him?"

"Gordon White. He still pesters me down the Kite even though I've told him I'm not interested."

Anna shot her gaze to Lenny. *Our Gordon White?* Lenny widened his eyes and jotted something down.

"He's one of your lot," Carys said, answering that question. "Bloody pervert. You don't want to know what he asked me."

Anna thought about Lenny's date with the grasshopper enthusiast and had to hide her smile. "Perhaps you should tell us. It might be relevant."

"He wanted sex inside one of those big wheelie bins behind the Kite, on top of all the dumped food. I mean, do I *look* the type?" She floated a hand in front of her to showcase her expensive clothing. "Then he banged on about us getting in a bath full of chopped fruit and doing things to me with bananas. I'm telling you, he isn't right in the head, that one."

"You said he pesters you. In what way?"

"Touching me up at the bar, his hand on my arse or tit, that kind of thing. Asking me to go out with him. Last night, he said he hated Matthew and Nigel because I'd gone with them and not him. You should speak to him. See where *he* was after the pub."

Anna pushed off the cupboard and paced. "Who did you go to the Kite with?"

"When, yesterday? Two women from work. Laura and Hannah Baker, twins. Before you ask, they live at number sixteen Woodham Gardens, round the back there. We shared the taxi. It dropped me off first."

"Thank you. So Gordon was in the pub?"

"Yes, and he was more handsy than usual. I told him to back the hell off and leave me alone. He was drunk. Seemed angry, too, even before I said that."

"Because . . . ?"

"He said he'd had a bad day at work. But that doesn't give him the right to rub my boob and grab my arse." Carys held up her breasts as if weighing them. "These cost me a fair whack, got them done as a present to myself when the decree absolute came through. There's no way he's getting his hands on them with my permission."

Lenny cleared his throat, and Anna looked at him. He was clearly thinking what she was: that Gordon might be the unnamed subject of that email from Placket. Could he have got so riled up about being suspended, and Carys flipping him off, that he'd snapped and gone after Nigel? Was Matthew next?

She needed someone to do a wellness check on him. "We'll leave you be for now. Is there anyone who can come and sit with you, or are you okay on your own?"

Carys eyed up the young PC who stood in the doorway. She licked her lips. "Is he staying?"

Anna resisted shaking her head. "He could do for a while, I suppose."

"Then I'll be okay."

Anna glanced at the PC. *God help you, mate.*

She said goodbye and left the house, slipping new booties on at the front step. She moved to the side of the tent to send a message to the team about checking on Matthew. For all she knew, he could have copped it overnight as well.

CHAPTER FOUR

The Remember Room

Matthew twisted the key in the lock and stepped inside. Tonight he was going to tell his wife it was over. It had been a long time coming, and he'd had to gather the courage to do it. But now he was ready, especially after that chat with Dad, who'd told him life was too short to stay with someone you didn't love. And specifically, who didn't love you.

"I should know, son. I mean, look at your mother and what we both went through there."

Matthew paused in the hallway, spotting a pair of familiar shoes. He shrugged. Maybe Nigel had popped in for a natter and had waited for Matthew to get home. That wasn't unusual. But shit, it would mean postponing his big reveal until after Nigel had gone. Unless Matthew did it in front of him. Yeah, maybe that would be better. Carys might not go off on one with him there.

After taking his boots off and putting them in the designated cupboard, Matthew hung his coat in the top section, ever mindful of how Carys liked to keep things nice and tidy. It had been a bit of a bind at first, learning all her ways, but he'd soon found that if he put away after himself he didn't get told off. Why was he bothering with that now, though? He was leaving, it didn't matter if she got pissed off with him putting his boots on the mat or, God forbid, wearing them in the house.

She hadn't always been this way. To begin with, although he'd found her behaviour outrageous — Carys was so much more outgoing than him — he'd thought her kind and polite. They'd dated for a short time, then married, a whirlwind romance. He'd known they weren't suited even back then, but he was just giddy that someone like her wanted to be with him — and who else would have taken him on? He was damaged goods, not that his wife knew that. He'd never told a soul about what he'd done to his mother, not even Nigel. The only one who knew the truth was Dad.

After the wedding, everything had changed. Carys had directed where he went and when, who came to the house and who didn't. They'd hosted parties, ones he hadn't wanted, but he'd relented because she was a social butterfly. He'd suffered through them, pretending to enjoy himself, even when the music got too loud, the chatter too much. He'd done whatever she wanted — happy wife, happy life — yet lately that still wasn't enough. He'd taken to helping Dad out more than he needed to so he could get away from her.

He checked in the kitchen. Neither of them sat at the table; the house was so still, as if no one was home. They had to be, though, what with those shoes, so he went into the living room, expecting to find Carys and Nigel flaked out on the sofas. Many a time Matthew had come home from being with Dad to find his wife and friend asleep, the telly on. No telly tonight, although they'd been drinking red wine — there were two glasses on an end table along with a bottle. Carys liked the drink. She overindulged all the time.

As it was a mild autumn, he reckoned they might be sitting out the back or even in the hot tub. Mind you, the outside spotlights hadn't shone through the window, so that was a puzzle. He returned to the kitchen and opened the back door quietly. Darkness greeted him, plus the snuffle of a hedgehog on the lawn, startled by the security lamp snapping on as it caught his movement.

He closed the door and walked upstairs, asking himself why he was even bothering yet knowing exactly why. Carys had always been a flirt, the same as Nigel, and when they'd all been in the Kite the other night she'd said it didn't mean anything, it was just the way she was. Matthew had lied, said he didn't mind so long as it didn't go anywhere, and she'd glanced over at Nigel and giggled. Matthew had had a bad feeling then but ignored it. Now it was back.

But they wouldn't do that to him, would they?

He held his breath on the landing and stood there, asking himself if he wanted to move towards the bedroom or go back downstairs. The squeak of the bed starting up told him a terrible story, one he didn't want to hear, because if he did it would mean The End. He'd taken all sorts of crap from his wife, but not that. He couldn't stand that.

A little voice urged him to go and see if his suspicions were correct. He'd be able to walk out guilt-free then, the wronged party instead of the one doing the leaving. He'd known from the start she wasn't the woman for him. The life they led was so far from his ideal — she didn't like reading or being quiet, she didn't understand why he preferred home to the pub.

She didn't like many things.

He walked forward and pushed the door open, and found exactly what he'd envisaged. Nigel, on top of Carys, oblivious to the fact that Matthew was there. Carys, though, she stared around Nigel's shoulder and smiled. It should have hurt more than it did, this betrayal, that smile, but hadn't Dad warned him she was a flighty piece, someone not to be trusted?

"If you were home more, I wouldn't have had to turn to Nigel," she said.

"What the fuck are you on about?" Nigel held still, stared at her, then peered over his shoulder. "Oh shit. Oh fuck. I'm sorry, mate." He leaped off the bed, grabbing his clothes.

Carys said other things, but Matthew tuned them out. In a trance, he watched his best friend hopping around trying to get his boxers and jeans on, his eyes seeing the truth, his mind in turmoil. He could accept what his wife had done but not what his buddy had.

Tears fell. All those years with Nigel by his side, gone. Nigel had been Matthew's salvation, a balm to his shitty life at home while growing up. Why had he thrown it all away? There would be no turning back, no forgiveness. Nigel knew how Matthew felt about betrayal, yet he'd done it anyway. That meant he didn't care.

Nigel zipped his jeans up and glared at Carys. "Shut up! Can't you see he's crying? Jesus, woman, he doesn't need you gassing on at him." He appealed to Matthew, shoving his head through the neck hole of his T-shirt. "I'm sorry, this should never have happened. It was only a fling. It didn't mean anything."

"What?" Carys screeched. "You fucking what?"

Matthew calmly collected a few clothes from the wardrobe and drawers while they argued the toss. He took a suitcase from the top shelf and went downstairs to pack. He didn't need to take anything else with him. Things could be replaced, but his heart couldn't. She'd wrecked it, ripped it into pieces, as he'd known she would eventually. A shock, though, that Nigel had gone along with it. What had happened to their promise to never fuck the other one over? What about their brother bond, the one Nigel had said could never be broken?

Carys screamed, and he found he didn't care if Nigel was hitting her up there. He didn't care about anything anymore other than getting revenge. He'd wait for that. Bide his time.

He hefted the filled suitcase off the sofa. Someone knocked on the front door, probably Terry, seeing as their houses shared an adjoining wall.

Matthew opened it.

"Everything all right, pal?" Terry asked.

"Carys and Nigel are upstairs." Matthew couldn't elaborate, the words hid inside him, and he shut the door for fear he would burst out crying.

Footsteps thudded on the stairs, and he turned.

Nigel shoved his feet into his shoes. "I'll say it again, I'm sorry. She's a fucking slag. Got me drunk on wine. I didn't know what I was doing."

Matthew wanted to ask if this was the first time but knew in his heart it wasn't. All those nights Nigel had been here recently. He wheeled the suitcase into the living room and closed the door. Stood by the window. The front door slammed shut, and Nigel stormed up the path as if Matthew was the one in the wrong. Maybe Nigel thought he was, seeing as he hadn't rolled over and accepted the apology. That's what stung the most, that he was thought of as a pushover.

30

Do what you want to Matthew. He won't do jack shit about it.
The story of his childhood. His life.

Carys continued screaming. She did that often for attention. So used to it, Matthew ignored her. She'd expect him to go up there and calm her down, tell her he forgave her.

Not this time.

Not ever.

He waited for Nigel to drive away, then took a couple of coats from the hallway cupboard, plus two pairs of shoes. He put his boots back on. He'd have to go to Dad's, to that horrible place he'd grown up in where the memories lived in the walls. He'd find a flat soon, start again, although he'd never trust another woman. Or a man.

He walked out, put the case in the boot and drove off.
The End.

CHAPTER FIVE

Matthew sat at his desk in the open-plan office, eyes gritty from lack of sleep. He'd downed a couple of energy drinks already, plus a strong coffee. His heart thumped erratically, his chest seeming hollow. A horrible sensation came over him: that people knew what he'd done. How could they, though?

A quick glance over at his colleagues put his paranoia to rest. Nancy and Zoe gossiped. Jason stared at his monitor, frowning, likely working out his sums. A chartered accountant, he earned more than Matthew, who hadn't passed that exam, yet they did exactly the same job. Another unfairness, one of many in his life.

Everyone else in the office seemed equally oblivious, and he relaxed somewhat. He stared at his screen, seeing nothing. He didn't want to work, didn't have it in him.

His boss, all pot belly and grey comb-over, came out of his private office and approached Matthew's desk.

Shit, have I messed up the Forge account? I bet he's coming to have a go at me.

Matthew smiled, hoping his fatigue wasn't obvious. "Everything all right, Roger?"

"Err, yes and no. Bit of a weird one, actually. Can we have a chat?"

Nervous that he'd get raked over the coals, Matthew followed Roger into his office and closed the door. "Have I done something wrong?"

"Take a seat." Roger gestured to one of the chairs at his desk.

Matthew sat, his nerves spiking.

"Are you okay?" Roger asked.

"Um, yes?"

"Only, I had a phone call from the police."

Matthew's stomach bottomed out. His skin grew clammy, and sweat sprouted on his upper lip. He casually ran a hand over his mouth to get rid of it. "What did they want? I don't think I've parked my car anywhere I shouldn't . . ."

"A wellness check. They wouldn't say why they wanted to know if you were all right. They went to your flat first, apparently. Why they couldn't come here instead of ringing me, I don't know."

"Bloody odd."

"Give them a bell. I was asked to pass on this number." Roger pushed a pink Post-it note across his desk. "Some detective or other."

Matthew picked the piece of paper up. Anna James. God, it must be to do with Nigel. Had she found out from Carys that they used to be mates? Was he safe if they were only doing a wellness check? Like, they thought he was next on the killer's list or something? Or was that a trick, an excuse to find out where he was so they could arrest him?

"I'll go and do it now," he said. "This is the last thing I need today. Been feeling under the weather lately."

Roger leaned back, his elbow on the armrest. "Go home. Get some kip. You look like shit."

Relieved, Matthew stood. "Cheers. I should be better by Monday."

He left and returned to his desk, shaking. He collected his phone and keys from the drawer, then saved his work and shut off his computer.

"You off?" Jason asked.

"Yep, not feeling well."

"I didn't like to say, but you look like sh—"

"Yeah, Roger's already said. Have a good weekend."

Matthew casually walked to his car but wanted to run. He got in and keyed the detective's number into his phone, his stomach rolling over. The ringing in his ear seemed to go on for ages, and he contemplated cutting the call.

"DI Anna James."

He jumped at the sound of her voice. "Oh, um, it's Matthew Brignell. I was asked to call you?"

"Ah, yes. Would it be possible for us to come and see you in about an hour?"

Jesus Christ . . . "What for?"

"A few questions regarding an incident."

"What sort of incident?"

"You haven't done anything wrong, so don't worry, but I'd rather not talk about it over the phone."

"Um, okay. I was at work but I'm on my way home. Not very well."

"Sorry to hear that. It's not catching, is it?"

What, tiredness from chopping up a body? No. "It's not Covid if that's what you mean."

"Good. It's, what, eleven now. We'll nip by your flat around twelve or thereabouts. Actually, make that two o'clock. I've got others to speak to first."

"Not a problem." *It's a massive problem.*

The line went dead. Annoyed that someone else had treated him like he didn't matter by not even saying goodbye, Matthew slung his phone on the passenger seat and drove home. She'd said it was nothing to worry about, but she could have been lying, so he didn't make a run for it. He'd known he'd have to go through this, but now it was happening he genuinely didn't feel well. Then again, if she had others to speak to it meant he wasn't a suspect, didn't it? If she thought he'd offed Nigel, she'd have turned up at work already and taken him down the station.

Indoors, he made a cup of tea and some toast to settle his stomach. Paced, clock-watching. He'd be a right old state by the time that Anna woman got here if he wasn't careful.

"Come on, get it together, for fuck's sake."

The early hours of the morning tripped through his mind, every minute of it, from the second he'd grabbed Nigel in that car park to when he'd got home. He'd covered everything, had nothing to worry about, yet a spiteful little voice whispered he'd forgotten something.

Would he trip up when he was informed about the incident? Show his guilt? And it had to be about Nigel, it couldn't be anything else. If the Transit had been sighted, say he'd gone over the speed limit, a detective wouldn't be involved in that. He thought of the earth in the pig pen. Any soaked-in blood would have been trampled down by now.

It would be okay. It would.

CHAPTER SIX

In the tent, Lenny beside her, Anna stared at the head. Bruises and bloating had ruined the face, but a mole on the chin married with what Carys had said. The long black hair hung in string-like snakes at the ends, which had once been wet, probably with blood, but the rest appeared bone dry and clean apart from a patch on the side where something had struck the skull. The nose, likely broken, leaned to one side; the lips were puffy, the top one split. He'd taken a nasty beating. God knew what the rest of the body looked like. And where was it? Would the parts show up in the coming hours?

Herman had finished his initial perusal and made notes, and the driver's licence had been placed in an evidence bag. It was Nigel's, but that didn't mean the head was his. It could be days before DNA results came back to get a definite ID. Which reminded her to ask Herman about the tattoo.

"Can you check behind his right ear for me, please?"

Herman used a baton, similar to a conductor's, and moved some of the hair. "Celtic cross."

"Right, then that's as close to a proper ID for now as we're going to get." Anna sighed. "We're going to have to speak to his next of kin, so we may as well do the death knock instead of uniforms."

"No parents," Lenny said. "Warren replied to my message about looking into Nigel. Mother and father died six months apart three years ago. He's got a sister, though. She's local. Julie."

"Same surname as her brother?"

"Yes, Fogg."

"So she's not married, then. Have you got her address?"

"Yep. She's more likely to be at work though. She's full-time at the hairdresser's down Southgate."

"Any verdict for us yet?" she asked Herman.

He leaned towards the face. "I'd say he's been kicked in the head. Possibly a steel toecap. It's a clean cut through the top of the neck, a sharp instrument. Perhaps an axe or machete, if that's any help."

Anna nodded. "It is. It tells me we've got a nutter on our hands. But *who* has either a machete or an axe handy, for Pete's sake? Premeditated, if you ask me. And is putting the head on a spike significant?" She sighed. "Come on, then, we'd better get going. We'll come back to speak to the neighbour who claimed to be Nigel's mate after, then go and see Matthew."

* * *

Stylette, clearly a top-end salon, stood between a B&M and Brunch, a popular sandwich shop. Being here reminded Anna to get her split ends cut off but, as usual, she hadn't had the time. She kept her hair long, no fringe, so she could pop it in a ponytail with minimal fuss. The only thing she did was dye it brown at home, using root spray when a few grey strands wormed their way out to tide her over until she dyed it again. That was about as far as she went when it came to what she looked like. Make-up and all that nonsense were for nights out. She didn't indulge in those much either, preferring to read at home. These ladies, though . . . She stared at them through the window. It was obvious they cared about their appearance. Nice clothes, polished nails.

Sod that.

Anna pushed the shop door open and was swiftly hit by the scent of something she couldn't identify, plus styling products and the sharp sting of hair bleach — a woman sat in a chair getting white-blonde streaks put in, her head covered in folds of tinfoil. On the other side, a nail bar. Maybe that was the strange smell. Anna had never had her nails done, so wouldn't know.

A tall, round reception desk stood to the left, the shape of a toilet roll cut lengthways. A young blonde woman of about seventeen was stationed behind it, dolled up to the nines. Anna smiled at her. With her back to the customers, she held her ID up, but not enough that it would alert any nosy-beak clients.

"Is Miss Fogg in today?"

The receptionist stared at the ID then at Anna. "Oh. Um . . . oh. Is everything all right?"

Why do people always ask that? It was their way of finding out gossip, and it annoyed her. She hid her irritation and smiled. "*Is* she in?"

"Yes, but the boss isn't, and I usually have to run things by her first."

"This is important. We can't wait for your boss to get back."

"Okay, I'll . . . I'll let Julie know you're here. Would you like to wait out the back in the staffroom? It's through that mirrored door over there."

"Thanks." Anna walked over and entered.

The space, as elegant as the salon, was clean and tidy. Black-and-white, arty and professional pictures of different hairstyles hung on the walls. A breakfast bar with several stools in front of it had a large bunch of fresh flowers in a blue vase, and behind it was what appeared to be a galley kitchen, set up to resemble a coffee shop, with its fancy machine and cakes beneath glass domes. Whoever owned this place cared about the employees.

"I could just do with a bit of Victoria sponge," Lenny said.

"Maybe we'll get lucky and she'll offer us a slice. I'm starving. I need the loo an' all." Anna glanced at another door with a plaque of a woman's body on it. "I'll ask if I can use theirs before we go."

The mirrored door swung open, and a woman with long black hair poked her head round it. "You wanted to see me?"

"Julie? Come and have a seat." Anna would rather have done this at Julie's house so she had privacy, but this was the hand she'd been dealt. They needed to inform the next of kin sooner rather than later, because with the number of neighbours who'd been on the Lock word would spread fast on social media.

Julie came in and pulled a stool out. She sat on it and gazed from Anna to Lenny and back again. Anna studied her. Did she resemble her brother? Was this similar to what he'd have looked like without all that bruising and puffiness?

"Could you confirm what the tattoo is behind your brother's ear for me?" Anna asked.

Julie frowned. "A cross. Celtic, I think. Is he okay?"

Anna took a deep breath. "I'm sorry to have to inform you but, going by the information we have at present, Nigel *may* have passed away. I said may because we haven't had a formal identification yet."

Julie blinked several times, her eyes watering, bottom lip wobbling. "But he can't have. He's . . . he *can't* have."

Anna sat on a stool. "He was found in his girlfriend's front garden earlier this morning. She believes it's him." She decided to keep "only the head" to herself for now.

"Oh God. What . . . but Geraldine never said a word."

Anna hid her surprise. "Geraldine?"

"Yes, Geraldine Simmons. Um . . . can you give me a second?" Julie stared at the floor, emotions playing out on her face. Confusion. Shock. Realisation. She lifted her head and stared at Anna. "He's *dead*?"

"I'm so sorry, but we really do think it's him. A DNA analysis will be done as soon as possible. We'll have to collect some of his hair from his house in order to do that, though, or his toothbrush."

"I have a key. He has one for my flat as well." Julie got up and went to a row of lockers disguised as a tall white wall unit. She took her bag out, fished for the keys and handed them over.

Anna popped them in her pocket. "Thank you. Excuse me while I arrange for an officer to collect them." She sent a message to Karen, then popped her phone back in her pocket. "So his girlfriend isn't Carys Brignell?"

Julie pursed her lips and stuffed her bag away. "*Her?* No, thank God. He *was* seeing her for a while, but that was ages ago. He's been with Geraldine for months."

What the hell? "Do you know where she lives?"

Julie rattled off the address and sat. "But she's not at home. She's out there, in the salon, getting her hair done. That's what I meant when I said she hadn't mentioned anything."

Oh, bloody hell's bells . . . "Okay, we'll speak to her in a moment." Anna detested this part, where she delivered such devastating news and then had to press on as if she had no sympathy and only wanted information. "I hate to ask this when you're upset, but do you know of anyone who'd want to hurt Nigel?"

"Hurt him? Why would they do that? You said he was dead, and I thought . . . I thought he'd had a heart attack or something. I told him he was overdoing it at the gym." Julie wiped her eyes with the back of her hand, streaking kohl towards her temples. A false eyelash popped free at one end, and she absently pulled it off and scrunched it into her fist.

40

"He was murdered," Anna said, gentle with her delivery.

"Oh God. What? Who?"

"We don't know yet, which is why we need to find out as much as we can about him. So as far as you're aware, there's no one who would have wanted to do this to him?"

"No! He's . . . what *did* they do to him?"

"We won't know until the post-mortem has been done." *And we've found the rest of the body.* "Which gym does he go to?"

"Big Fitness."

"Thank you." She turned to Lenny. "Get someone from the team over there." She focused on Julie again. "How did things end with Carys, do you know?"

"He was only seeing her every now and then. He does that between proper relationships. Sleeps around. Doesn't take anything too seriously. Honestly, he only went round hers for sex. I had a right go at him when I found out he was messing around with his mate's wife."

"Matthew Brignell?"

"Yes."

"What's the state of play there?"

"Matt caught them in bed. Moved out the same night. They don't speak to each other anymore. Bloody shame, because Nigel's been friends with Matt since they were little. He's kind of like my second brother, so it affected me, too, as I rarely see Matt now."

Julie seemed to have got a hold of her emotions regarding the death, managing to quell the tremors in her voice. But the mind had a way of protecting you, so maybe Nigel's murder had momentarily left her brain. It was too much to contemplate at the minute. Anna would keep talking to give her further respite.

"It was suggested that Matthew could have done this. Would you agree?"

Julie shook her head. "Absolutely not. Matt's quiet, never sticks up for himself. He didn't even do that when he walked in on them, just went downstairs and waited for Nigel to leave,

41

then went to his dad's. To be honest, Nigel bullied Matt a bit. Maybe not bullied, but he talked him into doing things."

"Like what?"

"Getting drunk, all that. Matt isn't really a drinker. He's more your 'cup of tea and a good book' type." Julie's breath shuddered out of her, and her face creased up.

There it was. Anna held her hand and waited for her to sob it out. Lenny went behind the breakfast bar and attempted to work the coffee machine. The little bugger put three slices of cake on plates and placed them on the bar. Coffee made, he dealt out the cups and took a bite of Victoria sponge.

"Have a drink and something to eat, Julie," Anna said. "They say sugar's good for the shock." *And bad for Lenny's teeth, the sod.*

Lenny passed Julie a napkin, and she dabbed her eyes and cheeks. Most of her make-up came off. She appeared dazed, as if the tears and sobbing had wiped all the joy out of her. She put her eyelash in the napkin and balled it up. Took a bite of cake. Anna did the same; it wouldn't hurt to have a moment of quiet contemplation, something she craved throughout any day she had to deal with other people.

It was longer than a moment. Before she knew it, the coffees had gone.

"Maybe it isn't him," Julie whispered. "Loads of people have the same tattoo. I can't believe I'm never going to see him again. He's all I had left."

"I understand your parents passed away."

"Hmm. Matt arranged the funerals. Me and Nigel . . . we were fit for nothing at the time. This is why I can't see Matt hurting my brother. He's too kind. Have you seen him? Does he know?"

"Not yet. We came to you first — after Carys, obviously. She really did seem to think Nigel was her boyfriend."

"I'm telling you, he isn't. She's been down the Kite when he's with Geraldine, so she *must* know what's what."

Interesting. "Okay, I'll go and ask Geraldine to come in now. Would you prefer to go home rather than sit through all this again?"

"No, she might need me. She's . . . delicate."

Gawd.

CHAPTER SEVEN

Anna left the staffroom and shut the door. A couple of women who'd been there before had gone, and she worried Geraldine was one of them. A PC entered, and she took the keys from her pocket and quietly explained what she needed. He left, and Anna scoured the salon again.

She called out, "Geraldine?"

A blonde woman having her hair tonged held up a hand and looked at Anna's reflection in the mirror. The stylist glanced Anna's way. She didn't do a good job of hiding her irritation at being interrupted.

"Would you mind coming for a little chat?" Anna asked, going for casual rather than pulling her ID out again in front of the other customers.

"Um, who are you?"

Anna didn't want to say. "I'll explain in a minute. Julie's with us, so . . ."

Geraldine stood and brushed her hands over her knee-length black skirt. She picked up her handbag from the floor and followed Anna into the staffroom, where she immediately caught sight of Julie.

"What's happened?" She rushed over and put an arm around her shoulders.

"You need to sit down," Julie said on a hiccup. "It might not be true, so don't go getting in a state yet."

"But *you're* in a state."

Anna passed on the bad news. Geraldine crumpled, her legs going from under her, and sank to the tiled floor. Anna crouched and held her hand, waiting for the initial shock to subside. It set Julie off crying again, so Lenny laid his hand on her wrist. That was the thing about being a copper. People rarely saw this side of it, where officers were locked into people's grief along with them, tears stinging, empathy flowing, lost for words.

A couple of long minutes passed before Anna composed herself and helped Geraldine to stand. She guided her to a stool and gave Lenny the nod to make her a cuppa. Anna dragged a third stool over, and they sat in a triangle.

"Please bear in mind that there hasn't been a formal ID yet," Anna said. "I apologise for having to ask questions, Geraldine, but I have to treat this as if it *is* Nigel. Any time wasted isn't good. When did you last see him?"

"Last night. He came to mine. We watched a film on Netflix."

"What film was that?"

"*Fall.* The one about the women stuck up a pole."

Oh Jesus. A pole. Karen mentioned coincidences this morning. "What time did he leave?"

"About one." Geraldine stilled, her mouth dropping open. "You can't park in my street — it's not allowed, too narrow — so he left his car round the back. You have to go down an alley to get to the parking area. Do you think . . . I mean, could someone have followed him and killed him there?"

"Only if they knew he was at yours." Anna glanced at Lenny.

He took his phone out and got on with sending a message to the team.

45

"We'll look into that," Anna said. "Did he stay at yours often?"

"Thursdays, Fridays, and Saturdays. He's busy with work and everything during the week, gets tired. Plus I've got a little boy. He goes to his dad's on Thursday nights until Sunday afternoon."

"What does your son's father think of your relationship with Nigel?"

"They get on. Kevin, that's my ex, he's got a wife and another child now. We've both moved on. No animosity or anything."

"Has Nigel ever upset any of your neighbours or other people that you know of?"

"Matthew Brignell."

"Yes, we know about the affair. Did Nigel ever mention his feelings about that?"

"Only that he wished he'd never gone with Carys because she's a nightmare. She instigated it, got him feeling sorry for her. She reckoned Matthew left her alone a lot. She pounced on Nigel in a weak moment when he was drunk. He saw her a few times, got caught, then that was it."

"You said a 'weak moment'. If he saw her after that first time, did he consider *that* weak as well?"

"No, he admitted he'd used her for sex after that. Said he hated himself for messing around behind Matthew's back, tried to say sorry a few times down the Kite and by sending texts, but Matthew ignored him."

Can you blame him? "We've gathered Matthew's the quiet type. Maybe he didn't want a confrontation, in public or otherwise. A clean break is sometimes best when it's clear a relationship is over."

"Maybe. I don't know him as such, I've only heard what went on, but that sounds about right. If he's ever in the Kite, which isn't often, he's generally on his own, being quiet and whatever. He reads in the corner."

A loner? A lot of time to think about and plan a murder? Or is he too busy for that with work plus the farm?

Geraldine shuddered and looked at Julie, then at the wall. "I can't think of *anyone* who'd want to . . . want to *murder* Nigel."

Carys? A woman scorned because Nigel didn't want a serious relationship with her? Could someone as slight as her wield an axe or a machete, though? Anna couldn't imagine it. Yes, Carys was at the Kite until eleven, but she could well have done a stalker act outside Geraldine's after the taxi had dropped her home. Their houses weren't far apart; both streets branched off Haldon Way. There might be an alley that connected the two.

"How did Nigel seem last night?" Anna asked.

"His usual self. Laughing and whatever. Oh God, this is so awful." Geraldine burst into tears again.

Anna appealed to Julie. *Help.*

Julie got herself together and hugged the woman. She stared at Anna. "Go. We'll be fine."

Anna stood. "We'll be in touch with any further information. Again, I'm so sorry to have brought you bad news." She didn't like asking, but it had to be done. Her bladder was protesting. "Is it okay if I use the loo?"

Julie nodded.

The call of nature didn't stop because a killer was on the loose, and Anna was only human. Despite that, she still felt guilty when she went into the toilet, Geraldine's sobs wrenching out right up until Anna had washed her hands. She exited and glanced across. Two women, devastated by their loss, their lives never to be the same again.

The common theme here was Carys and Matthew Brignell; but, if he was so kind, was he really who they were after?

But the quiet ones are always the worst, remember . . .

CHAPTER EIGHT

Warren Yates stood in the parking area behind Geraldine Simmons' house with fellow DC, Sally Wiggins. Prior to leaving the station, he'd checked DVLA as to whether Nigel had a car. It sat tucked in a corner, away from other vehicles. Each space had a number painted on it, the bowl base of a six visible beneath the silver Audi. The vehicle didn't appear to have been tampered with and, gloves on, Warren tried the driver-side door.

It opened.

"Oh shit," Sally said, a wisp of blonde hair streaking over her eyes. She brushed it away. "Looks like he left Geraldine's, unlocked his car, then he was snatched?"

"It's likely. No signs of anything untoward going on around here, though. The alley's clear, and there's no blood anywhere. His phone's in the cup holder." Warren crouched to check under the car. "He dropped his keys, though." He pulled them out, stood and held them up. "A Metallica fan." One of the keyrings had the band's emblem on it.

Sally took two small evidence bags out of her jacket pocket, and Warren dropped the keys and phone inside. They inspected the area one last time, then Warren called it in. As it seemed Nigel had been waylaid here, a couple of SOCOs would be sent along. They remained in the car park until two PCs arrived, leaving them to set up a cordon, a logistical nightmare if any residents needed their cars, but that wasn't his problem. Then two forensic officers turned up, and Warren handed over the evidence bags.

Walking back down the alley with Sally beside him, he ran a hand over his head and stared down the narrow, cobbled dead-end street. Slender houses sandwiched beside each other, perhaps two-up two-downs, no front gardens. Each boasted different-coloured facades — pinks, blues, and pale greens — and brick chimneys, a few with chubby pigeons perched on top. One cooed as if to tell them to bugger off.

"I'll take one side and you take the other?" he asked.

Sally nodded and set off.

Warren counted the homes. Five on each side, so not too bad as door-to-door enquiries went. He knocked on number three because a curtain twitched in the window to his right. A slim old lady answered, her blue eyes rheumy.

"I saw the police arrive," she said by way of greeting, and nodded to Warren's parked Ford, the patrol car, and the small SOCO van. "Vehicles aren't allowed down here, just so you know. There's a sign up and everything. Fifty quid fine if the warden comes along."

She's one of those. A do-gooder. "I'm sure an exception to the rule will be made in the circumstances."

Her snaggled eyebrows rose. "What circumstances?"

Warren indicated across the street using a thumb over his shoulder. "Do you know the resident of number six?"

"Geraldine? Yes. Lovely girl. And her fella, Nigel. Quite the gentleman, he is."

"Did you happen to see him leave last night?"

"I did, as it happens. About one o'clock, it was. I was up with my insomnia. Saw him through the living room window. He met someone on the corner there, by the alley."

Warren glanced that way. A streetlamp stood at the entrance. Was it working? If so, this old dear might have some interesting information. He returned his attention to her. "Did you see who it was?"

She sucked on her floppy lips. "No, they were just shapes. Didn't have my glasses on, see."

"Yet you saw Nigel clearly enough."

"*Yes*, because he wasn't that far away when he came out of Geraldine's." She rolled her eyes as if he should have worked that out for himself. "What are you asking for anyway?"

He smiled. "Did you see if they went down the alley?"

"Yes, although I can't see all the way down it from here."

"Did you hear any vehicles starting up after that?"

"A bit of a rumble, but I assumed it was Nigel going home."

"What time was that?"

"About five minutes after they went down the alley? I thought someone shouted before that but can't be sure. You must know what these young men are like. Some are a bit loud, aren't they?"

"Hmm. Can I have your name, please?"

"Ivy Rhodes, but what do you want it for?"

"You're a witness."

"To what?"

He didn't want to tell her the real reason. "To when Nigel left the house. Is there anything else you can remember?"

She held a gnarled finger to her damp bottom lip. "No, that's it. Oh, hang on. Geraldine's downstairs lights went off as soon as Nigel walked out, and the front bedroom one came on shortly after. It flicked off about a minute or so later. And *he* was awake, him at number four, outside smoking a cigarette. He's not at work today; he's talking to that woman over there."

"Who is *he*?"

"A pest, that's who. Mr Davis. I don't know his first name, but it begins with an F. He keeps getting his parcels delivered to me while he's at work. I don't know, people see I'm at home all the time and expect me to be the bloody postman. He didn't used to come to collect his parcels, he waited for me to drop them over, but I soon put him right. Now he gets them off me himself, but he's rude about it." She folded her arms. "I might well tell the driver to put them on his doorstep in future. If they get nicked, that's his lookout."

Eager to get away from her, Warren gave his thanks and walked across the road. A wide man, Mr Davis almost filled his doorway. A stain punctuated the front of his white T-shirt, perhaps mustard. Warren refrained from speaking as he'd arrived mid-conversation.

"Did you recognise him?" Sally asked.

"No, but it was definitely a bloke. Had a hoody on. Black I'd say, or navy."

"How long was he there for prior to Mr Fogg leaving number six?"

"Two fags' worth of time. Ten minutes or so? He stood under the streetlight, hands in pockets, head down. I thought it was a bit weird, him being there, which is why I had the two ciggies instead of one. I thought it was one of those gang kids selling that spice crap. Once I saw Nigel knew him, I relaxed."

"Sorry to interrupt," Warren said. "DC Yates, by the way."

"Freddie Davis."

Warren acknowledged that with a nod. "I was just talking to your neighbour and—"

"Yeah, I saw. Fucking old bat."

Warren hid his smile. "She said there may have been a shout, then an engine starting up. Did you hear that?"

Davis sniffed. "Nah, I had my earbuds in. I listen to podcasts to get me to sleep. A shout? Blimey. Did something go off out the back, then?"

Sally took over to save Warren having to divulge anything. "How well do you know Mr Fogg?"

Davis shrugged, his meaty shoulders almost touching his ears. "Not well. I say hello if I'm out here having a smoke, but that's about it. Has he done something or what?"

"We just need a timeline of events," Sally said. "How tall was the stranger?"

"Five something. Closer to six feet, now I come to think of it. He was a bit shorter than Nigel. Odd how you notice shit like that. I spotted it when they walked off together."

"Did you hear any of their conversation, if they even had one?" Sally asked.

"Yeah, Nigel said, 'What the fuck do you want?' I thought that was a bit off myself, but there you go."

"Off in what way?" Warren queried.

"Nigel's never been rude whenever I've spoken to him, but he could be being polite, I s'pose."

"Did the man answer him?" Warren prayed for something that would give them a lead, although knowing someone had been in the street was a big one by itself.

"I think he said they needed to talk, then they went down the alley and I didn't pick up anything else."

Warren wrote that down. "Is that all you can remember?"

"Yeah."

"Did you see anyone else around that time?"

Davis indicated Mrs Rhodes's house. "Only her, nosing through her bloody window. She doesn't even have any nets up, look. Doesn't care who sees her when her curtains are open. I'm not happy with her. She had a go at me the other week about my parcels. It's not my fault the delivery bloke leaves them there."

Sally looked at Warren and frowned. Warren shook his head, letting her know it wasn't anything to worry about.

"If that's all, then," Sally said.

Davis nodded. "Yep, that about sums it up."

They walked away from him. Warren glanced over his shoulder. Davis sparked up a cigarette, clearly settling in to watch any proceedings. They split up again to knock on other doors. Finding no one else in, Warren nipped back to the parking area to let one of the PCs know which residents still needed speaking to. With nothing left to do, he led the way back to his car.

Inside, Sally settled beside him.

He started the engine. "Lunch?"

She nodded. "I'll update Anna on the way."

He drove off, pondering what they'd discovered. Whoever that mystery man was, he had something to do with Nigel not getting into his Audi. Hopefully, someone else along that street would offer up some information later. In the meantime, a bacon bap from Brunch called his name.

CHAPTER NINE

The Remember Room

Matthew didn't normally stand on street corners like some weirdo, but he did tonight. Nigel had a new lady friend, which wasn't unusual — the man collected them, notches on his bedpost, although she'd lasted longer than the others. Matthew had seen them leaving the Kite on the nights he'd sat outside in his van. He'd got rid of his old car a couple of years ago so Carys and Nigel wouldn't recognise him. He liked to sit and watch the pub, see if they went home together again, rekindling their romance. They hadn't since the night he'd caught them, although they copped off with others. The pair of them were filthy. Didn't care who they gave themselves to, who they hurt.

Nigel and his newest woman had got a taxi and Matthew had followed in the Transit. The cab had dropped them at the entrance to a car park behind some houses. Matthew had stopped and turned the engine off and watched them walk down an alley. Quickly, he'd gone after them, his footsteps light, them too drunk to hear him, too busy laughing. He'd caught sight of them just as they'd entered a house.

Now, he waited for Nigel to leave. His ex-mate had never been one to stay overnight, to have the full experience of intimacy and snuggles. Nigel always said women were for fucking, not loving. That poor woman he was with, Geraldine. Did she know that? Know she was being used? Did she care? Or was she like Carys, only after the same thing?

Two hours passed. But Matthew was a patient man. He'd waited for two years as it was, so however long it took tonight didn't matter.

He'd received the odd message from Nigel, who'd tried to build bridges, but Matthew had ignored them, same as he had whenever Nigel had come up to him in the Kite. That's why Matthew had changed his phone number and didn't visit that pub unless he knew his old pal wasn't there. Confrontation had never sat well, and he'd had to gear himself up in order to do it tonight.

Two years was a fair while to think about everything that had happened. But he'd had all his life to think about the other things. Specifically Mum and how she'd got into his bed at night when he'd been a teenager and expected things from him no mother should. Dad had been either asleep or out, none the wiser until Matthew had got the balls up to tell him. It was because of Mum that he'd known pigs could eat a body within minutes. He'd been eighteen.

He hadn't meant it.

It was an accident.

A happy one, Dad had said months later.

The police had come. They'd asked Matthew numerous questions, going on and on, trying to see if he or Dad had killed her. He'd forced himself to remain calm, like he always had. No good came of being angry, Mum's treatment of him and her death had shown him that. If he hadn't been angry, she'd still be alive. He'd promised never to get that irate again, yet here he was, only this time he meant *to commit murder.*

He pushed those thoughts away. Jolted at the sound of a door opening. Prepared himself for the planned attack. Keeping his head down, he glanced up. Some bloke came out of the house next to Geraldine's and sparked up a cigarette. Matthew moved slightly, so his face would be in shadow, the light from the streetlamp behind him. If he walked away, it would look off, so he took his chances and remained where he was.

The man smoked two fags, then Geraldine's front door opened. Nigel crept out, a thief in the night — a thief of that poor woman's emotions, the robber of Matthew's.

Nigel walked towards him. "What the fuck do you want?"

"We need to talk."

Nigel stormed down the alley, Matthew jogging to keep up.

"So now you want to chat, do you?" Nigel muttered. "What about all those times I got hold of you and you ignored me? How come I have to wait two years for you to finally give me the time of day? Go and get fucked."

Matthew waited to see red, but nothing happened. He panicked. He needed to let the anger out, but it remained inside him like it had always done until that night in the pig barn with Mum.

Nigel clicked his key fob. The indicator lights of his Audi flashed, once, twice. He opened the car door and bent over to put his phone inside. He stood upright and gave Matthew a nasty smile.

At last, spurred on by Nigel's arrogance, his utter disregard, Matthew rushed forward. Anger flooded him, so hot and fast it startled him for a moment. He shoved Nigel, the momentum taking him down to the ground with him. They tussled, both trying to get the upper hand. Matthew got a lucky break and elbowed him in the nose. A faint crack, Nigel shouting in pain, then silence save for their heavy breathing.

Matthew got up, shut the car door with his foot, and kicked him in the face several times, once in the head, subduing him enough that he could drag him out of the car park to the Transit in the street behind. He dumped him on the pavement and snatched some cable ties out of his pocket, snapping them around Nigel's wrists and ankles. All the while, Nigel groaned, and, in the light of a lamp post, his eyes swelled, one more than the other. Matthew pushed him in the back of the van and got going. He drove around the houses for a bit to go through his plan again, then headed to Hawthorn Farm. At this hour, no one was about.

He parked in the old barn and closed the large doors. Switched on a torch he'd already put on a shelving unit.

He hauled Nigel out of the van. "Get on that table."

"Fuck you, man."

"I'm warning you . . ."

"You're out of your bloody tree if you think I'm getting on there." Nigel stared at the tools on a trolley with the eye that had a partial slit. "Come on, pal. Pack it in now. I get that you're angry, but it's been two years, for Pete's sake."

"It's the anniversary tonight."

"The anniversary of what?"

"The night you two wrecked my life. The night you took the decision away from me. The night I was going to end it, but you couldn't even give me that, could you?"

"Aww, piss off. I did you a favour. You got to look like the poor bastard who'd been duped instead of the wanker who left his wife for no reason."

"I know, but it didn't give you carte blanche to help make that happen, did it?"

"I showed you who she really is. I told you not to marry her."

"You broke the trust between us. That kills me more than her being a slag."

"I've said sorry for that a few times. Can't we move on?"

"No. Get on the table."

"Sod off."

Matthew grabbed a hammer from the trolley and whacked it on Nigel's knee. The man went down, screeching, and Matthew gripped him under the arms and swung him onto the steel surface.

"All that pain you gave me is coming your way." Matthew grinned. "Then I'm feeding you to the pigs."

CHAPTER TEN

Matthew rented a ground-floor flat and had sole use of the back garden. While worrying about what the police would say, he'd come up with the perfect idea to throw them off the scent. He checked his surroundings — high firs either side of the lawn and at the bottom. Washing he'd not long hung out flapped in the chilly breeze, a pair of trousers still in the basket, one leg draped over the side as if he'd been disturbed mid-job.

He turned and faced the building. Braced himself for what he was about to do. Clenched his fists, his leather gloves tightening. Drawing his head back, giving his hair a mean wrench, he shot forward and nutted the window frame. Pain erupted, sharp and awful. But he did it again and again.

The moment he sensed the forehead skin split, he shouted, "What did you do that for?"

He punched himself in the face. Not hard enough. He walloped his cheek a second time, then his mouth. The taste of blood seeped onto his tongue, and he swallowed it. Blinked as blood dripped from his forehead.

"Leave me alone, please . . . please, what do you want from me?"

Staying behind the side gate and out of view of the homes opposite, he opened it and left it ajar. Jogged on the spot to create hard, echoing footsteps as if someone was running away.

A moment or two to catch his breath, and he sidled back into the garden. Woozy, he walked inside to look in the bathroom mirror.

"Jesus, what a mess."

He used his shirtsleeve to wipe away some blood, put his gloves away and made a cup of tea.

Everything would definitely be all right now.

CHAPTER ELEVEN

At the kitchen table, Anna and Lenny sat with Terry Newman, the neighbour who'd claimed to be friends with Nigel. Thankfully, he'd got dressed. He'd provided cups of tea and ham sandwiches. Something of a surprise but a welcome one. As they ate, he chatted.

"Look, people are going to say he was nice an' all that, and don't get me wrong, he was, but he could also be a bastard when it came to women or getting his own way. A tad manipulative. Nigel liked the ladies — he'd only recently settled on a girl called Geraldine."

"Yes, we've spoken to her," Anna said.

"Poor cow. She must be gutted. Anyway, the setup he had with Carys was a bit . . . well, a bit odd. She told my missus they were an item and that they'd be getting married, but *he* told *me* he was just shagging her. I was inclined to believe him, to be honest, because the shit that comes out of Carys's mouth . . ."

"Do you know her well, then?"

"Nah, Debbie tells me all sorts."

"Is that your partner?"

"Wife, yeah. They chat over the garden fence out the back from time to time. Debbie reckons Carys is a sandwich short."

"What sort of things does she say?"

"Like how they were going on holiday to the Maldives, yet they didn't. How Nigel bought her this engagement ring — emerald, I think Debbie said it was — but Nigel said she'd got it herself from Argos for fifty quid. Little lies she doesn't have to tell. Maybe she feels the need to big herself up, lacks self-esteem, wants Deb to like her, but Jesus, she's full of bullshit. Her telling you she's Nigel's girlfriend, it's all bollocks."

Maybe she doesn't like to admit she's had two failed relationships recently, so told us a white lie.

Anna finished her sandwich. "Going back to Nigel not being nice sometimes. What, exactly, did you mean by that?"

Terry scrubbed a hand down his face. "I feel rotten, talking about him like this when he's dead, but it's nothing I haven't said to his face . . ." He winced. "Bad choice of words, but you know what I mean."

Anna's earlier conversation with Karen came to mind, and she suppressed an inappropriate smile. "Carry on."

"He could be a bit unfeeling. You know, didn't read the room, or if he did he couldn't care less if what he said upset someone. Could be classed as ribbing, winding people up. Like when we worked together, he'd always comment on my weight, say I needed to get down the gym. It got a bit wearing after a while. If I'm honest, it hurt."

Anna cocked her head at him.

His eyes widened. "Now don't go thinking *I* killed him, because I didn't."

"Where were you last night?"

"I was down the Kite with Deb. We had dinner there and stayed on for a few pints. Left after that mad bint next door went home."

"Carys?"

"Yeah."

"Sorry, jumping back a bit. Are you a solicitor as well?"

"I used to be. I switched jobs because I always seemed to be representing scum, getting guilty people off. I've gone into social work."

Anna's mind zipped back to the pub topic. Now Terry had mentioned Carys's proclivity to lie, she wasn't sure if she could take what she'd said about Gordon White seriously. *Was* he a pervert? Was the work email a coincidence?

"Was Carys with anyone last night?" she asked to double-check the woman's alibi.

"Yeah, two birds, twins, and this fella spoke to her for a bit. Blond-haired chap in a suit. He was feeling her up. She spoke to another one an' all."

"Right."

"I've seen her with the latter before, a few weeks ago. They were out the back of the pub by the wheelie bins, kissing."

Anna had the shocking image of them getting inside it. Carys had seemed grossed out by Gordon's supposed suggestion, but had she lied about that, too? If so, what was the point? For attention?

"Is Debbie at work?" Lenny asked.

"Yeah."

"Is it possible to phone her so we can have a word about that man? Put it on speaker?"

"Could do. She's in an office by herself, so it'll be fine." Terry drew his phone across the table and prodded the screen.

It rang out, then a woman said, "What are you up to, sexy?"

Terry blushed. "Err, pack it in, love. I've got the police here. We're on speaker."

"Shit, sorry. What about? You *did* pay that parking fine, didn't you?"

"Yeah. Listen, I wasn't going to tell you until I picked you up later, but something's happened. The police want to speak to you."

"Are you okay?"

"Yeah, it isn't about me. You know Nigel?"

"Of course I do."

"Someone's only gone and left his head on this wooden stake thing in Carys's front garden and—"

"*What?*"

"I know. Poor bastard's dead, obviously. Anyway, Carys is saying he's her boyfriend. So, that bloke we saw her with last night, the older fella. They want to know about him. Has she said anything?"

"Only that she sees him on and off."

Anna cut in. "Hi, Debbie. I'm Detective Inspector Anna James. Has Carys mentioned the man by name?"

"She doesn't know it, just has sex with him. There's this other one called Gordon, though. What does this have to do with Nigel being dead? God, I can't get over this."

"It's a line of inquiry." *Like whether Carys asked Gordon to murder Nigel.* Stranger things had happened, so Anna wasn't going to dismiss that out of hand, although a copper doing the killing might be a bit of a stretch. "How well did she say she knew Gordon?"

"She didn't. He has a thing about her, apparently, keeps asking if she'll go round his and tidy up."

"Come on, love," Terry said. "We should take whatever she says with a pinch of salt."

"True, but she can't lie *all* the time."

"Is there anything else you think we should know?" Anna asked. "Relating to Nigel this time."

"No. I didn't really know him. He said hello or waved when he turned up at Carys's, you know, if I was outside or whatever, but nothing more than that. Terry had already warned me not to get pally with him because he can be rude."

"Okay, well, thank you for your time," Anna said. "If you could keep this conversation to yourself . . ."

"Will do."

"See you later," Terry said.

"Yep. Tarra."

He ended the call. "She's my everything, she is."

63

Anna smiled. "She must be if you protected her from anything Nigel might have said to her."

"Yeah, well, if it got *me* down, imagine what it'd do to her."

"Was he like that with Carys?"

"Not that I saw. There were a few times we were all in the Kite and she seemed pretty happy in his company. So did he. I felt bad that she was seeing him behind her husband's back."

"Did you know Matthew?"

Terry nodded. "Bloody good bloke. Got to know him when he lived next door. It was disgusting what those two did to him. He didn't deserve that, working what amounted to two jobs, Carys bawling him out for it. I was awake the night he caught them at it. It was summer, and everyone had their windows open. Our bedroom is next to hers, so the voices carried."

"What did she say?"

"That it served Matt right that he'd caught them because, if he was home more, she wouldn't have had to turn to Nigel. The fact that she'd zoomed in on her husband's best friend was a bit below the belt, in my opinion. She went on and on, laying the blame at Matt's door. He didn't say anything back, not that I heard anyway. Nigel told Carys to shut up, couldn't she see Matt was crying. He said she was only a fling, she didn't mean anything to him, and Carys screamed."

"She was screaming?"

"Yeah, like she was being hurt. I got up, went round there in case Matt had walloped her, but he opened the door straight away. He held a suitcase, I remember that because it was a bit sad, know what I mean?"

"So far, people have said Matthew is meek and calm. This is the first time anyone has said he might have hit her."

"Considering what was going on, even the calmest of men might snap at seeing their wife in bed with their best mate, no?"

"Hmm. What happened next?"

"I asked if everything was all right. He said Carys and Nigel were upstairs, then shut the door on me. He'd been crying, I know that much. I went home, stood by the living room window. Nigel walked out, got in his car and fucked off. About two minutes later, Matt came out with the suitcase and drove off an' all. Carys was still screaming after he was long gone."

Anna frowned. Why scream when neither man was in the house? Had she been *that* angry that both had left her? Was she the type to go off the rails if her plans didn't work out?

"Okay, thanks. So, despite your worry that he might have hit his wife, I take it you don't think Matt would have had anything to do with Nigel's death."

"Nope. He's not the type. He moved on with his life quietly, no fuss. I admire him for his dignity."

How on earth had Matthew ended up with a woman who sounded so highly strung? *They say opposites attract, but bloody hell!*

Anna stood. "We'd better get going. Thanks for lunch. It's really appreciated."

"Not a problem. I know what it's like, racing around at work and not being able to stop for food." Terry got up and went first down the hallway.

"Do you like social work?" Lenny asked behind him.

Terry opened the front door. "Yeah, much more rewarding. I work with kids in care."

"That's got to be tough," Anna said.

"When no one's available to foster them after their mum and dad have had a barney, yeah, it's tough. Me and Deb are going to adopt this lad. He's only six, but no one wants him. Too troubled."

"We need more people like you in the world." Anna smiled. "Good luck with that. If we have any more questions, we'll be in touch."

She stepped out into the sunshine, a nippy breeze attacking her cheeks. A SOCO came out of the tent and nodded to her. Herman's car had gone, as had the second forensic van.

65

Steven Timpson also left the tent and walked down the side of it to speak to Anna and Lenny as they reached the point where a hedge bisected Carys's garden and Terry's.

Anna gave him a hopeful look. "Anything?"

Steve tugged his face mask down. "The wood for the spike is years old, so it's anyone's guess where it was purchased. However, it's been in the ground at some point before now. Discolouration, and it's weathered. We might get lucky with embedded soil samples in the grain. It'll give us an idea of where that wood's been."

Anna, always amazed at how the forensic lot came to their conclusions, let out a sigh of relief. "It could narrow it down to Marlford?"

Steve nodded. "I'm praying for spores specific to plants here."

"Ever the optimist," Lenny said.

Steve smiled. "That's me. Who the hell were you with in the Jacobean last night, by the way? Wouldn't have thought she was your type."

Lenny's cheeks turned red. "Don't ask."

Anna elbowed him in the side. "Tell him about the grasshoppers."

Lenny glared at her in mock annoyance, then laughed. "One, they have ears on their bellies."

"What?" Steve pulled a face.

"Apparently," Lenny said. "Two, they existed before dinosaurs. And what's the other one she mentioned? Oh, they spit to defend themselves."

Steve folded his arms. "Who told you all this?"

"My date."

Steve laughed. "She was trying to bin you off, pal. Bore you to tears."

"I gathered that." Lenny slid his hands into his pockets and cleared his throat. "Anyway, moving on . . ."

"Hmm," Anna said. "Probably best. Your dating exploits are atrocious."

Steve took a step back and jerked his head at the tent. "Any news on who could have done it yet?"

"We're off to see the man whose name keeps cropping up. Carys Brignell's ex-husband."

"Ah, boyfriend's head on a spike to make a point?"

Anna shook her head and whispered, "According to some, he wasn't her boyfriend."

"Oh." Steve nodded knowingly. "She plays around, does she?"

"Seems so. Right, we'd better get on."

They said their goodbyes, Anna's mind already on how she'd tackle Matthew. Quiet types usually took a bit of coaxing to get them talking, but they had all afternoon. She wasn't leaving his place until she'd got his measure.

CHAPTER TWELVE

Matthew jumped at the sound of the doorbell. He'd been expecting it, but still. A quick glance in the mirror above the fireplace, and he winced. Shame he'd had to mess up his face, but he *had* to protect himself. Getting the blame for murder wasn't in the plan.

At the front door, he took a deep breath, let it out, and opened up.

"What the hell happened to your *face*?" a forty-something woman blurted, her ID held mid-air, eyes wide. "Sorry, that was a bit of a shock. DI Anna James and DS Lenny Baldwin."

"Come in," Matthew said, less nervous now he'd seen these people looked so *normal*, not like the police at all. "I'll tell you about it over a cuppa. I assume you want one." He moped down the hallway, shoulders slumped to give them the idea he was the tragic recipient of a beating he hadn't deserved. "Someone jumped me in my back garden."

"What? Did you phone the police?" she asked behind him.

"No, I knew you were coming, so . . ." He flicked the kettle on, having filled and boiled it not long ago for something to do to calm his waiting-game nerves.

"I'll make that," the man offered.

Baldwin. The name matches his head. "No, no, you take a seat. I like to keep busy."

"But you said you were poorly when we spoke on the phone," Anna said. "It's fine, let Lenny deal with the drinks. I think you should come and sit down, tell me what went on."

So someone actually listened to me, then. She remembered my poorly comment. Matthew didn't know what to do with that so enjoyed the glow of it while he could. It reminded him of how he'd felt after he'd killed Nigel. He stuffed *those* thoughts away and sat opposite Anna at his little white table with two chairs.

"Start from the beginning," she said and leaned back, hands clasped over her tummy.

"But you're meant to be here to talk about an incident." Matthew frowned.

"That can wait. I'm concerned about your forehead. And this attack might be related anyway, so tell me."

No one had shown him this much concern since Carys at the start of their relationship, and even then that was bullshit. In reality, she'd only cared about *herself*. It had been a ruse to get him to go out with her, so she could spend his money and not her own. Once they'd married, she'd flipped a switch and life had changed.

Trying to contain himself, he adopted a suitably pained expression. "I was hanging the washing out and heard the garden gate click. When I turned, this man stood there."

"What did he look like?"

"Tall, like me. Black jogging bottoms and a hoody. The hood was up and pulled low, so I couldn't see his face. Slim." He'd described himself on purpose. That man smoking a ciggie had seen him in Geraldine's street and might tell the police about it. "Gloves."

"Did you recognise him?"

Did she ask that to trip me up? "I didn't see his face, remember?"

"What happened next?"

"I was going to ask him what he was doing in my garden, but he grabbed the back of my hair and dragged me over to the kitchen window." Matthew turned his head slightly to show Anna where some of his hair had been wrenched out. He'd remembered to get the gloves back out of the drawer and picked some strands off them and dropped them outside. He doubted forensics would come here about this, but he'd sorted it just in case.

She stood and inspected his head. "Ouch. So he pulled you across the garden pretty hard, then."

"Yeah."

She sat and thanked Baldy, who'd brought the teas over.

Baldy returned to the worktop and stood against the sink unit, cup held at his chest. "Did you try to get away from him or shout for help?"

Matthew shook his head. "I couldn't. It was all too quick. He smacked my face into the window frame three times. I asked him what he'd done that for, then he punched me in the face twice. I said something like, 'Leave me alone, what do you want?' He didn't answer, instead running down the side of the flats. I went inside — the gate's still unlocked, I didn't shut it — and had a look in the mirror to see what he'd done. I've got a bit of a headache now, and one of my teeth split the inside of my lip, but I'll live."

"What time did this happen?" Anna asked.

"I'm not sure. It was after you rang me, I know that much."

"Your forehead looks like it needs stitches," Baldy said.

"I'm not bothering the hospital with that, they've got enough to do. I've got some of those Steri-Strips. I'll be all right."

"We can't force you," Anna said, "but I advise you to get that looked at."

Her concern felt forced on him now, as if she was trying to back him into a corner. Like Mum used to. Matthew grew uncomfortable. Annoyed. His emotions always swung

70

back and forth like that, and he'd never got a handle on it. Still, used to hiding how he felt, he stuffed it deep inside. "Honestly, it's fine."

"We'll file a report on the attack, and I'll send someone to take an official statement, plus get people round to see if any neighbours saw or heard anything." She looked at Baldy. "Can you organise that for me, please?"

Baldy put his cup down and took his phone out.

Matthew's stomach cramped. He'd wanted this to happen, but it was all going too fast. "You said this might be related to the other incident. What's happened?"

Anna took a sip of tea. "I'll preface this by asking where you were last night."

He knew how this went and had anticipated telling her he had no solid alibi, but, if he'd changed his evening routine up until the point he went to bed, someone round here might have noticed. He'd switched all the lights off at his usual time, plus his phone.

"I was here."

Anna sat straighter. "Can anyone vouch for you on that?"

"No, I live on my own."

"Okay, what time did you go to bed?"

"Ten, like always. I prefer routine."

"What did you do before that?"

"Played *Piggy Kingdom* on my phone." And he had, before going upstairs and lying in the dark until he could go to the farm.

"What, *all* evening?"

"From about seven. I got home from work at around quarter to six, made dinner, had a shower." He'd done that, too, then put his black clothes and hoody on.

"When was the last time you saw your ex-wife?"

"Oh. Is this what it's about? Is she okay?"

"She's . . . well, she's as okay as she can be in the circumstances. So, when *did* you last see her?"

"Probably in the Kite. Can't remember when exactly. Not recently, though. I haven't been in there for a while."

"When did you last see Nigel Fogg?"

"Again, likely in the Kite."

Anna ran a fingertip around the rim of her cup. "I'll be honest and say we've found out about the affair between Nigel and Carys. How do you feel about that?"

"Gutted at the time, obviously, but she clearly wasn't happy if she was seeing him behind my back. I wasn't going to force her to stay with me, so I left."

"What are your feelings towards them now?"

"I've had a lot of time to think about it — we split a couple of years ago — and I'm at peace with it. We make mistakes, and these things happen for a reason. We should never have got married. We weren't suited. She's a high-maintenance party girl, and I'd rather sit and read a book or go on long walks. I should have told her I wasn't interested the first night we met and let Nigel get a look-in instead. He saw her first, but she fancied me. God knows why."

"Why *didn't* you walk away?"

Matthew shrugged and went with the truth. "I was chuffed a woman liked me instead of him, even if I *did* work out. It's because of my job and how much I earn. It explains why she went for my ugly mug. But Nigel's always overshadowed me with women. They prefer him to me. I allowed it to cloud my judgement. I convinced myself her crazy ways would calm down, that I wouldn't get a woman like her ever again so I'd better make a go of keeping her. I mean, look at me, I was punching above my weight."

Baldy snorted. "I know how *that* feels."

Matthew gave him a "plain men unite" smile. "Yeah, it's tough finding someone to even glance at you once, let alone twice. Carys is so pretty. Sadly, that's all she's got going for her." He hadn't meant to say that.

"What do you mean?" Anna asked.

Fuck. "She can be spiteful, cutting, and she lies a lot. That's a bit alarming for me as I tend to go with the truth."

"What kind of lies?"

"Stupid stuff, like she told someone she'd been skydiving when she hadn't. I asked her about it later, and she moaned I wasn't home enough to know *what* she was doing, so how would I even know? But something like skydiving, you'd be excited, wouldn't you? You'd tell your husband about that."

"Hmm, I would. Why do you think she tells lies?"

"She puts on this front, like she's a super-confident person, but maybe she doesn't feel she's interesting enough so makes up all those wild stories. Her mum and dad expect her to be perfect. Maybe she's desperate to come across that way, as someone who's got it all going for her. She wouldn't talk about her life before I met her. If I asked her about it, she said it was an invasion of privacy. She doesn't see her parents often, and there's no brother or sister. Whatever it is, I'm glad to be out of it. Living with her was . . . hard work. I'm an introvert, see."

"Same," Anna said. "Does Nigel have any distinguishing features?"

Matthew frowned at the abrupt change of subject. "Bit of an odd thing to say."

"Humour me."

He sipped some tea. "He's one of those pretty boys. Looks like Johnny Depp. Long black hair, a few tattoos, those black-and-grey sleeves everyone's getting at the moment. Got a mole on his chin, but the ladies seem to love it. What's going on?"

"Going by the visual ID we have, and confirmation from his sister regarding a tattoo behind his ear, I'm afraid we think he's deceased."

Matthew stared so hard that tears formed. "What?"

"Sorry to have to tell you that. We know you were close friends at one time."

"Oh my God. Julie. Is she okay?"

"She's devastated, as you can imagine."

"I'll need to help her with the funeral. She wasn't up to it when their parents died, and she's got no one else now. What . . . happened to Nigel?"

"We're not sure yet, but it's definitely murder."

"*What?*" Matthew rubbed his chin. "Bloody hell! I know we're not talking, but I wouldn't wish that on him."

Anna finished her tea. "Do you know anyone who'd want to kill him?"

Matthew shook his head. "Not kill him, no. Punch him in the face, yes, and there are several who'd do that. He's not good with tact, put it that way. He's offended loads of people over the years. No one's ever given him a wallop, even me, yet he hurt me the most. He's got a way about him where he says below-the-belt stuff, then brings you round to thinking he's joking."

"A prankster?" Baldy asked.

"More like a wind-up merchant."

"Right." Baldy wrote that down.

Matthew stood. "I need to see Julie. She'll be in bits."

"Two seconds," Anna said. "She's with Geraldine at the moment, so she'll be fine. We haven't finished here yet."

"Oh." Matthew sat.

"Is there anyone you've both offended? You *and* Nigel?"

"I try hard not to offend *anyone*. I'd rather walk away than get into a confrontation. And I haven't spoken to him in two years, so why would anyone associate me with him *now*? I've ignored him every time he tried to speak to me. And who the hell would wait that long to kill him and attack me anyway?"

"That's what I'm struggling to get my head around. What about boyfriends after you and Nigel? Know any of them?"

"I don't have a clue who she's seeing at the moment or why they'd have a problem with me. We're divorced, it's over, end of story in my eyes."

Anna stood. "Okay, that's it. Any wooziness, you get straight to the doctor, all right? We'll make a note that you refused to take our advice."

"That bad, is it?" he asked. "Having to cover your backs like that?"

Anna smiled. "We'll be in touch if we need to question you again."

He showed them out.

Two PCs stood at the front doors of the houses opposite.

Shit, that was quick, and all because of me.

It was weird, yet enthralling, to be so important.

CHAPTER THIRTEEN

Anna studied the area outside the three-storey block of flats, wishing she'd used Matthew's loo. If his attacker left via the side gate, he could have been spotted out here. A row of houses stood opposite and two officers were chatting at their doors.

Lenny came up beside her. "What do you think about him?"

"Seemed pleasant enough. Nothing to write home about. I understand the calm description now."

"Too calm?"

"As in he tried to come off as unruffled?" Anna shook her head. "No, it struck me that he really is that laid-back. Apart from his worry for Julie. He showed some proper emotion then. If we believe what we've been told, she's like a sister to him, so naturally he'll be concerned."

"A little strange he's *that* laid-back when it came to him being attacked. What I mean is, he waited for us to arrive instead of reporting it. He didn't fight the man off. He didn't display any unease when telling us about it. Don't you think that's weird?"

"You don't buy the calm facade?"

"No, it's not sitting right with me. Almost like he's coached himself to be that way before we arrived. I don't know, maybe he had a tough upbringing so he shields his feelings, keeps them hidden, but it's still off."

Anna messaged the team for them to poke into Matthew's past. "What do you reckon about Nigel and Matthew being targets? Carys is the common denominator."

"I thought the same. It can't have been her who whacked Matthew, though. He said it was a bloke, plus she'll still be at home. Or I'd have thought she would be, what with this morning's events."

Anna drew her coat fronts together and folded her arms over them. Although the sky was a lovely blue and the sun out, that wind was cruel. "A recent boyfriend who got the hump?"

Lenny sighed. "Enough to kill someone, though? Really?"

A worm of unease wriggled. "We're going to have to speak to Gordon, you know that, don't you? Even if just to warn him he might get punched next. Or murdered — he needs to be careful."

"It'll need to be a delicate chat, given that email from Placket. If it's even him."

"Especially when I ask him about the sex-with-food thing."

"Carys could have lied about that, too."

"It's outrageous enough for that to be a possibility." Anna couldn't hack standing around talking. She itched to get moving. "Let's put some booties and gloves on. Have a nose in that garden."

Suitably protected, she walked down the side of the building. A matching block of flats stood to her left, forming an alley with Matthew's. She took a photo of the gate so there was a record of how it had been left open, then went through onto textured patio slabs. The secluded area gave complete privacy, so there was no chance that any residents at the back behind the trees would have seen anything, but those on the second and third floors of the flats might have. Washing had been hung. There was a pair of trousers still in the basket on the grass.

She turned to study the kitchen window and jumped at seeing Matthew at the sink, washing the cups they'd used. She smiled at him and diverted her attention to the frame. Blood marred the white-painted wood in a smear, likely where his forehead had met it, and a droplet sat on the sill. She glanced down. A couple of small splashes on a mossy slab, dripped from a height, creating the familiar starburst pattern.

She argued with herself about what to do. Budgets and costs aside, she felt the garden could do with being checked over by SOCO. Resources were already stretched with forensics being at Carys's and in the car park behind Geraldine's, but the killer may have left something of himself behind here.

Matthew said the man had gloves on, though.

Still, she phoned it in.

"Good call," Lenny said.

"I thought the same. Come on, we'll help uniforms out by knocking at the flats — I want one of them to take Matthew's statement."

They split up, Anna organising the statement and then going upstairs in Matthew's block. The tenant on the second floor didn't answer, and, on the third, the lad hadn't seen or heard anything because he'd been asleep. He worked on the night shift at the chocolate factory, and she'd woken him up.

Back out on the street, she strode up to Lenny. "Any luck?"

"No one was in, but one of the PCs said there's a lady over the road who was out doing her weeding all day. She said no one left the alley but then admitted she'd had her back to the flats at one point."

"So our man could have waited down the alley until she turned away. Okay, I'll let the PC over there know to wait at the end of the alley for SOCO. I don't want to risk anyone else going into that garden. Stay put while I tell Matthew to remain indoors." She entered the flat foyer and knocked on his door.

He opened it and frowned. He'd put Steri-Strips on his forehead wound. "Did you forget to ask me something?"

"No, I just nipped by to say not to go in the garden. Forensics will be here shortly."

"So you're taking this seriously, then? Listening to me?"

Anna frowned back at him. "Why wouldn't I? You've been attacked, and it could be linked to a murder. I'd be a fool not to."

He nodded. "Thank you. For caring."

"It's my job."

"A policeman's here, taking my statement."

"Brilliant. Bye for now."

She emerged onto the street, pondering what he'd said. Didn't people usually listen to him? With evidence to show he'd been assaulted, of course she bloody would.

She spoke to the second PC about manning the alley, then got in the car and phoned Warren.

"All right, boss?" he asked.

"Yep, you?"

"So-so. Peter's been to the gym to ask about Nigel. No one there seems off. And Sally's had a nose into Carys's past. No priors. She's clean. She's currently having a look at Matthew."

"Okay. Before I forget, I need one of you to get on the ANPR cameras and check which vehicles left Spruce Way this morning — all morning, please, as I don't have a specific time to go on. If there are no cameras near the street itself, list cars and whatnot coming or going from that direction and find out who the drivers are. Someone's attacked Matthew Brignell in his garden."

"Bugger. Will do."

"Can you do me another favour? Time's running away with us here. Can you and Peter nip to the Kite and speak to the landlord and anyone who was at work there last night? I need you to ask about all the people me and Lenny have

chatted with today. I'll message you a complete list in a minute, plus what time they said they left."

"What are your thoughts so far? So I know which direction you're going in."

"I mainly want the lowdown on Carys Brignell, Matthew
Brignell, Nigel Fogg, and Gordon White."

"*DI White?*"

"Um, yes."

"Blimey. What's he got to do with this?"

"He's apparently interested in Carys. We're visiting him
next. After the pub, can you call in on Laura and Hannah
Baker, Carys's colleagues? I want to know which taxi company
they used. Find out as much as you can about all of them. Oh,
before I go, can you get me Gordon's address, please?"

The clacking of a keyboard, then Warren gave her the
information.

"Cheers."

She ended the call just as Lenny got in the car.

"Gordon's place?" he asked.

"Yep. I suppose we'd better see if he's at work or not first."

"If he isn't, he could be the station pervert." Lenny took
his phone out.

Anna got the engine going and drove away. Lenny put
Karen on speaker.

"I've nipped away from the front desk," Karen said. "I
was supervising a booking-in — some lout's been mouthing
off at us. Day drinking and assault on another customer in the
Horse's Hoof. I can have a quick chat because the duty sarge
has calmed him down. What can I do for you?"

"Is Gordon White in today?" Lenny asked.

"He was first thing," Karen said, "then he signed out.
Everyone's been speculating, if you know what I mean."

"Yep." Lenny gave Anna his devious look. "Out of interest, did anyone else sign out early?"

Anna slapped his arm and smiled. He was a sod when it
came to wheedling information out of people.

"You know I shouldn't say," Karen said, "not when there's an ongoing investigation and an officer is standing not three feet away from me. Blimey *O'Reilly*, it's got everyone talking."

"Thanks," Lenny said.

O'Reilly? He doesn't strike me as a perv. Anna filed that away for later.

"Fair's fair," Karen said, then whispered, "so now it's your turn to share. Why the interest in Gordon?"

"His name's cropped up in this case."

"Bloody hell, you think you know someone . . . What's he got to do with a murder?"

"He might not have *anything* to do with it," Lenny said.

Anna butted in. "Know him well, do you, Karen?"

Her heavy breathing filled the car. "Hang on, I'm going somewhere else. Johnson's in the staffroom." A clatter, a creak, then silence. "Right, I'm on my own now in the broom cupboard — the shit we have to do around here for a bit of privacy. Look, between us three, as soon as that email came in I knew it'd be Gordon, even before he signed out."

"How come?" Anna asked.

"I brought a salad in for lunch once and he asked if that was *all* I used a cucumber for."

"Oh, nasty," Anna said. "He's never said anything inappropriate to me."

Karen laughed. "I doubt *anyone* would. You'd soon put them in their place. Anyway, I told him not to be so disgusting, and he said he wasn't, he was about to give me some good advice."

Lenny clenched a fist on his knee. "Which was?"

"That Sainsbury's was cheaper than Ann Summers."

"Fucking arsehole," Lenny muttered. "Did you report him?"

"Did I heck," Karen said, "but I told him if I heard him saying that sort of thing to anyone else, I would. He probably thinks it's me who's dobbed him in. He gave me a filthy look when he left here earlier."

"A pervert masquerading as a joker," Anna said.

"The worst kind, if you ask me." Karen sighed. "I'd better get on. I'll let you know if I hear anything more. Are you down the Hoof after work?"

"Depends if anything crops up," Anna said, turning into Gordon's street. "But the way it's going at the moment, it's a lot of talking to a lot of people and not much else. The usual."

"Fair enough. Chat soon, my lovelies." Karen ended the call.

"Cucumber?" Lenny said. "How old is he? That's schoolboy humour. Can't say I've ever heard him saying anything inappropriate when I'm around either."

"Maybe because he knows you'd tell me and I'd give him what for."

Lenny smiled. "Glad I'm on your side, that's all I'm saying." He glanced out of the window. "Is this it?"

"Mmm, the house with the white door."

"Nice place."

Twenty-one Copse Court presented as a cottage but was more likely designed that way. It looked too new to be original, and, if she remembered rightly, this street was only about ten years old.

"Suppose we'd better go and see if he's in, then," Anna said. "But I'm warning you, if he says anything even slightly pervy towards me, I might lose my shit."

Lenny smiled. "Noted."

CHAPTER FOURTEEN

It was funny how kids from the same class could go such different ways when they got older. DC Peter Dove stood at the bar in the Kite and looked at his old mate behind it. Alfie Finch — aka Wheels, a former getaway driver for the Northern Kings gang — smiled, his gold tooth standing out among the white veneers.

"I see we're both baldies these days," Wheels said. "I shave mine by choice, though."

Wheels in fact knew Peter all too well, so this was for show in front of Warren. The secret between them lingered, and, at times like this, Peter wondered whether their connection was obvious. It was hard, being two people. Living two lives. He wasn't sure he wanted to do it anymore. His duty to the Kings had been overridden by his duty to the law.

He ran a hand over his head. "I had a monk spot that someone kindly pointed out. It had to go."

"Fucking tragic what age does to you. I see you brought a pal with you."

"Warren," Peter said. "A colleague."

"So you're here on official business, not to catch up after, what, more than thirty years?"

Another lie to hide the truth. "Afraid so."

"I'd never have pegged you as a copper. Couldn't believe it when I heard." Wheels poured two Cokes from the soda hose. "Especially after you nicked Todd's trainers that time."

"Because you dared me to," Peter said, his cheeks growing hot.

They were the only thing he'd ever stolen. He'd wanted to be a part of the Kings so much back then. Mike had started the gang when they'd been twelve, and all the lads had been desperate to belong. Sadly, it became more sinister than a few boys hanging around the park drinking canned lager and smoking robbed fags. They weren't people you wanted to mess with. Burglaries, beatings, drug dealing, you name it, all done below the radar. None of them had been nicked for their gang-related antics, although a few had been nabbed for doing shit on their own. A lad ten years younger than Peter and Wheels had been back and forth to prison so many times he'd earned the nickname Parole. As for Mike, known as Trigger — well, his nickname said it all. He dealt in guns, although where he kept them hidden had never been established. It hurt Peter that he'd never been privy to that information, as if they didn't trust him. Yes, he was a copper, but he was *their* copper.

"So, what d'you want?" Wheels asked. "I've retired from the Kings now, so if you're thinking of pinning anything on me you can get fucked."

"Yeah, right. You'll always take orders from Trigger. You never leave the Kings, even when you have."

So true. I'm still with them, albeit on the quiet.

Wheels nodded. "We made a pledge back then. *Some* of us stuck to it."

"I couldn't carry on once things went dark," Peter said to Warren, aware his colleague had perked up at the turn of the conversation. "I was only in the gang as a kid. Placket knows."

Warren shrugged. "Not my business." He stared at Wheels. "We're here with questions relating to a murder."

Wheels held his hands up. "Fuck all to do with me."

Warren snorted. "No, I doubt the MO is your style. His face wasn't slashed for a start."

"Your lot worked that out, did they? Our trademark." Wheels chuckled.

"Hmm." Warren glanced around. "Is there somewhere we can chat in private? It's busy in here. Too many ears wagging."

Led through the bar hatch into an office out the back, Peter leaned back on a hard wooden chair and Warren stood by the door.

Wheels walked round the desk and sat behind it, propping his feet on the top. "Ask away."

Peter listed the people who'd said they'd been in the Kite and what time they'd left.

Wheels nodded. "Yep, all correct. What else?"

"We have concerns about a man called Gordon White. There have been allegations of inappropriate behaviour. That shouldn't be passed on, by the way."

A bellow of a laugh came out of Wheels's wide-open mouth. "Gordon, the copper? He's no pervert, but O'Reilly is."

Peter hid his surprise. "Cormac O'Reilly?"

"Yep. Trigger's been watching him for a while, and so have I. I'm *that* fucked off with him. He pesters women, bugs them for sex. Touches them when he shouldn't. I've warned him to keep his hands to himself. I'll be teaching him a nasty lesson if he keeps on. His current fascination is with that Carys Brignell tart. *Her* current fascination — or it was until recently — was with Parole."

"So she's been cheating on Nigel with him?"

"Eh? She hasn't been Nigel's bit of stuff for yonks. Carys is in here every night, trying to cop off with whoever will have her. She tells her bullshit stories to anyone who'll listen if it means she gets to spread her legs. She's a sex addict, I reckon, or one of those people desperate for an emotional connection. What's this really about? You mentioned murder. Who's dead?"

"Nigel."

"Oh, fuck me sideways." Wheels lowered his feet off the desk. "And you think one of the Kings did it, is that why you're here?"

"No," Warren said, "but did they?"

"Like I'd tell you."

Peter took over. "How did things end between Carys and Parole?"

"He packed her in. She lied to him, so that was the end of that. If he wanted to get back at her, he'd have slashed her face, not gone after one of her blokes. You're barking up the wrong tree, pal. I'd have heard about this if it was Kings business, not that I'd ever admit it to the police if it was one of our hits. But it actually wasn't. You'll be wanting to have a nose at that O'Reilly fucker. Take a look at this."

Wheels brought his computer to life and accessed a file. He turned his screen round so they could see and opened a browser window. CCTV footage of inside the pub. He fast-forwarded to a specific point, then paused it.

"Now, I knew exactly where to stop on this because I checked the time it happened last night. I planned to black-mail the bastard with it." Wheels pressed play.

O'Reilly, talking to Carys at the bar, grabbed her breast and squeezed. She appeared disgusted and snatched at his wrist, yanking his arm away from her. He then went for her backside, taking a big handful, and she slapped his arm and said something.

"Did you hear what she said?" Warren asked.

"Told him to keep his filthy paws to himself, or some-thing to that effect. Oh, and to back off and leave her alone. Watch what he does when she walks off." Wheels hit play again.

O'Reilly took his phone out and appeared to be filming her.

"If that isn't pervert material, I don't know what is," Wheels said. "I'm telling you, he's a dangerous bastard."

Uncomfortable at seeing a colleague behaving like that, Peter shook his head. "I'll need a copy of that."

Wheels smiled. "Thought you might."

* * *

Laura and Hannah Baker worked as architects in the Gear Hub down Southgate. The only way Peter could tell the difference between them was their skirt suits. Laura's was pink, Hannah's blue. They'd been shown into a spare office, the twins sitting on a sofa, Peter and Warren in front of them on desk chairs. Their identical faces gave him the creeps. Twins always had that effect on him.

"Do you know why we're here?" Peter asked.

Hannah nodded. "Carys phoned in earlier, said she couldn't come to work today because her boyfriend's head was in her front garden. It had been chopped off or something. Is she bullshitting again?"

"Unfortunately not. Who's her boyfriend?"

"We don't know his name," Laura said. "Neither does Carys, but she's been seeing him every now and then. Only for sex, though." She blushed. "She said one marriage was enough to put her off for life, so she prefers to sleep around, no strings. What do you need to see us for?"

"We won't keep you long," Peter said. "We need to verify a couple of things. Did you go to the Kite with her last night?"

"Yes, straight from work," Hannah said. "We didn't even want to go. This is going to sound horrible, but we don't want to be associated with someone like her."

"What do you mean by that?"

"Erm, she's a slag."

"Hannah!" Laura slapped her sister's arm.

"Well, she is!"

Peter jumped in to prevent the squabble going further. "So why *did* you go?"

Hannah crossed her arms. "She's pushy, and she can be persuasive. That's why she's our top architect. She convinces customers to choose her way instead of theirs so she doesn't have to amend her designs. I don't like bullies, which is what she amounts to. It was easier to go than argue with her, though. I was too tired to get into a spat with her."

"Did you stay all evening?"

"Yes. We got a taxi about eleven. We asked the driver to drop her off first because we couldn't wait to get rid of her."

"What taxi company did you use?"

"ABC."

"Did you see any men acting inappropriately towards her?"

"Yes, that man called Gordon. She said he won't leave her alone and wants her to do rude stuff with food. To be honest, we're never sure whether to believe her because she's always lying."

Laura nodded. "We've caught her loads of times. We set traps to catch her out. Mind you, she was telling the truth about Gordon and the food. He said something about it to her last night. When he touched her boob and bum, I thought she was going to go apeshit. We're not fond of her, but she doesn't deserve to be mauled, even if she *is* free with her favours."

"Did she say anything else this morning when she rang in?"

"No. She told us about the head then put the phone down."

"Has she ever mentioned whether she feels animosity towards Nigel Fogg, a previous boyfriend?"

"Oh, is it his head, then?"

"It is."

"She was annoyed when he ended it. She'd been having an affair with him, and her husband caught them. She thought Nigel would marry her when she got divorced, but he stopped seeing her way before that. I doubt very much she'd do anything other than key his car or burn his clothes, to be honest."

Peter stood. "Okay, thanks for your time."

He and Warren left the Gear Hub and returned to the car.

"I thought Gordon was married." Peter started the engine.

"He is, but his wife left him, so the rumours say. Maybe he's having a mid-life crisis, going with a younger woman."

Peter shook his head. "Best get back to the station and put all this on the whiteboard. D'you reckon he's the perv in Placket's email?"

"God knows."

"I wouldn't have had him down as a deviant."

"Me neither, but some people are good at hiding things. Like the fact you ran with the Kings."

Peter swallowed. He'd been up front with his bosses from the start about that. "I explained earlier, and you said it was none of your business."

"In front of Wheels, yeah. I didn't want him to know it had shocked me. He said you haven't seen each other for thirty years. Is that true?"

"Of course it is." *Bollocks, is it.* "I wouldn't jeopardise my career by going back with that lot."

"Are you doing a Carys on me?"

Peter frowned. "What?"

"Lying."

Peter laughed. "Piss off, mate. The Kings are in my past. I was a kid when I left. I got out as soon as the bad stuff started. I said that earlier."

Warren stared out of the passenger window. Peter looked ahead, worried his cover might be blown. He'd joined the police because Trigger had told him to. They'd needed an inside man. Now Warren would be watching him like a hawk.

Fuck.

CHAPTER FIFTEEN

Gordon scowled upon seeing Anna and Lenny on his door-step. He crossed his arms in a defensive stance and glared at them, his eyebrows lowering. "I see the rumour mill's been working like the clappers, then. Placket's sent you to get inside my head, has he? Fucking typical."

Anna pulled a face. "Err, don't know what you're on about. We're here to get your insight into a woman called Carys Brignell."

Gordon appeared confused for a second. "Oh. Right. Well, in that case you'd better come in. Excuse the mess, I'm not the best housekeeper. The place has gone to the dogs since the wife left."

They assembled in his kitchen. Laundry in a pile on the floor, mainly whites, his work shirts. Washing up, stacked high in the sink — must have been there for a few days, the sauces dried. The place had a nasty smell to it, musty, and she wrinkled her nose.

"You've got a dishwasher there," she said. "Why not use it?"

"Haven't had the time nor the inclination." Gordon flumped onto a dining chair. "You of all people know what it's like, the job sucks everything out of you."

Anna, used to order and tidiness in her home, walked over to the window and opened it. A nice breeze wafted in, diluting the stench. She moved to a sink set in a centre island.

Despite him possibly being a pervert, she'd help him out, if only to calm her mind, which felt as cluttered as her surroundings. "Now don't go getting ideas, but this is doing my head in — I can't think in this mess. I'll sort the kitchen while we talk, but you're on your own with the rest of the house."

"Cheers." Gordon smiled, although it came across as sad. "Make us all a cuppa, will you, Len?"

Lenny hated being called that, it made him feel old. Anna bent to look under the sink, hiding her grin. She found some rubber gloves, checked there were no spiders inside — she'd been caught out before — and got on with rinsing the plates to loosen the dirt. Lenny reached over and filled the kettle, giving her a nudge while he was at it.

"If he calls me that again . . ." he whispered.

Anna ignored him else she'd laugh. "Right. Carys. What's your take on her, Gordon?" She stared across the island at him.

"Why do you even need to know?"

"Bear with me on that. Tell me what she's like." She started putting things in the dishwasher next to her.

"She's a rare breed. A good laugh when she wants to be. I've shagged her a few times."

Anna hid her distaste. "When was the last time you slept with her?"

"Last night."

Anna paused, a plate held mid-air. "Oh, right? Okay . . . What time was this?"

"I went round there after I'd been to the Kite. Thought I'd chance my arm, seeing as she'd been flirting with me. I got to hers about half eleven. I walked."

Anna carried on stacking. The kettle rumbled behind her. "Did you notice anything odd when you arrived?"

"Nope, everything looked the same. What sort of odd are we talking about?"

She dipped into the cupboard again and found a dish-washer tablet, dropped it inside and pressed the start button. There was too much crockery to fit in there, so she'd wash the cups by hand. Hot water on and a squirt of Fairy into the bowl, she said, "Someone lurking about."

"In Bishop's Lock? Not likely. They're all too Neighbourhood Watch posho types, so they'd have phoned it in if they'd seen someone."

Lenny took the tea over to the table and moved some hunting magazines so he could put the drinks down.

"Cheers, Len," Gordon said.

"It's Lenny."

"Right. *Lenny.*" Gordon smiled. "I only said it to wind you up, pal. Jesus." He glanced across at Anna. "What's she done, then?"

"Nothing illegal as far as we know." The cloth Anna had stuffed inside a cup squeaked as she twisted it. "These need bleaching. I don't know how you can stand drinking out of stained mugs." She found a bottle in the cupboard and squeezed some into the water, adding the cups one by one. She wrung a cloth out and wiped the island, already feeling better for putting a dent in the mess.

"The missus used to do all that," Gordon said.

"Obviously. Okay, what do you know about Carys's ex-husband, Matthew?"

"Bit of a loner. Quiet. Wouldn't say boo to a goose. It's the other one you ought to be worried about. Gobby little shyster."

"Nigel Fogg?" Lenny sat at the opposite end of the table to Gordon.

"Yeah, him. Thinks he's a comedian, except he isn't funny. Total twat. You know the sort, says what he thinks regardless of how it makes people feel."

Anna rinsed the cloth and gave Lenny one of her looks: *Watch him.* She turned to wipe the other worktops, her back to the men. "Funny, because we heard the same about you today. A lot of inappropriate chatter about sex with food."

"Eh? Carys said that, did she?"

"Two people, actually." Anna spun round in search of some spray cleaner and took it over to the cooker. "Is it true that you asked someone to get in a wheelie bin with you and have a bath with fruit in it?"

"Did I fuck! Who said *that*?"

Anna smiled, glad he couldn't see it. "You know I won't divulge that. So you're saying it isn't true?"

"No, it bloody well isn't."

"Thanks for establishing that. I had a feeling one person in particular was lying." She scrubbed at a stubborn piece of dried gravy. "What time did you leave hers?"

"About midnight."

"Just a quickie, then?"

"That's all I ever go there for. She's not relationship material."

"In what way?" Hob finally clean, Anna threw the cloth in the bowl and put away a few things — cereal boxes, a packet of sugar and the like.

"She's into partying, likes a drink, isn't the sort to settle down. I need a new wife, as you can see, and she's not it. I asked her if she'd come here and tidy up for me, and she said she never gets her hands dirty. Employs a cleaner."

"So you're on the lookout for a replacement, and in the meantime Carys will do for sex?" Anna returned to the island and checked the cups, then sorted clean water so she could rinse them off. She glanced up when Gordon took too long to answer.

"Yeah, we have an understanding."

Why didn't she say Gordon had been to hers? It would have established her alibi better. Why lie and make out he gave her the creeps?

93

"Someone told us you were angry in the Kite last night," she said.

"Err, nope, although I'd had a bad day at the office. I expect you'll be asking me about it next if Placket's opened his gob. He'd better not have."

"We all have bad days at work. I'm not interested in what went on, just whether you were angry enough to commit murder." She eyed him to catch his reaction.

Casually, he leaned back and picked his cup up. "Now I *know* you're taking the piss. Me, murder someone? What the hell would I even do that for?"

"Jealousy?"

"Jealousy regarding who?"

"Carys."

"Aww, come on now. You've met her? Seen what she's like? She's a good-time girl, nothing more. If she shags other people, that's her business. Like I said, we have an understanding."

"So you weren't in a mood because of her? You didn't tell her you hated Matthew and Nigel?"

"No! She's a liar. I haven't even told her my name, I wanted to keep things anonymous in case the wife comes back, so how the hell would she know it?"

That gave Anna pause. "We were definitely told it."

"Listen, you may as well know. I got signed off for six months today. Depression, but that's between us, all right? Since the wife left, I haven't been myself. Haven't wanted to do anything much, even work. Yesterday was particularly bad, and I fucked up. I snapped at someone we were interviewing, called him inappropriate names. He made a complaint, so I got myself a phone appointment in the afternoon with the doctor and told him the lot. I went into the station today to hand in my sick note. I wasn't angry last night, more like down in the dumps, so whoever said I was arsey is wrong. Maybe Carys got me mixed up with someone else. There's another Gordon who goes in that pub."

"We were told your surname, too."

Gordon appeared stumped.

Anna added, "And that you're a copper."

"I've never said what I do for a living to anyone in there, so this is all bollocks." He shoved a hand through his hair. "Hang on, O'Reilly uses the Kite. He's been sniffing around her. I saw him last night. He touched her arse and tit. Fucking lecher."

Anna made eye contact with Lenny, then switched to Gordon. "Did you receive the mass email this morning?"

"I never checked, too busy getting signed off. I had to hand in my work phone, and Placket said he'd change my email password until I came back because someone else will need to man the account."

"So you don't know about the investigation into sexual misconduct?"

"Jesus, no, I don't. Who is it?"

"They've been suspended. Only you and O'Reilly signed out around the time the shit hit the fan."

"And you thought it was *me*? Thanks for that. Who else will? Christ, I'm not a pervert! This is all I need when I feel the way I do. I'm meant to be taking it easy, sorting myself out."

"What if O'Reilly's been using your name?" Lenny asked.

Gordon slapped the table. "If that arsehole's been telling her he's me . . ."

"Calm your tits," Anna said. "Let's think about this for a second."

"There's nothing to think about," Gordon blustered. "O'Reilly's a filthy bastard and has been blaming it on me. Fucking Nora!"

"If we can put that aside for a minute." Anna sat at the table and sipped her tea. It had started going cold. "Did you see anything off when you left Carys's?"

"No. Look, what's this all about?"

"Someone put Nigel's head on a stake in her front garden during the night."

"You what?" Gordon shot up and paced. "It wasn't me! If she said it was, that's another lie."

"She didn't." Anna gulped her tea until it was all gone. "I'm going to need to use your loo. Is it as gross as the kitchen was?"

Gordon blushed. "Sorry."

"I'll clean that for you, seeing as you're struggling, but get someone in to do the rest of the house if you're not up to it. The mess won't be helping your mindset. Lenny, call Warren and get him to ask about O'Reilly while he's in the Kite." She checked the time. "Bugger, they've probably left by now."

She nipped off to the loo, cleaned it and the sink, then did her business. The towel hanging from a hook on the wall smelled decidedly iffy, so she didn't bother drying her hands and took it to the kitchen. She stuffed the pile of washing into the machine and set it on a hot cycle, pressing the button for it to switch to dryer mode afterwards.

"You're a good woman, Anna," Gordon said, back in his seat. "Fancy a husband?"

"Err, no."

"Shame."

Lenny shook his head at them. "Warren and Peter have already left the pub, but Peter said he'd ring the landlord and ask."

"Okay, so to recap." She looked at Gordon. "You have casual sex with Carys but nothing more."

"Right, and I won't be doing it again. I was warned she's a Bella Bullshitter but didn't listen. I'll go to the Hoof from now on an' all. So who the hell's killed Nigel, and where's the rest of his body?"

"No idea," Anna said. "One more thing, I'd advise you don't make any lewd remarks concerning cucumbers or anything of the sort, because people will get the wrong idea."

"Karen. That was a *joke*, ages ago."

"But you can see how it looks now that email's gone out, so watch what you're saying." She smiled to ease the sting. "Are you going to be okay when we leave?"

"I'll have to be. Got to get this sorted." He tapped the side of his head.

"No chance of your wife coming home?"

"No, she's sick of my hours. Got herself a flat."

"Which is why I'm not married." Anna collected the cups and washed them. "I can't be doing with being nagged. Okay, we're off. When that machine beeps, take that washing out and fold it so it doesn't get crinkled."

Gordon smiled. "You sound like my wife. God, I miss her."

Or you miss her doing the housework. "Things will get better, they usually do. I'll subtly let Karen know you're not the station pervert."

"Ta." Gordon stood. "You've given me a lot to think about. Not only with Carys but this place. It didn't even take you long to clean the kitchen. I'll have a bash at the living room when you've gone."

Anna felt sorry for him, but she'd done what she could, and now it was time to get back to work. A visit to O'Reilly was in order. Then she'd drive to the station and get the whiteboard updated. After that, home time. Or the Hoof for that drink. She needed to let Karen know Gordon wasn't a complete and utter filth-bag.

CHAPTER SIXTEEN

DS Cormac O'Reilly lived in one of the ex-council homes on a run-down estate in Northgate. Forty-two Blythe Crescent wasn't as tatty as its counterparts; at least, the outer pebble-dash walls were painted bright white, making the neighbouring homes appear shabby in comparison. Still, the Rowan estate had always been a place to avoid if you didn't live there. It was a strange little community where people either banded together to keep their secrets or shut certain folks out if they didn't "belong". The spice-heads roamed more abundantly in this area, gormlessly wandering the streets or acting up, depending on how the drug took them. That O'Reilly lived here was a shock. He always presented himself as "better than", peering down his nose at people. A disguise, then, to hide where he really came from?

Why stay here if he doesn't like being associated with it?

Anna was very much in the camp where, if you didn't like something, change it. Don't piss and moan then stay rooted in the same place. There was always a way out, even if it seemed you were surrounded by roadblocks.

She glanced at Lenny to get his take on it.

98

"Why's he living in this bloody dive?" he whispered at the front door. "No one *chooses* to stay on Rowan."

"Maybe he grew up here." Anna pressed the bell button. The chime was dull from inside. Furniture deadening the sound? "He might have an emotional attachment to it. Lots of memories."

Her childhood home sprang to mind. A council house in Westgate, the better part of the city. Nice and tidy, Mum houseproud, always cleaning and doing the washing. Anna had grown up safe and loved, the right balance of freedom and rules in place. She had no hang-ups from her upbringing, no trauma, no bad memories to hinder her adult life. She'd had it good, grateful to have been given the opportunities she had. A few might say she couldn't possibly understand some offenders, those with unsettling childhoods, lives that led inevitably to crime. But she tried to empathise, to put herself in their shoes in order to see why traumatic experiences affected their decisions.

Her phone bleeped, and she glanced at the screen.

Peter: *Been to the Kite. O'Reilly is a person of interest.*

Anna: *Funny you should say that. We're at his now.*

Peter: *Got CCTV for you. Catch you later.*

She showed Lenny the messages.

"Jesus," he said.

A shadowy figure approached the mottled glass in the door, and she tensed. Now they knew Gordon wasn't the pervert, O'Reilly was very much in the frame. Or had the real perv been told not to sign out of the station so no one suspected him? Innocent until proven guilty, that type of thing?

The door swung open, and O'Reilly rolled his bulging eyes. He'd always reminded Anna of a frog.

"Come to arrest me, have you?" he barked.

Anna frowned for effect. "Err, nope."

O'Reilly's features relaxed. "Oh. I thought Placket had sent you."

Knowing O'Reilly's penchant for being bolshy, Anna chose the path of least resistance. "No, we're here to pick your brains regarding a case we're on. Got a spare minute to chat?"

O'Reilly nodded and folded his arms. "Go on, then."

"Inside?" Anna prompted.

He glanced over his shoulder, then back at her. His cheeks stained pink. "Can't it be here?"

"It's delicate. I don't want your neighbours hearing anything regarding our inquiry."

O'Reilly sighed. "One word to anyone about my house, and I won't be happy."

"We haven't come here to see the house." Anna put one boot on the threshold.

O'Reilly stepped back, turning to walk down the hallway. A mixed pile of trainers and brogues sat on a shoe rack to the left. He led them into a living room. Anna sucked in a sharp breath. Where Gordon's place had been untidy, O'Reilly's was a hoarder's paradise. Junk filled the space, apart from a small area saved for a grubby brown recliner and a clear alleyway through the mess leading to it. Stacked cardboard boxes, four or five high, reminded her of the homeless quarter in Eastgate, towers constructed to ward off the inclement weather. In between lay shoeboxes, some of the lids open to reveal trinkets, papers, and God knew what else, as though O'Reilly had recently rooted through them.

Her head buzzed amid the clutter. Too much stuff made her uncomfortable, and she concentrated hard to ignore it.

O'Reilly sat on the chair. "Not a word." A six-foot wooden giraffe peered down at him, a green blanket draped over its back, emulating a saddle.

Anna and Lenny remained inside the doorway, their shoulders touching due to the lack of room. She itched to put things in order, but understood that to muscle in on a hoarder's possessions wasn't the way to go. These things would be precious to him, even if she deemed it unnecessary crap. And besides, she didn't think O'Reilly was as receptive as Gordon when it came to accepting help. But really, no one needed this many lamps, cushions, and crocheted blankets.

"It's all my mum's," he said. "I haven't got round to chucking it yet. I've made a start by having the outside painted, but that's as far as I got. This is her house — was. I grew up here. Hated it because people thought I was scum. You know what they say about the Rowan estate."

"Why live here, then? Why not sell it?"

He cleared his throat. "I moved back in when she . . . when she died."

"How long ago was that?" Lenny asked.

"Ten years come Christmas."

Anna sensed O'Reilly had only offered the explanation so they didn't go away and pick his life apart, supposing this and that about him. Time to get off the subject. "Sorry, but we need to crack on. What do you know about Carys Brignell?"

"What, the little slapper down the Kite?"

Anna glared at him. "The *woman* who goes to the Kite, yes."

"She's a prick-tease."

Christ, he's one of those *men.*

"Is that the sole impression you got from her?"

"You could say that."

"Why is she a tease?"

"She wants me, I know she does, but she makes out she doesn't. Plays hard to get."

And I suppose if women didn't wear short skirts, they wouldn't be raped. "Have you ever discussed sex in wheelie bins and baths of food with her?"

He chortled. "Yep, to see how easy she was. You know, whether she'd spread her legs for just anyone, no matter how odd they are."

So she wasn't *lying?* "Did you tell her your name is Gordon White?"

O'Reilly laughed. "Wow, she *has* been talking, hasn't she? Yes, I did. I thought she'd correct me, but my suspicions were right. He's fucking her but hasn't told her his name. Wants to keep it quiet in case his wife comes back. Prat."

"Did you sexually assault her last night in the Kite?"

"I touched her boob by accident, if that's what you're referring to. I reached across to pick up my pint, and my arm brushed it."

"Did you accidentally touch her backside, too?"

"Now hang on just a minute. Has she made a complaint about me?"

"Not an official one, no. It came up in conversation. What time did you leave the Kite?"

"About half ten."

"Where did you go?"

"To the kebab van on Church Street in Southgate."

"Did you walk all the way into town?"

"Yes. Got there about eleven. CCTV will be your best friend and my ally."

Smug bastard. "What did you do after that?"

"Got a taxi home, 123 Cabs direct from the rank. Arrived here around ten past. Ate my food, watched two episodes of *The Tower* on Apple TV. Went to bed. Got up for work, got called in to see Placket, who informed me that another accidental brushing of my hand on PC Jahinda's tit in the canteen yesterday had resulted in immediate suspension while an investigation takes place. I'm sure you've heard about that."

"Seems you accidentally brush people's private areas a lot," Anna said. "Can anyone verify you were home all night?"

"Nope, but I suppose that will be held against me, too."

"There are witnesses to you inappropriately touching Carys. Were any people present with Parvati Jahinda?"

"One or two."

"Unlucky for you. Do you know a Nigel Fogg?"

"One of Carys's old fuck buddies. A dickhead."

"Did you know he's dead? Murdered?"

For the first time, O'Reilly's cocky demeanour faltered. He blinked several times and stared at her. "Are you accusing *me*?"

"Did I say that? I asked if you were aware of him."

"Yes, I am. And no, I didn't realise he was dead."

"Do you know her ex-husband?"

"What, that weird twat, Matthew? Yeah, I've seen him in the pub a time or two, but not for ages."

"Why do you say he's a twat?"

"All those bookworm types are. Fucking weirdo. Living inside a fabricated world so he doesn't have to face the real thing."

"I'm a weirdo as well, then," Anna said. "Good to know. I really had no idea until you informed me. So . . . going by what you've said and how you come across as disliking Matthew and Nigel, where were you this morning?"

"I got sent home from work and went to Sainsbury's, the one in Bridge End shopping centre. Had some lunch at Five Guys, again in Bridge End, then went and had my hair cut in Jack of All Fades."

"Also in Bridge End?"

"Yep. I arrived home just before you two turned up. CCTV and ANPR will be your buddies again there."

Anna felt whatever she said he'd have a response for it. Where he'd been, what he'd done, what he'd watched on TV — he couldn't be tripped up. Of course, he could be innocent of murder, but as for sexual misconduct he was guilty as sin.

She smiled tightly. "We'll check all that out, obviously. Thanks for your time."

"What, you're not going to tell me what Meek Matty has to do with your line of questioning? Has he been bumped off an' all?"

"No. He was assaulted in his garden today by a man matching your description."

"Righty-ho, so it *must* be me, then." He shook his head. "Look, I know how this works, how you'll be desperate to pin this on someone and wrap things up, but it's sod all to do with me, all right? I've got the sexual assault bullshit going on — and it *is* bullshit — so now you want to kick a man when he's down. Been there, done it myself with suspects. But I'm telling you, I went nowhere near Matthew's place. I don't even know where he lives. Check the database at the nick to see if anyone's looked him up before today. You'll find they probably haven't, so no, I didn't use police resources to see where he lived so I could go and do whatever to him. I didn't touch Nigel either. One thing stands out in all this, though. Carys. Maybe poke into her a bit more. She's a loon and a half."

Lenny scoffed. "So why chat her up?"

"She's an easy lay. Got to get it where you can, haven't you?"

"Have you ever had sex with her?" Anna asked.

"Nope."

"Do you have a grudge against Nigel and Matthew? You supposedly said you hated them for being with Carys. What's that all about?"

"I meant that she'd gone with them when she wouldn't even give me the time of day."

"I've got to clear something up." Anna couldn't let what he'd implied go by without pulling him up on it. "I don't appreciate the inference that I want to wrap cases up quickly regardless of whether we have the right man. That is *not* who I am. I'm also not in the habit of kicking a man while he's down. I'm here to ask questions because your name came up in our investigation, and that's *all*."

"Touchy," O'Reilly said. "But then you always were."

"No, I'm straight as an arrow, always have been, and someone saying I'm bent pisses me off."

"Everyone's fit for turning. Are we done?"

"For now." Anna couldn't wait to get out of there. She'd known O'Reilly was a smug, self-absorbed bastard, but she

104

hadn't realised how much until today. Or that he enjoyed playing mind games.

No wonder Carys dislikes him.

Anna walked out, relieved to smell fresh air rather than the accumulated dust in the house. She got in the car and waited for Lenny, processing everything that had been said.

One thing was for sure. That man wasn't safe to be around. She hoped PC Jahinda's accusation stuck.

CHAPTER SEVENTEEN

Anna sat at her desk for a moment to recalibrate, the door to her office closed. She'd been on the go all day and her throat was tight from so much talking, her mind buzzing with all the information, not to mention the residual memory of O'Reilly's cramped house.

Sometimes, she needed a second to breathe, to be alone. She made a good show of hiding her introversion, otherwise she'd never get things done, but people tired her out, as did pretending they didn't. Humans were energy thieves, some of them vampires of joy. Plus O'Reilly's insinuation about her had hit a nerve. She was a good woman, would never twist the facts to benefit a case, and the idea that he thought she might do that upset her. Did other people see her that way, too? Or was he just a dick when it came to women and liked to cast aspersions, toying with their emotions?

She leaned her head back on her chair and closed her eyes. She did one of her meditation exercises to centre herself. Blanked her mind. Listened to the stillness within. And peace flooded over her.

Until O'Reilly's jibes barged into her head again and ruined it all. *Fucking weirdo.* She'd been called that many times while growing up, but, like Mum had said, better to be that kind of weirdo than the other. Better to read books than go out and hurt people.

Anna's love of mystery fiction — starting with the tame Famous Five books by Enid Blyton and *Scooby-Doo* on the telly — had influenced her career choice, no doubt about it. All those secrets to solve, the clandestine nature of it. She loved the big reveals, how everything came together, and hoped it would happen with this case, too.

A quiet tap on her door, and she opened her eyes. Lenny peered through the glass wall, his face sliced into three segments by the vertical blinds. He held a cup up, and she nodded, rising to open the door and join him in the incident room.

She took the coffee from him. "Thanks."

"Thought you'd like one to go with your contemplation. Sorry to have disturbed you. I know how much you need the space."

"It's fine, I feel better for having a couple of minutes. It all gets a bit much sometimes."

"Gordon's and O'Reilly's gaffs. They did your head in, didn't they?"

"They did." She strode towards the whiteboard at the front, and her professionalism took over. "Right, let's have a recap so we're all on the same page." She placed the cup on a grey filing cabinet beside a pot of thick marker pens of various colours. "First, what happened at the Kite?"

Peter stretched his legs out under his desk. "Everyone who said they were present last night told the truth, right down to the times they left. The landlord, Wheels, said Gordon isn't our pervert, it's Cormac O'Reilly. Trigger's had his eye on him for a while."

"Christ," Sally said. "I had a feeling it was him. He's always looked at me funny."

Anna sighed. "I thought Wheels had retired from the Northern Kings? I assume he told Trigger about O'Reilly."

"Yep," Peter said. "Although he *says* he's retired now, he's still in with Trigger. Everyone knows that, which is why most people behave in his pub. Wheels is naffed off that, despite him warning O'Reilly, he keeps pestering the female punters. Reckons he's going to teach him a lesson if he keeps on."

Anna winced. "I hope he doesn't. I don't want to have to visit him if O'Reilly turns up here to report a beating. Saying that, the Kings work under the radar so we can never pin anything on them, so I doubt Wheels would drop them in it by association. He wouldn't want to upset Trigger. Maybe it was bluster, Wheels chatting shit."

"Maybe," Peter said. "We've got a copy of the CCTV from the pub. I've passed it on to Placket so it helps with the misconduct case at the station. It clearly shows O'Reilly touching Carys inappropriately, on purpose, so if he tries to worm his way out of it we've got proof."

Anna pursed her lips. "O'Reilly told us different, didn't he, Lenny?"

Lenny nodded. "Reckoned it was an accident."

"Absolutely not," Warren said. "He's the station perv, all right."

"He admitted as much to us," Anna said. "I wouldn't usually bandy someone's name about in this situation but, as it could pertain to the case, the lady in question regarding his suspension is Parvati Jahinda, but we will *not* put her name on the board in case anyone wanders in here and sees it. I want to protect her privacy."

"Shit, poor Parv." Sally let out a long breath. "She's so sweet, too. Good for her on reporting him."

"I've checked," Lenny added, "and she's still on duty today."

"Maybe she was advised to continue working so no one put two and two together when they noticed she wasn't on shift," Anna said. "We'll keep that info to ourselves, but bear it in mind if O'Reilly's looking likely to be our murder suspect. He certainly matches the height and build description Matthew gave of his attacker."

Lenny stood and stretched. "Carys has been with Nigel and Matthew. She's our link, although obviously we should be open-minded as to whether it's a coincidence."

Warren chuckled. "What, a coincidence that her boyfriend's head was left in her front garden and her ex-husband's had his face smashed against a window? Come on, pal."

"We can't get tunnel vision, that's all I'm saying."

"I agree," Anna said. "Let's not forget she went with Gordon, too. Is there anyone else we need to be worried about?"

Peter held up his pen. "Wheels said Carys kept going home with some bloke from the Kings recently, Joshua Cribbins."

Anna rolled her eyes. Parole. "Christ, what was she doing with him? He's a crook, has tatts all over his face. Doesn't seem her type."

"Danger?" Sally suggested. "Notoriety? His sort has a certain allure."

Peter tapped his pen on his thigh. "It didn't last long, a few nights over a couple of weeks."

Anna's stomach turned over. A lead? "So he could have killed Nigel?"

"Why go after her exes, though?" Warren asked. "The Kings are better known for going directly for the person who pissed them off. Targeting Nigel and Matthew isn't their style."

Anna tilted her head. "Is that your perception or something Wheels said?"

"Wheels outright told us, if Parole had something to do with wanting to get back at Carys, he'd have more than likely slashed her face."

"Still, it's worth speaking to him anyway to tie up any loose ends," Anna said. "But that can wait until tomorrow. Parole also fits the description of Matthew's attacker, bar the tattoos. Matthew didn't see his face, which might be why the hood was pulled low, to hide the inkwork. What else did you get?"

Peter picked up his cup. "Nothing except Carys is a regular. She's in the Kite every evening, telling her 'bullshit stories' to anyone who'll listen — Wheels's words, not mine."

Anna checked the whiteboard. It had been updated already. Lenny must have added everything while she'd been taking a moment to herself. A photo of Nigel had been placed at the top on the left-hand side — Sally had probably found it on social media — and Anna's assumption that he'd looked like his sister was correct. And yes, he had a Depp air about him. Next to that, Matthew's and Carys's pictures. In the second half, Gordon, O'Reilly, and Parole. All five men had Carys in common. She plucked a name for the case out of the air and wrote it at the top. *Operation Jewel.*

Anna summed it up. "Everyone who was in the Kite told the truth. I see on the board that the times Wheels said they left match what they told us. Anything back yet on the car park behind Geraldine's house?"

"An email came in saying his Audi has been taken in," Warren said. "Ivy Rhodes, an old lady opposite, heard a vehicle starting up. She assumed it was Nigel's car, but as that was still there it had to have been the killer's."

"What about CCTV?"

"Nothing yet," Sally said. "There are no cameras around Bishop's Lock or in the vicinity of Spruce Way, where Matthew lives."

Anna clenched her fists. "So we're dealing with someone who either knows where the cameras are to avoid them or got lucky both times."

"I roped a uniform in to help me. He's still on it, going over all the footage again."

Anna released a breath. "Right, so we've got sod all with regards to who this could be. Lovely. What about Matthew's past? Did you have time to check that, Sally?"

"I did. He went to Westgate primary then Westgate secondary. No criminal record. Grew up on Hawthorn Farm. Mother deceased when he was eighteen. Eaten by pigs."

"Erm, *what*?"

"I don't think you were here when that happened."

Anna had done a stint at Nottingham nick once upon a time. "Probably why it's news to me, although now I'm thinking of it I've got a vague recollection of it being in the papers."

Sally smiled. "Placket was the SIO on that. It was put down as accidental death on account of how pigs behave. I checked, and they can be nasty little things. Who knew? The father's still alive. I got hold of one of Matthew's secondary school teachers who still works there, an old boy, and he said Matthew was always eager to learn. I'm looking into his friends, but it seems he's a generally nice bloke."

Does he even have friends if he's a loner and he stopped speaking to Nigel? "Julie Fogg has known him for years because of his friendship with her brother, and she said he's a good man. Maybe I'm guilty of thinking something that isn't there. He could just be a normal bloke with a tragic death in his past, nothing more. He could have taught himself to regulate his emotions in order to cope with what happened to his mother."

"Imagine that," Peter said. "Pigs eating your mum."

Anna clapped. "Right, let's go through everything else and then call it a day. With forensics and Herman busy on this, we haven't got much else to do until we get any news from them. We'll pay a visit to Parole tomorrow. We'll all be doing weekend overtime, obviously. What did you get from Laura and Hannah Baker, Carys's colleagues?"

Peter picked up his notebook. "They only went to the pub with her because she railroaded them into it. They normally avoid her because she's a fibber — seems everyone feels the same way — but they left in a taxi together. They asked the driver to drop her off first because they didn't want to spend any more time in her company."

"Why couldn't they have just said no, they didn't want a drink with her?" Anna asked. "If you don't want to do something, just bloody well say so."

Lenny laughed. "We've had this convo already today, me and you."

Anna remembered him talking about his date. "Hmm. We're obviously all made differently. I'd say bog off, no thanks."

They discussed everything else and watched the CCTV from the Kite. O'Reilly was a definite pervert, and it churned Anna's stomach.

The clock ticked over to half five, and she thanked them for their work today. "Is everyone up for going to the Hoof for a quick one?"

"I can't," Sally said. "I've got to pick my son up from after-school club."

"Me and Peter are playing squash," Warren said. "Court's booked for six."

"You were hopeful we'd be finished on time." Anna smiled.

"I took a punt."

That left Lenny.

"Are you coming?" Anna asked.

Lenny nodded. "Do wolves howl?"

She laughed. "I shouldn't have even asked. I suppose you'll want a lift home an' all."

"Do bears shit—"

"Pack it in!"

She nipped into her office to switch off her computer. When she came back out, the team had gone, so she checked everything had been powered down and met Lenny in reception. Karen stood beside him, her fur-collared leather flying jacket zipped up, a red scarf tied tightly.

"Got any goss?" Karen asked.

Anna nodded. "We did."

"Oh goody."

They all walked down the road to the Hoof, Karen babbling about her day. In the pub, Anna ordered the first round — she'd be having lemonade as she was driving — and they sat around a table away from other officers.

"Shit," Anna said. "I forgot to pop in and update Placket."

"Oh, he left at three," Karen said. "Reckons he had a dentist appointment."

"Reckons?" Lenny queried.

Karen smirked. "Someone phoned and asked for him ten minutes before he buggered off. A woman. She sounded like she was disguising her voice. All of a sudden he's telling me he's got to go have a filling done. Must be hiding something, no? So, what's the deal with Gordon?"

Anna lowered her voice. "It isn't him. He said the cucumber thing was a joke."

"So, who is it, then? O'Reilly?"

"Yep." Anna sipped her lemonade. "He admitted it to us, although he's basically saying it's a misunderstanding."

Karen's eyes widened. "Who was he pervy to?"

Anna nudged Lenny's knee under the table. "That we don't know."

Karen shook her head. "Bloody hell, that's a turn-up for the books. O'Reilly always seems so up his own arse that he'd never do anything like that."

"Men like him are good at acting one way while thinking another," Lenny said. "I don't buy the accidental brushing story."

Karen frowned. "What are you on about?"

Anna whispered, "This must stay between us, okay?"

Karen nodded. "I only gossip to you two, you know that."

"Well, we've got him on CCTV at the Kite, touching up one of the people involved in Operation Jewel."

"The head-on-a-spike case?"

"Yes. He can't wriggle his way out of this one." Anna got a whiff of food as a server walked past with two plates.

Tiredness overcame her, and the thought of cooking didn't appeal. "Sod it, I'm having my dinner here."

Lenny rubbed his hands. "It's my turn to pay."

Karen gulped some of her lager and lime. "Not for me. I've had a beef curry in the slow cooker all day."

"What are you having, Anna?" Lenny asked.

"Steak pie and chips."

Lenny got up to order, and Karen dived into a story about an offender who'd been brought in for stealing someone's knickers off the washing line. Anna didn't miss those days, dealing with people like that. She preferred the grittier side of things, a proper puzzle to solve.

Well, she definitely had one of those at the moment.

CHAPTER EIGHTEEN

Matthew parked the Transit a street away from the Kite. Hood up, head down, he walked to the pub, conscious that at this time he'd be seen. Quarter past seven on a Saturday night might be inviting trouble, but when he nabbed his target it would be darker, and any sightings of him now would be forgotten; he was "just some bloke" off for a bevvy.

He'd left his phone at home, powered down. It wasn't unreasonable for the police to assume he'd gone to bed early. After all, he'd supposedly been poorly and sent home from work, plus he'd been attacked.

He stood down the side of the Kite at the corner of the building. From there, he could poke his head round if anyone left the pub or dip backwards into the shadows if someone approached. He had a long wait on his hands, but that was okay. It would give him time to stir his anger. He couldn't afford to have the same thing happen that had occurred with Nigel, where his rage had threatened not to show itself.

He zoned out and visited the place inside his head where the memories lived. Lots of anger resided there, enough to fuel him tonight if he could harness it.

CHAPTER NINETEEN

The Remember Room

Matthew walked through the alleyways of his past. None of them were in chronological order, they linked together like word association, only instead of words it was emotions or images or events. He opted for the route towards his biggest bout of anger prior to finding Carys and Nigel in bed together. Anger that had grown in layers through his childhood to explode in one shocking moment.

Mum had been using him for five years, whispering filthy things, telling him to do what no son should to his mother. He'd been confused by how she could want to do this when she'd always made it clear she didn't like him. He'd also been confused by how his body had betrayed him the first time, that, even though he didn't want to, he'd become excited. She'd always touched him down there as far back as he could remember, drying him after a bath long after he could have done it himself. But this, this touching was different. More. Wrong. A viler form of control.

It had happened most nights, while Dad, tired from working the farm, napped on the sofa. Matthew envied him his oblivion, a great ball of jealousy knotting in his stomach because of it.

As isolated as he'd been growing up, only leaving the farm to go to school, Matthew had lived by Mum's rules, doing whatever she said. She'd moulded him into an automaton, he could see that now, quickly erasing any anger that reared its head inside him, forcing him to meditate to remain calm, to accept what she did. He'd been conditioned, her training him to be the man she wished she'd married, someone without a temper.

Matthew veered down another alley, the word "temper" changing his path. This alley had tall buildings either side, so high they seemed to go on forever, kiss the sky, the dark clouds greeting the incoming storm.

Ahead, Dad worked on his harvester in the yard, the farmhouse beyond. It had broken down on the way to one of the fields, stalling on the country road and creating a tailback, the engine spluttering. A recovery lorry had brought it back, and Dad muttered about the inconvenience and how, if he didn't get it fixed, he risked losing his potato crop. He had a specific day each year to dig them up, something about tradition and superstition.

"I bet it was that fucking bitch," Dad mumbled in the cab, head bent near the controls. "She's snipped part of the bloody wires, look. Shit . . . I should have just bought her that stupid bracelet she wanted instead of standing my ground."

They must have snapped while Dad drove. Maybe his knee had snagged them and broken the connection.

Matthew drew closer, leaving the alley and stepping into the grey-drenched area, how he always saw his thoughts. A rumble of thunder rolled through the air, a faraway spear of lightning jabbing a bulbous, black-bottomed cloud. Fat droplets of rain came on suddenly, drenching him.

"What the fuck are you standing there getting soaked for, kid?" Dad shouted and jumped down from the cab. "In the house, quick."

Matthew dashed after his father, the rain hard, pelting his head, his back, seeping through his checked shirt. They toed off their boots in the mudroom, then lumbered into the kitchen. Mum stood at the Aga, stirring something on the hob.

"Did you fuck with my harvester?" Dad stalked up to her and folded his arms.

117

A smug smile stretched her pretty face.

"You did it to mess with my head, didn't you?" Dad asked. "You know how funny I am about harvesting on the right day. What did you want to achieve? To prove my spuds would be okay if they're pulled up tomorrow? To prove me wrong? Or is it over that bracelet?"

What a strange conversation. How stupid for two people to war over something that in all honesty didn't matter. Dad digging his heels in, Mum wanting to make a point. No one else could have clipped the wires, it was only the three of them at the farm. Dad wouldn't have sabotaged anything, and Matthew certainly hadn't.

"The potatoes will still be fine tomorrow," she said.

"This is that control thing, isn't it?" Dad said. "You've always got to orchestrate everything. Well, like I told you, the farm is my business, I know it better than you, so back off."

"There's a new set of wires, I bought them, and tomorrow morning I'll give them to you."

Matthew frowned. This was what she did, played God. She pulled their strings, tugging them into doing what she wanted. At eighteen, Matthew had left behind the boy who'd always wanted to please her, instead growing to hate her, to hate who she'd made him. Someone who craved his mother's touch yet detested it at the same time. Hanging around with Nigel at school, then college, and now uni had shown him that his mother wasn't right in the head.

And he'd had enough.

Mum gathered heaps of vegetable peelings and put them in a carrier bag as though Dad wasn't looming over her, as angry as the storm in the heavens. She cooked in batches, freezing portions to eat throughout the month. "I'm going to feed this to the pigs. It'll give you time to calm down. You should take a leaf out of Matthew's book on that score. Anger doesn't suit anyone."

She turned the heat down under the huge saucepan and breezed past Dad, who caught hold of her arm, swinging her back round to face him.

"We need to talk," he said. "This can't go on."

Mum smiled. "You know it's pointless trying to threaten me, I'm going nowhere. Your secrets could land you in trouble."

"I should never have told you."

"If I hadn't found it, none of this would be happening. You wouldn't have had to confess. But here we are!"

What was "it"?

She swaggered into the adjoining mudroom. Matthew stared after her. She stuck her feet into her wellies and shrugged on her raincoat. Paused at the door to look back at him, at his crotch, a gesture to warn him that she held all of his secrets, too, ones she'd engineered into existence.

Ones he no longer wanted to share with her.

She opened the door, admitting a bellow of thunder, then she was gone.

Matthew turned towards Dad.

"She touches me," he blurted. "She makes me have sex with her."

Dad's face contorted, and he staggered to the side, bumping into the unit beside the Aga. "W-what? What? That fucking evil bitch . . ."

It happened so fast. Dad stomping into the mudroom, putting his boots on, no coat. Flinging the door open and flying into the yard. Matthew remained calm, hating that calm, because that was her legacy living inside him. He tried to shirk it off, to feel the same anger Dad did, but the serenity wouldn't leave. He wandered into the mudroom, slipped his boots on, dazed, the whispers in his mind telling him Mum would be in for it. Dad's temper could never be tamed once it was up, and there would be no going back now. Whatever secret his parents kept between them would be cast aside. Dad was too incensed not to do something.

Matthew stepped out into the stair-rod rain and closed the door. He ran across the small field towards the pig barn, Dad halfway there, Mum just going inside. Another belt of thunder vibrated the ground, shivering up Matthew's legs. He called on the anger again, but it ignored him. Dad had reached the barn and disappeared through the doorway. Matthew pushed himself harder, going faster, barrelling inside.

Mum stood on the middle rung of the pen fence, bending over, the carrier bag held upside down, peelings falling. Pigs trotted over, snorting, scoffing the food, some going without and squealing their annoyance. She'd shed her coat, which hung on a fence post.

Dad walked up behind her, shouting, "What have you done to my son?"

Mum turned her head to stare down at him, then glanced at Matthew. For the first time, fear flitted across her face, then it vanished, replaced by her smugness. And he knew, he fucking knew she was going to try to point the finger at him. Why, though, when she always said she hated being married to Dad? Why was she about to say Matthew was a liar so her husband wouldn't hit her with that clenched fist of his? Was it the control Dad had mentioned? Did she love it that much she was prepared to live here in misery?

"What are you talking about?" she asked, likely enjoying her lofty perch. She probably thought it established the hierarchy around here.

"You've been . . . you've been abusing him."

"What?" She trilled a laugh. "He told you that? And you believed him?"

"He wouldn't make something like that up. He's a good lad."

Mum sneered. "I think you'll find it's him abusing me. He waits for you to go to sleep, then comes into our bedroom. He forces me, he pins me down, he—"

Matthew had rushed forward and pushed her without registering it. The anger had overtaken the calm at last. She tipped over the fence and landed on a pig called Black Spot. It scrabbled out from under her, stared down as though possessed, then bit a chunk out of her face. Never would he have believed those animals were capable of such violence, yet, now one had started, the others followed its lead. Mum screamed, bringing her hands up to shield her face, then she vanished from sight, the pigs converging, hiding her.

Matthew stared at Dad.

Dad stared back.

"Leave her, son. Let them have her."

And another secret was born.

CHAPTER TWENTY

"Get out and stay out. You're barred!"

Matthew poked his head around the side of the Kite. Bathed in the light of the lamps above the pub sign, the landlord stood with his arms by his sides, hands clenched into meaty fists. No one messed with him, he had an affiliation with the Northern Kings, so the man on the ground must have done something bad to piss him off. Maybe Wheels had the same issue with him as Matthew did.

"If I see you within half a mile of this place, I'll have you," Wheels said.

The target got up and ran his hands down his clothes, an obvious, subconscious act of brushing off his embarrassment. Matthew recognised it as something he'd done when Mum had left his bedroom. He'd drawn his quilt over his used body and smoothed it.

The target stalked across the car park, reached the pavement and turned left. Wheels muttered something and went inside. Matthew waited for a few heartbeats, then followed the man, rushing to catch up.

"What the hell was that all about?" he asked, coming abreast of him.

"Something and nothing. I don't like that pub anyway, so it's no skin off my nose if I don't go back."

"He said you're barred. Bit harsh."

"Yeah, well, he thinks he owns this part of town, always has. Prick."

"D'you want a lift home?"

"Could do."

"I'm parked in the next street." Matthew dipped down a connecting alley and glanced over his shoulder. "I've always wondered why none of that lot ever get arrested for the stuff they do. I mean, it's obvious it's them."

"The Kings answer to no one, and they're good at what they do. You can't arrest anyone without proof."

That's good to know.

Matthew reached the Transit and unlocked it. He had two choices here. Wallop the target now and bundle him in the back, or let him ride shotgun and convince him to go to the farm for a nightcap. He sifted through his emotions to see whether going to the Remember Room had stirred enough anger. It simmered below the surface, so, as the man approached the passenger side, Matthew elbowed him in the back of the head.

He didn't flop to the pavement as Matthew had imagined, instead staggering into a bush bordering someone's front garden, letting out a shout of surprise. Matthew checked the houses for anyone watching, then lunged forward and pulled his target up, throwing him to the ground and getting down there with him. The man curled into a protective ball, arms over his face, like Mum with the pigs.

"Why the hell are you doing this?" the target asked, voice full of panic.

"You slept with Carys, you filthy pervert."

"What? I didn't!"

"You would say that."

"I swear to God, I never touched her."

"You did, I *saw* you."

"All right, all right, I touched her, but not like *that*."

Had Matthew got it wrong? Had he assumed this prick had slept with her? Could he believe him? Yes, it seemed the bloke was being honest, he was clearly too frightened to even think of a lie, but it was too late to back out now. Things had gone too far.

Matthew wrapped his hands around the bastard's throat and strangled him until he went limp.

He checked his surroundings again. Dragged the inert body to the back of the van. He tossed it inside and got in with it. Closed and locked the doors. He flicked on the battery-operated light mounted on the side panel and found his cable ties. Trussed the body up. Stuffed a cloth in its mouth.

He climbed through to the front, again scoping out the street, and drove away. Two years it had taken him to become the master of his emotions instead of Mum conducting them from beyond the grave. Two years of planning and retraining himself to use his anger. It was to his advantage, the time lapse. No one would think he'd wait *that* long to exact his revenge.

No one would suspect the laid-back man who wouldn't say boo to a goose.

He'd imagined putting Mum's head on a pole many a time when she'd been alive. Back in the old days, heads on spikes signified treason or treachery. The faces, displayed for all to see, showed everyone they'd done something heinous. He'd wanted so much for Mum to be shamed for her actions.

Matthew had read a lot in his lifetime, garnering strange little facts that no one in his circle found interesting, like the one about the Durham women who'd washed the heads, brushed their hair, as was the custom, and were rewarded for doing so with a cow.

What was Matthew's reward?

A nugget of satisfaction. A sense of regaining control after years of relinquishing it to his mother. He hadn't washed Nigel, nor had he combed his hair, and he wouldn't do it for his latest victim either. *These* men deserved to appear as the filthy, stinking bastards that they were. They deserved to have ravens swooping down to peck out their eyes, but, in this case, the police would get to them first. It didn't matter that he couldn't replicate history exactly — after all, he wanted to *change* history, to erase all those who had ruined his heart and fucked with his head. There were still three to go and five days left before Dad came home.

He could do it. Fix everything.

Dad had been so much happier since Mum had died. Matthew had noted it, and his plan to remove all those who'd hurt him had sprouted wings. With them gone, *he'd* be happier, too.

He pulled into the farm barn and smiled.

CHAPTER TWENTY-ONE

Working on a Saturday was never a good thing in Anna's book, but then murderers didn't take the weekend off either. She stood outside a trendy block of apartments in Westgate. It appeared crime did, in fact, pay. She'd looked Parole up on the system, and he owned a Porsche. She glanced back at it, parked near the lake, its red paint gleaming beneath the sun.

"Shame we can never catch any of the Kings in the act," she said to Lenny.

He gestured to the building. "We're clearly in the wrong job."

"Never," she said. "I'd rather be on the right side of the law than the wrong. The fact these are called apartments and not flats tells me he's raking it in, though. With a view of that lake, we're talking a hefty price tag to live here."

"Makes me wonder how a bloke who was always in and out of prison for stupid things ends up living it so large."

"He was younger back then. He's learned to be savvy. To not get caught. I expect Trigger's trained him up, pushed him through the ranks so he earns more."

They walked into the foyer. A middle-aged security guard sat behind a glass-topped desk. He looked up, frowning, then his face evened out at the sight of Anna holding up her ID.

"Anna James and Lenny Baldwin, here to see Joshua Cribbins."

The bloke held his meaty hand out for them to shake. "Ken Marshall. You know who he is, don't you? And what he does?"

"Yep." Anna smiled. "But thanks for trying to warn us."

"He's a nice fella to be fair, never gives me any hassle, but I don't like the idea of people walking into the lion's den, so to speak. I have to keep an eye out, management said, watch the comings and goings. If anyone comes to see him, I have to ask what it's for and report back."

"No one's likely to tell you if they're also dodgy," Anna said.

"True." Ken folded his arms. "Still, I do as I'm told. Management don't want any trouble here. This is a high-end place."

"We're here to ask for his help, actually," Anna lied, "so nothing for your boss to worry about."

"You ought to be careful," Lenny advised. "If he finds out you're giving people a heads-up about him . . . His type think they own everyone, including you, and he could get shirty."

Ken's cheeks grew pink. "I hadn't considered that. I don't like the thought of anyone getting hurt, that's all."

Anna stared over at a sofa by the doors, a tall potted plant beside it. "Keep your head down. Be polite. Stay off his radar. If you spot something iffy, let me know on the quiet." She glanced around. "I see you have cameras. Anything caught on them would also be handy. Certain fish are a bit too slippery for us to catch without help."

Ken winked and puffed his chest out. "I get you but, as far as I've seen, he doesn't conduct 'business' here."

"Well, if he does, phone it in."

Anna walked to the lift and pressed the up button.

Lenny stood beside her and whispered, "Has he got a death wish or what?"

"Seems like it."

The lift took them to the seventh floor, and Anna stepped off and marched to Parole's door. She knocked, made a mental note of the camera above the lintel and steadied her nerves. The intercom to the side crackled, and she held up her ID.

"Oink, oink. Two rashers of bacon," Parole said. "To what do I owe the pleasure?"

"We need some info on Carys Brignell," Anna said to the intercom. "Can you help?"

"Depends whether you're here to try and get me in the shit. I've been fooled that way in the past, sent down for something I didn't do."

They all say that. "It's not that kind of situation. We're not interested in what you get up to, only what you can tell us. Can we come in?"

Something buzzed, and the door unlatched. Anna pushed it open and walked inside. Now *this* place wouldn't mess with her head. The open-plan living area, not to mention the floor-to-ceiling windows occupying the whole right-hand side, gave her a sense of peace. Shiny flooring, some kind of fancy tile, reflected the furniture — black leather sofas, glass-and-chrome coffee and dining tables, a lovely white kitchen, glossy cupboards. Doors to the left that must lead to the bedrooms and bathroom. No Parole in sight.

Lenny closed the door and whistled. "Blimey, this is a nice pad."

"Glad you like it." Parole appeared from behind a white room-dividing shelving unit that separated the living area from the diner. Various items filled the shelves. Books, plants, some tasteful silver ornaments.

She took the man in. He didn't just have tattoos on his face. They covered his chest, neck, and arms, and his muscles were the type only acquired in the gym. His low-slung jeans left little to the imagination, and Anna refocused her attention on his eyes in case he got the wrong idea. She'd only ever seen him fully dressed before, and from a distance, so his appearance had come as a shock. A face full of inkwork made it difficult to see who he really was. Disconcerting.

"Fancy a coffee?" Parole strolled across to the kitchen, his feet bare.

"That would be lovely, thanks." Anna slipped her professional aura back on and stood in the dining area in the top-right corner.

She stared down at the vast expanse of Jubilee Lake, the water dark blue and rippling. People out on paddleboards enjoyed the autumn sunshine, others sat on the banks in their coats. An ice cream man leaned out of his van, clearly touting for the last dregs of business before winter came along in its leaden boots and stomped all over the unseasonably good weather. Someone sailed a small boat, and a drone hovered around it.

"Must be lovely to sit here and watch the world go by," she said and turned towards the kitchen. "I'd love to live here. It's calming."

"Yeah, it's all right." Parole took a cup from beneath a posh barista coffee machine and placed it on the side for Lenny. He added two more under the spouts and pressed buttons.

"How much did this place cost?" Lenny asked. "I'm genuinely curious."

"Three quarters of a mil. I didn't buy it. You know who my grandparents are, right?"

"No," Lenny said.

Parole smiled. "So you didn't look into me before you came here? Fuck off!" He chuckled.

Lenny shook his head. "We checked where you lived, obviously, and had a look at your record and saw how many times you've been in the nick, but as for your personal background, no. Like Anna told you, it isn't that sort of visit."

"Good to know."

"Who *are* your grandparents?"

"They own the chocolate factory."

"Ah, right."

Parole jerked his head at Anna. "Coffee's ready." He put hers on the worktop. "I'm glad this is only a casual chat. I don't fancy being put back inside. I haven't been arrested for ten years. I promised my grandad I wouldn't get caught again — he reckons it would be bad for business. If I do, all this gets taken away. He's basically bribed me to behave. I haven't done that, I've just learned how to not get caught. What do you want to know about Carys?"

Anna walked over and collected her coffee. Frothy milk sat on top. "You've been seeing her?"

"For sex, and it's over now."

"What did you make of her?" Anna sipped. The drink was better than the popular outlets people went dotty over.

"She's good in the sack, but if you want intelligent conversation she isn't your girl. For serious relationships, I prefer a woman with a bit about her, know what I mean?"

Anna stared at a tattoo on his forearm — a crown nestled among surrounding roses.

He saw her looking. "A new thing. All the Kings have them."

Anna battled with her embarrassment at being caught. "How come you ended things with Carys?"

"You saying I ended it tells me you already know, but I'll indulge you so you can't say I wasn't cooperative. She lied to me. I don't do liars, so I binned her off."

Anna smiled, hating herself for liking this man. For all the tales she'd heard about him, he didn't come across as a nasty person. "Indulge me again. What did she lie about?"

"Something rotten. That she has a sister with leukaemia. That was on the first night I met her. I had someone look into her, and she hasn't even *got* a sister. I wasted my sympathy on someone who doesn't deserve it. I asked her what she was playing at, and she swore blind she was telling the truth. It got me so angry I told her to keep away from me."

"Did she ever tell you about her feelings towards her ex-husband, Matthew, and someone called Nigel Fogg?"

"Nah. Why?"

"Nigel's head was left on a spike in her front garden, and Matthew was attacked."

"I heard about that." Parole rubbed his chin. "Is this one of those times where you tell me I need to be careful?"

Anna nodded, although that wasn't the purpose of this chat at all. She wanted to put the feelers out to see if *he* was their man. "We've had to warn someone else as well."

"I can take care of myself," he said. "As you likely know."

"Have you heard anything about Nigel and Matthew from anyone else?"

"I know Nigel's a mouthy prick and Matthew's quiet. I see Nigel often enough in the Kite, although Matthew isn't there on the regular." Parole's focus swerved to the lake. "Hang on, are you saying Carys might have had something to do with what happened to them? She's as thin as a whippet and even less dangerous. How could she kill or attack anyone?"

"Appearances can be deceptive."

"There are ways for a man to tell." He looked at Anna, his gaze too penetrating. "She hasn't got the strength in her to fight anyone off."

Ah. She didn't want to go down the route of dissecting his bedroom antics, but she had to check. "It's always consensual, though, yes?"

"Yep. I'm not in the habit of forcing women to do shit." He studied her even more. "I like you, Anna James, so I'm willing to help out. The Kings might have a rep but we're not complete bastards. I'll do a discreet bit of digging."

Anna took a card out of her pocket and passed it to him. "Thanks." She returned to the window wall to drink her coffee and watch the lake. "We need to know who killed Nigel, so, if you hear anything, let us know. It's looking like the same person attacked Matthew. Tall, black clothing. A hoody."

"I'll see what I can do."

His voice sounded close, and she sensed him at her back, annoyed with herself for not picking up his footsteps. She relaxed a little — Lenny was here and wouldn't let her get hurt — but still, her nerves danced. Parole had an energy about him she couldn't put her finger on. What had Sally called it? An allure.

He stood beside her and leaned to the side, closer to her. "Are you single?"

He'd said it so quietly she could have misheard. "What?"

"Are you single?" he repeated.

"I am. Not looking to be part of a pair either, even if you do make good coffee."

He laughed. "Shame. Relationship aside, we could do with a copper on the books."

"Then that isn't me. And I'd have thought you'd already have one."

"We do, but one more won't hurt."

"I don't suppose you'll tell me who the bent copper is, will you?"

"Nah."

She thought of the phone call Placket had received yesterday, the supposed dentist appointment. Filed it away just in case.

Her senses had gone skew-whiff with Parole being so near, and she didn't like it. "You're standing in my personal space."

He took one step to the side. "I apologise. Never been fond of people doing that to me either."

Lenny appeared on Anna's right. "Is this a private party, or can anyone join in?"

"Anyone," she said, relieved he'd picked up on her discomfort.

Parole inhaled a deep breath. "You came to deliver a warning, and I appreciate that. What if Carys got someone to pick off all her exes for whatever reason?"

"It's a possibility," Anna agreed.

"Stupid bitch." Parole walked off.

"You okay?" Lenny whispered to Anna.

"Yep."

They finished their coffees, Anna contemplating what Parole had said. It *was* possible Carys had sent someone after Nigel and Matthew, but what for? And why now?

"We should go and see her," Anna said under her breath.

"Carys?"

"Hmm. Ask her why she didn't tell us about you-know-who going to her place on Friday night."

"Who went to her place?" Parole asked.

Anna turned. "Bloody hell, bat ears."

He smiled. "You need to be able to listen in my line of work. Whispers cause a lot of trouble."

Anna raised her eyebrows. *He'd* whispered to *her*, and yes, he was trouble, someone she didn't need in her life in that way, even if she *did* find herself drawn to him. "Know anything about a Gordon White?"

"Might do."

Her shoulders slumped. "Aww, he isn't your copper, is he?"

"Nope. But there's one you need to know about. O'Reilly. He tells people he's Gordon White. We've been watching him for a while. Poked into him and found out his real name. His card's marked."

"So we heard."

"Who from?"

"Wheels."

Parole scratched his ear. "O'Reilly's a bad dog. Deserves to be put down."

"I'd advise you not to get involved." Anna took her empty cup to the sink. "Thanks for the coffee and the chat. And any help you can give us."

"I'll do my best." He stared at her again. "But only because it's you."

She backed away. "Stop it."

"What?" He laughed. "Go on, sod off. I've got the gist. Flat-out rejection. I'll give you a bell if I hear anything."

She walked towards the front door, confused over her reaction to him. He was a top-end criminal, and she was a copper. He was stupid to think it could ever work.

And so was she.

CHAPTER TWENTY-TWO

Lenny's stomach had been rumbling ever since they'd left Parole's, so Anna pulled into a parking space at McDonald's at the edge of Westgate. It was in a service area beside the dual carriageway, with a Costa, a WHSmith, and toilets inside a glass-fronted building. A van along the way sold jacket potatoes and pasties.

Lenny went inside. Anna paced beside the car, needing to get her steps in. Several people ate in their vehicles, and she wished she'd asked Lenny to pick her up a couple of bacon rolls, not just a coffee. She clicked the key fob to lock the car and went into McDonald's. At the self-service screen, she ordered some breakfast, nipped to the loo and met Lenny in the queue.

"We'll pop to Carys's after this, then go back to the station," she said.

A young man in front turned around and stared at her. He had the air of a spice-head about him — pasty skin, red-rimmed eyes and the general look of being unkempt and half asleep.

"Station?" he said. "Are you coppers?"

"We are," Lenny said.

"Ah, maybe you can help me, then."

"What with?" Anna took one step back to create more distance between them. The man didn't smell too nice, as if he'd slept in his clothes for days, and spice-heads were unpredictable.

"There's something you should know, man. I mean, it's fucking crazy." He laughed. "Like, *proper* mental."

"When did you last use?" Anna asked.

"Last night. What's that got to do with you?"

"Just checking."

"I'm not a fucking liar."

"I'm not suggesting you are," she said.

"Two hundred and five! Two hundred and six! Two hundred and seven!" someone behind the counter called.

"The last one's me," Anna said.

Lenny moved forward to collect their bags. Mr Spice did the same. Lenny came back and nudged Anna for them to leave, and they walked outside.

"He might have something for us," she said. "Let's wait."

Lenny sighed. "He's on a downer. I wouldn't be surprised if he tells us he met God or was abducted by aliens or something."

"But what if he doesn't? What if it's something important?" Anna took a bacon roll out, removed the paper and bit into it. "There's something about these. Bloody lovely."

Lenny placed the drinks tray on a nearby wall and took a sausage bap out. "I disagree. These are better."

They ate for a moment, Anna staring through the double doors. Mr Spice leaned against a pillar, ramming something into his mouth.

Lenny tutted. "See? He's already forgotten he spoke to us."

"I still want to wait."

She'd eaten her second roll by the time Mr Spice weaved his way outside. He stopped, gawped at them and frowned.

"Do I know you?" he asked.

"We're the police officers you spoke to inside," Anna said.

Mr Spice's eyebrows arched. "Oh yeah. You need to come with me. Seriously."

Anna recalled what he'd said, that it was something "proper mental".

"What's the problem?"

"I saw this head, right? A fucking *head*. Don't look at me like that! I know you think I'm making it up, but I swear it was there. No one in Maccy D's believed me."

Anna's stomach rolled over. "Where was this?"

"On my way here."

Frustrated, she gritted out, "But *where*?"

"That field over there." Mr Spice pointed. "Well, not *in* the field exactly, but on a fence pole."

"Where did you cut across the field from?"

"Eastgate. I'm in the homeless quarter. Mum kicked me out."

While she felt sorry for him, she could understand where his mother was coming from. Spice altered people's personalities and wreaked havoc, breaking families apart. "Take us to the post."

Mr Spice's mouth dropped open. "You believe me?"

"Let's just say I'm curious. Come on." Anna took her coffee and dropped the holder and her rubbish in the bin.

Lenny walked ahead with Mr Spice, through the car park, past a line of trees that separated the services from the field, and out onto rough ground in front of a three-bar wooden fence.

Mr Spice trundled off first. They had to walk in single file along the fence line. Anna's nerves got the better of her, and she entertained the scenario of the drug addict turning nasty on them once they got to a more remote location. But he stopped short and pointed.

"See it? Up there."

Anna moved to the side to peer past him and Lenny. Something round did appear to sit on top of a fence post, about waist height.

"Okay, you stay here," Lenny said to him. "You might need to give us a statement."

"Will I get lunch if we do it down the nick?" Mr Spice asked. "Only, I'm a bit short as I used my last few quid on breakfast."

"Yep, and you can have a shower while you're at it," Anna offered. "I'm sure there's a spare tracksuit knocking about an' all."

Lenny marched off.

Anna scooted past Mr Spice, giving him a wide berth, and jogged to catch up with Lenny. She glanced over her shoulder. Mr Spice had curled up on his side on the ground by the trees, probably taking the chance to have a nap. She shook her head; the drug had really got its roots firmly into the vulnerable people of Marlford.

"Oh fuck." She paused where Lenny stood and stared at the head. "That's O'Reilly."

No busted face like Nigel's. No bruises or broken nose. His tongue poked out, staring eyes, petechiae underneath. Strangulation? With the absence of a neck, it was hard to tell.

"Jesus Christ." Lenny got his phone out and called it in.

Anna turned away from the head. It didn't just sit on the post, the square top of the wood was *inside* the head, as if flesh and bone had been carved out to make room. She battled rising nausea and checked out the area. The services would have cameras, but would they have picked anything up this far along? And would the killer have been stupid enough to use the car park as an access point? The tree trunks, so dense and close together, would obscure any view. The field itself, bordered by high hedges on the other three sides, didn't have any track lines where someone had walked over the grass. It hadn't been cut for a while, and bent over in a sudden gust of wind. Had the killer risked parking on the hard shoulder just before the exit for the services?

It felt ominous, that wind, and Anna shuddered. If they weren't dealing with Nigel's head, too, she'd have put money on this being retaliation from someone who knew what O'Reilly had done to Parvati. But this *had* to be related to Carys. Why had

O'Reilly been targeted, though? He hadn't had a relationship or sex with her — unless he'd lied about that — so it would have to be because of him touching her up. Or was she way off the mark there? And there was no way Parole would have got to O'Reilly so quickly. There had only been fifteen minutes between leaving his apartment and arriving here.

Someone knew about Carys's life, who she saw, who'd annoyed her. If it wasn't Carys herself getting someone to do this, who would have taken it upon themselves to go as far as murder? Who *cared* enough to want to defend her honour? And why had Matthew only been attacked, not killed?

Lenny slid his phone into his pocket. "They'll all arrive shortly." He nodded towards Mr Spice. "Looks like he's gone to sleep. Fancy getting into that state."

"Are you talking about that kid or O'Reilly's head?"

Lenny laughed. "The kid."

"I know. I thought some dark humour would lighten the mood a bit."

"*I'll* tell you something dark." Lenny moved closer. "I don't feel bad that O'Reilly's copped it. Do you?"

"I don't like *anyone* dying, no matter who they are or what they've done, but I get what you mean."

"Perverts ought to be castrated."

Anna grimaced at the image. "Parvati might take this badly. I doubt very much that she wished him dead. She's not the type; she'd just want him dealt with by the law. She's soft-hearted, and this might haunt her."

"Depends what he did to her. Even softies can imagine bad things, you know."

"There were witnesses, so he can't have gone *that* far with her."

"No, thank God."

Anna walked back to check on Mr Spice. He was breathing steadily, hugging himself for warmth, so she picked her way through the trees and into the car park. She meandered to the road that led to the services. Thoughts of someone scooping out the innards of O'Reilly's head intruded, and she blanked them out. Drank some coffee.

Five minutes later, a police car swung into the turning. She waved them over to a space by the trees and waited for the officers to get out.

"Reported by a spice-head," she said. "Another murder. Can one of you go and stand on this side of the trees to prevent anyone going through? The other of you needs to go and get the witness. I didn't ask his name, but he's asleep just along there. He'll be more receptive if you take him to the station for his statement. He's had breakfast, but he'll need more food and a shower. Give him a tracksuit while you're at it. It'll be warmer than what he's got on right now."

"Since when did we become a hotel?" one of them grumbled.

"Since I said so." Anna glared at him. "Sometimes we need to bend the rules and go one step further. He's been kicked out of his house and lives in the homeless quarter. I want him to have a proper kip before his statement's taken so his mind's clearer. Where's your compassion?"

Another police car rolled up, and PC Watson got out.

"Actually, I'll ask Ollie to deal with him. He's more of a bleeding heart." Anna walked away from them and smiled at Ollie as he left the car. She explained what she wanted him to do and led him to where Mr Spice rested.

"Poor sod," Ollie said, staring down at him.

"I know. So I'll leave him to you, then?"

"Yeah. I'll have a root around and see if there's a spare bed for him in one of the homeless places. I'll let control know we need another copper or two out here, seeing as I won't be staying." Ollie peered between two trees. "Looks like we've garnered a bit of interest. The rubberneckers are out in force."

"It'll be worse when SOCO and Herman turn up."

She left Ollie to it and went to her car. She picked out some booties and gloves from the box in the back seat and took them to Lenny.

"I know we've already walked over the scene," she said, putting them on, "but it'll save Steve having a pop if he catches us without gear on."

"This is rank," the PC said and jerked his head at the fence post.

Anna recognised him as the one in Carys's house yesterday. She couldn't recall his name. "Did Carys offer any more information after we left?"

His cheeks coloured. "Err, no. She was more interested in trying to get me to go out with her. I said I was married, but she kept on. I changed the subject, tried to get her to tell me more about Nigel, but she wasn't having any of it. The conversation turned to sex. I actually think she's obsessed with it. In the end, I walked out. Can't be doing with that business."

"I don't blame you." An image of Parole came to mind, and Anna pushed it out. *She* couldn't be doing with that business either.

CHAPTER TWENTY-THREE

The tent had to be cut down the middle on both sides so it could straddle the fence. The pieces flapped in the wind, and a SOCO was in the process of stabbing holes in the fabric and pushing long cable ties through them to keep the material together around the middle bar. Anna, standing in front of the head in full protective gear, drew her attention away from the SOCO and to the pathologist.

"What's your take on this?" she asked.

Herman crouched and looked up at the base of the head. "Whoever it is has the tools to scoop the neck free of flesh and remove the top of the spine."

"Bloody barbaric," Lenny muttered. "There's a lot of hatred there if they were prepared to do that."

"Not enough to beat him up, though," Anna commented. "Nigel had been battered."

"Because he put up a fight?" Lenny suggested. "He needed to be subdued? O'Reilly may have been tricked and gone willingly."

"Or possibly strangled from behind so he didn't get the chance to retaliate," Herman said. "Petechiae present, as well as broken veins in the whites of the eyes. Protruding tongue.

Without a neck and no finger and thumb bruising, without lungs to check for drowning or the rest of his body to inspect, this is a guess." He peered round the back. "Ah, a small lump, so he was hit from behind."

"I came to the same conclusion regarding strangulation," Anna said. "I thought we'd have had more phone calls about scattered body parts by now, though. I envisaged Nigel being cut up and spread around for some reason."

"Who can blame you for thinking that?" Herman said. "We've seen so much depravity in this job. The mind conjures the worst-case scenario. At least it does for me until I can prove otherwise."

Anna glanced at a SOCO who had picked something out of the grass and held it up. He shook his head and bagged it.

"What was that?" Anna asked.

"A Fruit-tella wrapper, so unless we've got a sweet-eating killer . . ."

"Okay, we're off. We need to find out who the next of kin is." Anna left the tent, took her protectives off in the designated area and returned to the car park. In the car, Lenny spoke to the log officer, while she phoned the team number.

Warren picked up. "Morning, boss. Did you get anything from Parole?"

"Not much, except he was seeing Carys but dumped her when she lied to him. That's not my concern at the minute. Bit of a shocker here for you. We've found O'Reilly's head on a fence post at the services in Westgate. Either a coincidence or fate sending us this way, but a spice-head overheard us talking about the station and said he'd seen a head."

"Fuck me. What are the odds?"

"I know. The universe is bloody weird the way it works."

"You're telling me. There's a clear pattern forming here: men who've had anything to do with Carys are being offed. So how come Matthew's still alive?"

"Exactly what I want to know. Maybe the killer intended to murder him but got disturbed. Maybe someone saw him.

That reminds me, can you check whether all the reports are in on that? We left Spruce Way without speaking to all the residents. PCs were going to finish the job."

"Two secs." Warren's keyboard clattered, and his breathing coasted down the line. "All residents were spoken to by eight p.m. last night. No one saw anything."

"So why did he get spooked, then? We'll have to come back to that. The reason for my call is I need to know O'Reilly's NOK. His mother's dead, he told us that, but is there anyone else?"

"I'll access his employee file, hang on."

Anna wiped some dust off the dashboard with the flat of her hand.

"He hasn't got anyone."

"No one at all? No cousins or anything?"

"Nope, I've run a wider search."

"Bugger. Okay, me and Lenny will go to the Rowan estate and speak to his immediate neighbours. We might get lucky and find one he was friends with. Can you arrange for PCs to get down there an' all? That whole street needs talking to. O'Reilly may have been abducted from there. I want one of you to phone Wheels and see if O'Reilly went to the Kite last night. You know the drill."

"Placket's in. Shall I let him know what's going on?"

"Please. Tell him I couldn't update him yesterday as he'd gone to the dentist. Pass on everything that's happened. He'll likely focus more on speaking to Parvati to let her know the score. I'm gutted for her that she didn't get proper justice."

"Sod's law that someone like him would get away without facing charges."

"Luck follows some people. Okay, I'm off. Chase up Nigel's DNA test, and let me know if you find anything interesting on O'Reilly."

She ended the call and smiled at Lenny, who clipped his seat belt in place. She put hers on and drove away.

"O'Reilly's a Billy No-Mates. No family, nothing," she said.

"So where are we going?"

"To speak to his neighbours." She filled him in on what the team were doing. "There's naff all else we can do until we get a break."

* * *

"He went out around seven," Mrs Knowles said, a boy of about five kicking her calf beside her. "Pack it in, Sammy, for God's sake. These are coppers, and if you keep on they'll take you away."

The boy ran off, shrieking.

"Do you often frighten him like that?" Anna said.

"I've got to do *something*," Knowles retorted. "He's a right little bastard."

Those words took Anna back to her PC days when she'd had to deal with the likes of Knowles every day. Those on Rowan were a law unto themselves. Mum said they'd been slung up, not brought up, and it wasn't any wonder they acted the way they did.

Anna spotted the lad peering at her from around a door-frame at the end of the hallway. She smiled and gave him a wave. He stuck his middle finger up at her.

Bloody hell.

She returned her attention to his mother. "So, seven, you said."

"Yeah."

"Did he go in his car?"

"Nah, he got a taxi. Cam's Cabs."

"What was he wearing?"

"A grey suit, white shirt. Same poncy gear he puts on for work. What's he done, then, grabbed someone's tit? He's known for that around here. When he's down the Plough, he's got a habit of touching women."

"Why didn't anyone report him?"

Knowles laughed bitterly. "And get told to fuck off because he's one of your lot? You all stick together, you pigs."

"It would have been taken seriously," Anna said.

"Whatever."

"Are there a lot of people around here who don't like him?"

"*No one* likes him on account that he's the filth."

"Do you know of anyone who'd want to harm him?"

"Take your pick. Go and ask around at the Plough. You'll get told some stories, I can tell you."

"We will, thanks. Did you hear him come home?"

"Nah. He wasn't back by ten, and I'd know because he always slams the fucking door. I reckon it's to piss me off. We had a barney about it once when Sammy was a baby. All I asked was that he be a bit quieter, and he told me to knob off. Called me a fat cow an' all. Nasty piece of work, that one."

Blimey. "Did you see anyone else in the street around the time Mr O'Reilly left?"

"Now you come to mention it, there was this van. One of them Transit types. White. It had a company name on the side. Can't remember what it was, but it was to do with plumbing because it had a picture of a tap. When the taxi pulled away, it followed. Could have been a worker leaving one of the other houses, though. Give me two secs and I'll find out. All of us bar O'Reilly and Stan Bates belong to a WhatsApp group. Stan doesn't even own a phone, he must be heading for his hundredth birthday, and it stands to reason why O'Reilly wasn't invited."

She took her mobile out of her bra and thumbed the screen. Anna glanced around. Three PCs stood at doors, and Lenny spoke to an ancient man weeding his garden. Stan? SOCO had arrived a couple of minutes ago and were gaining access to O'Reilly's house.

A volley of message pings rang out. Anna smiled. People round here were quick to pick up their phones if they thought

145

gossip was on offer. They'd have seen the uniforms and gathered something was going on.

"No one had a plumber round," Knowles said. "If it helps, the Transit was parked outside Sasha's over the road. Number ten. She might know more."

"You've been brilliant," Anna said. "Thank you." She handed a card over. "If you think of anything else, drop me a text or ring me. Someone will be round to take a proper statement."

"What's the perv done?"

"He was murdered." Anna studied the woman for a reaction.

"Good." Knowles moved back and shut the door.

Anna walked across the street to number ten and rang the bell. The door whipped open almost immediately, as if Sasha had been watching her approach through the window.

Blonde, a little grubby and with greasy hair, Sasha smiled, her eyes lighting up. "The plumber's van. It arrived at half six and stayed there until the pig went out."

"Did you get a look at the driver?"

"I think it was a bloke. He had a hoody on. Couldn't see his face, like."

"Did you get the number plate?"

"Yep. I wrote it in my notes app." Sasha produced a phone from her pocket and prodded the screen. "I always do that ever since Lisa's kid got snatched that time."

"The Bardwell case? Alex?"

"Yeah. You just don't know who's about, do you? Here you go." Sasha turned the screen around.

Anna opened the team chat app and put in the number. She added a message to say what it was about and sent it. "You've been really helpful. I appreciate it. As you're opposite Mr O'Reilly's, did you happen to see anything else?"

"He went out at—" Her phone bleeped. She glanced down at it. "Fuck me, he's been bumped off?"

Knowles has been spreading the news, then. "Yes. You were saying?"

"He left at seven in a taxi. The van went after it. Cor, that must be the killer. No one down here even had a plumber in."

"It could be a coincidence," Anna said. "Did you happen to see or hear anything after that? O'Reilly coming home? Anyone loitering about on foot?"

"If they'd been loitering like that, I'd have come out to give them what for. Told them to sling their hook. We don't let anyone fuck about down here because of what happened to Alex. If it wasn't for my quick thinking back then, that kid would be God knows where. Abroad with a paedo ring, most likely."

Gordon had been the SIO on that case. A paedophile had abducted Alex from his front garden, and a woman had come out and stood in the middle of the road, preventing him from leaving. Other neighbours had joined her, and a man had hauled the paedo out of the car and given him a kicking in the road.

"You were the one who stopped the car?" Anna asked.

"Yep. Call me Miss Marple and be done with it."

Anna smiled. "Please be mindful of your own safety when doing things like that, will you?"

"Nope. If it involves kiddies, I don't give a shit about myself. As for that pig across the road . . . Couldn't give a stuff that he's dead. Ruddy perv. Did you get told about him?"

"I did, and I'll be investigating those claims."

"What's the point? It's not like he can be slung in the nick now, is it?"

"For his victims. They may need help in coming to terms with it."

Sasha eyed her. "You're all right, you are." She paused. "For a plod."

"I try to be. Thank you for your time and the information. Someone will come along shortly and take a formal statement."

"Did he suffer?" Sasha asked.

"I should imagine so."

"Grand. Have a nice day!" Sasha slammed the door shut.

Anna wandered across to the garden where Lenny was chatting to the old man. Both women seemed delighted that O'Reilly had copped it. What must he have been like outside of work? He sounded a right deviant monster.

They walk among us in plain sight.

Lenny finished speaking to the man and joined her on the path. Anna guided him towards the car, away from listening ears. Several neighbours had come out to chat over their garden hedges.

"He went out in a taxi at seven," Lenny said.

"I got that much information myself. Plus a Transit, a plumber's van, followed the cab." Anna's phone trilled and she accessed her messages. "Shit, the plate must be stolen. It belongs to an Audi." She replied to Warren, asking him to check whether any Transits had been spotted on yesterday's CCTV trawl. "What else did the old boy say?"

"Stan, his name is. Used to be a pawnbroker down Southgate years ago. O'Reilly didn't come back at any time before two a.m. Stan went to bed at midnight. His room's at the front, and he doesn't close the curtains so would have seen any headlights. He was reading until two."

"So O'Reilly could have been collared elsewhere. We'll leave the rest of the door-to-door enquiries to the PCs while we have a nose inside the house. And I need them to get statements before we go."

At the end of O'Reilly's path, they suited up, signed the log at the door and entered. The familiar, cloying scent of dust flew up Anna's nose, dulled somewhat by her mask. She found Steven in the kitchen surrounded by more boxes.

"Why not put it into storage if he couldn't face sorting through it?" Lenny said behind her.

"He might have liked having her things around him. Couldn't let her go," Anna said.

Steve's eyes crinkled over his mask. "Always seeing the other side of the coin, you are, Anna."

"We all should in this job. Got anything for us?"

"Despite the hoarding, I can't see any signs of a struggle. The boxes and whatever might cramp the place up, but it's orderly."

"I doubt he was accosted here," Anna said. "Witnesses have said he left at seven in a taxi, and no one saw or heard him coming home."

"Thank God for nosy neighbours, eh?" Steve gazed around. "We'll do the usual here anyway. Cross the t's an' all that."

Anna's phone went off again.

Warren: *O'Reilly went to the Kite. Wheels has rung me to say he kicked him out for being a perv again.*

> Anna: *Cheers. We'll go there now. Can you or someone else nip to the Plough on the Rowan estate, please? O'Reilly had a rep there as a bit of a sex pest. I want all the info you can get.*

Warren: *Will do.*

She sighed and looked at Lenny. "We need to go to the Kite. Speak to Wheels."

"Shit."

"I know. The things we have to put ourselves through, eh?"

CHAPTER TWENTY-FOUR

Matthew woke mid-morning, a pounding headache crushing his brain. Two nights in a row with minimal sleep. He'd have to watch himself. Catch up during the day so tonight he'd be alert enough to carry on with his plan. The next target on his list was a trickier customer, and an elbow to the face wouldn't work.

He'd have to take the hammer.

He made porridge for breakfast, adding extra sugar and a squirt of honey because Mum had never allowed that. He did a lot of things now that went against her teachings, just because he could. He thought back to how he'd been with Carys, basically letting her fill Mum's shoes, organising his life, his feelings, his everything. He was used to it, and in a way it was a comfort to have someone else governing what he did. So easy to slip back into old habits.

He'd snapped out of that fugue and had planned to leave her, but she'd thwarted him by having sex with Nigel, knowing Matthew could come home any second. She must have wanted to end their marriage, too, but instead of saying so she'd let her actions do the talking for her. Perhaps she'd guessed his intentions and wanted to get there first. Mum all over again.

Dad warned me, but I ignored him.

He washed his bowl and spoon, staring into the garden, where forensic people had picked over his grass and checked his washing for clues. They'd bagged something, hopefully the hair he'd dropped, and swabbed the window frame, then knocked on his door to say he was okay to go out there because they'd finished.

He worried that the police would wonder why he hadn't been killed. Why Nigel and that O'Reilly fella had been offed during the night yet he'd been attacked during the day. Would they be asking why the change of MO?

Mistakes were easily made, especially when panic set in. And he *had* panicked at the idea of Anna and Baldy coming to speak to him, hence beating himself up to throw them off the scent. He should have told them he'd scared the attacker off so it was a more plausible scenario. He should have waited until it got dark, hurt himself, *then* phoned Anna to report it.

Shit.

He channelled his mind to tonight. Someone had probably found O'Reilly's head by now, so the police presence in Marlford would be heightened, fears of a spree killer on the loose. This could be a problem — residents would be on their guard, watching, wanting to spot something and become the hero.

But it was too late to back out now. To stop. He was almost halfway to giving himself the peace he deserved. Doing this had quickly become addictive. The power, having full control.

He almost understood why his mother had remained in her marriage and ruled his and Dad's lives. To hold all the cards when it came to another human being was the biggest rush ever.

So much so, he wondered if he'd stop at five kills.

CHAPTER TWENTY-FIVE

The Remember Room

"What did she have over you?" Matthew asked Dad, his breathing ragged, his chest tight from his furious heartbeats. "What's the secret between you?"

The pigs had ripped Mum's clothes, shredded them, eaten them, biting at her, even dragging her legs out of the wellies. They'd devoured all of her apart from her teeth. They stubbornly remained in the gums, her jawbone exposed either side. The animals had lost interest and wandered off to the other end of the pen, some of their heads poking through the fence to take a drink from the water troughs. Thirsty work, eating a human.

"I'll never tell anyone, not even you, son."

Matthew stared at Mum's grin lying on the muddy floor, wishing the pigs had scoffed it. She still taunted him, even in death. "I won't tell anyone."

"That's what she said, but she held it over me every day." Dad rubbed his eyes. "Much as I could do without them snooping around here, we're going to have to phone the police."

Matthew's stomach lurched. "And say what? I mean, I killed her. I pushed her in there."

"No, that first pig set the others off. It only takes one rogue to lead the way. They follow by example."

"I didn't know pigs could be like that."

"Why do you think I told you never to come in here?"

"Will the police want to know why we didn't get in there to save her?"

"I'll explain it all to them. Black Spot is three hundred pounds. Times that by thirty of the buggers. And you saw how quickly they stripped her down. No, we won't get any blame. As far as they're aware, we wondered where she'd got to and walked over here to see if she was okay. We found her teeth, end of story." Dad moved towards the doors. "Come on."

They tromped back to the farmhouse, Matthew cold and shaking. Dad phoned the police. No wonder he'd never allowed Matthew into the pig pen. Right from when Matthew had been small, he'd always said it was too dangerous, that pigs had a way about them. You had to be careful.

While they waited for the officers to arrive, Dad turned the heat off beneath the cooking food and boiled the kettle. He popped a pot of coffee on. "They'll want a cuppa. They'll be here for a while. Probably spend the night fucking about in the barn. I'll have to put a divider up in the middle of the pen so the pigs don't go on the attack again. The coppers will have to get in there, see."

Matthew nodded. "But they might attack you."

"They might."

"I'm scared."

"So am I, but we stick to the story, all right?"

"Yeah."

"When they've gone, you can tell me all about it if you like. Her. What she did."

"No. I can't."

Dad sighed. "I'm sorry. I didn't know."

"It's all right."

Dad wiped his tears. "It isn't. It fucking isn't."

* * *

Dad climbed out of the pen at the far end. The pigs were cordoned off at the top. He'd hammered a middle fence into the boggy floor, something

153

he did when cleaning them out so he could work in peace. And, now Matthew knew all too well, so they didn't bite or attack him. Steel panels leaned against it so the pigs couldn't see the police. Matthew stood in the barn doorway with a copper in uniform, shaking, goosebumps all over his arms despite him having a thick jacket on.

Officers in forensic clothing, including two detectives, stood in front of the pen, one of them about to climb over and get inside to retrieve Mum's teeth and do whatever it was the police did in these situations. She appeared nervous, and glanced at the steel panels.

"It'll be all right," Dad said. "They might poke at the steel and knock it over, but they can't leap the fence. Too fat, and their legs aren't long enough."

The detectives turned from their colleague to face Dad.

One, DI Placket, jerked his head towards the doors. "We'll chat over here."

Matthew stiffened. What if they asked him questions and he fucked it up?

"Explain to me why those pigs ate your wife," Placket said, deadpan.

"They get aggressive to establish dominance over the others. Black Spot is the king, for want of a better term. The lack of food causes fights. She didn't bring enough peelings for all of them, and by the time Black Spot got there it had all gone. He attacked her instead of the other pigs. It happens. He's nigh on three hundred pounds, so she didn't stand a chance. Plus she didn't put the cardboard box in the pen before she jumped over."

"Cardboard box?" Placket asked.

"Pigs seek novel objects, they like to explore. If she'd have put the box in there, they'd have automatically gone to investigate, giving her time to put the food down and get out. Although why she didn't throw the peelings into the pen, I don't know. I don't understand why she got in. She knows how pigs behave. They're used to me, they see me as one of them — I'm their feeder, the giver of water, see? But I still have to distract them before I get in. Pigs are mainly okay if they're all used to each other, but I introduced a few new ones this morning, so that'll be the cause of Black Spot acting up."

"Acting up?" Placket repeated. "That's putting it mildly."

"It's to establish dominance over the newbies. If you get a moment, go and have a look at some of them. The recent additions will have *lesions where they've been bullied and bitten. Takes about twenty-four hours for them to accept dominance. Black Spot will still be in an agitated state. It's like having strangers come to stay in your house. He attacked my wife instead of another pig. As he's the king, the others joined in, kind of like his soldiers wanting to show him their support. Sounds daft, but it's the way it is."*

"Fascinating," Placket said, "if disturbing."

"I suspect I'll have at least one lame newbie come the morning. Black Spot will have been picking on the weakest one. Nature's cruel sometimes."

"Did you warn your wife about the new pigs before she brought the peelings here?"

Matthew held his breath.

"I did. I also told her there weren't enough scraps, that the pigs would get antsy if they didn't get any. I told her to throw them over the fence." Dad looked at Matthew. "That's what I said, wasn't it? Words to that effect?"

"Yes." Matthew folded his arms. "But she said Dad was teaching her to suck eggs."

"This must have been an incredible shock to you, Matthew," Placket said.

"I . . . we came out to see where she was and . . ."

"Let's talk about it in the house, all right? Standing here isn't helping matters." Placket walked out.

The other detective followed. Dad put his arm around Matthew's shoulders and they trudged towards the farmhouse, the PC close behind them. Matthew's mind swirled with a new possibility. Had Dad let Mum go out there on purpose, hoping Black Spot would turn on her? If Matthew hadn't got to the barn when he had, if he'd been a few seconds later, would Dad have been the one to tip her over the fence instead? Had he wanted *Mum to die?*

All questions for later. For now, they faced a barrage of questions to establish whether there had been any foul play. But, without a body to check for any bruising Matthew may have caused when he'd shoved her, there was no proof they'd done anything wrong.

No proof at all.

155

CHAPTER TWENTY-SIX

Anna stood at the bar in the Kite and glanced around. The place was packed, some of the Kings sitting at a large round table on the dais. Many on this estate didn't work and came here to save being at home on their own, craving company. Others who could afford meals out and plenty of drinks sat away from their poorer counterparts as if they might catch something if they got too close. A couple of families sat having a full English breakfast. A little girl was trying her best to win a teddy from the grabby machine.

The complexities of Marlford's quadrants were different in each section. Northgate, and especially Rowan, housed what some would consider the dregs of society, the "chavs". Westgate, the more affluent. Southgate was the main hub, with the town centre and people who got on with their lives in anonymity — no "love thy neighbour" going on there. And Eastgate, with the Kite and Bishop's Lock, was a mix of the well-off and those who just got by, plus the homeless quarter.

The tidy people paid Anna and Lenny no mind, but the scruffs eyed them warily. The latter could sniff out a copper a mile away, or so they claimed.

Wheels came out from a doorway behind the bar and caught sight of them, Anna with her lemonade, Lenny holding a Coke. His wide face broke into a knowing grin, a gold tooth glinting at the front. He jerked his head towards a door to Anna's right, the move revealing a tattoo on the side of his neck, the same crown Parole had on his forearm. The Kings' logo. He walked to the end of the bar, lifted the hatch and walked through the doorway. Anna followed, Lenny at her rear. She gazed around, surprised by how nice it was.

Two long cream sofas opposite each other against the left and right walls. Black-and-white photos hung above them, similar to those at the hairdresser's salon. At the back, a kitchen station with a kettle, coffee machine, and stacked cups, all matching. Beside that, a fridge and a shelving unit with baskets of crisps, prepacked sandwiches, and chocolate bars.

"Look after the staff and they'll look after you." Wheels plonked himself down on a sofa. "Help yourself."

Lenny went straight for a Snickers. "Do you want a brew, Alfie?"

Wheels grunted. "It's Wheels. Coffee. Three sugars."

Anna sat on the other sofa and popped her lemonade on the floor by her feet. "You phoned Warren about O'Reilly."

"Yep. Fucking dirty prick."

"Did you notice what time he came in?" Anna glanced up at Lenny, who handed her a bag of Maltesers. "Thanks."

"Of course I fucking well did." Wheels took the coffee Lenny passed to him. "I always note when he comes in, what he does while he's here, and when he leaves. He's a pest. Or was. I hear he's copped it. About sodding time."

"Who told you?"

"I've got eyes and ears all over the ruddy shop, told them to listen out more carefully since Nigel was killed. It's all over the Rowan estate."

"Right. When did O'Reilly arrive?"

157

"Ten past seven. He left at eight when I grabbed him by the scruff and chucked him out. Told him not to bother coming back an' all. Said I'd have him if he came within half a mile of the place."

Lenny sat beside Anna. "Why, what did he do?"

"Upset Sandra, one of my workers. She was collecting glasses, and he slapped her arse, then asked her what she was doing after work. I'm not having that kind of behaviour in here anymore. I let him be previously but, as my missus said, I'm basically allowing the women who come here to think I agree with that shit when I don't. Enough is enough, and, if me kicking him out meant someone got hold of him and killed him, good."

Anna bit her lip. "This isn't public knowledge yet, but it relates to the murder of Nigel Fogg. If you can keep this to yourself . . ."

"Depends on whether the Kings can help you. I'd have to explain things to them, see."

"Okay, but don't tell anyone other than the Kings. O'Reilly's head was found on a fence post. Nigel's was on a post in Carys's garden. Do you have any idea what that could mean, both of them found like that?"

"What, like an MO?"

"Yes. Do you know of another gang or anyone who's ever said they'd behead someone and stick it on a spike?"

"Nope. What's your line of thinking?"

Anna didn't know how much to share with him.

"Look," he said, "I get that you need to keep shit to yourself, but you'll get no better help than from the Kings. We can get info out of people, frighten them when you can't. If someone's going round offing Carys's men, we've got a vested interest. We want to find whoever it is so they don't go after Parole. Whatever you say will remain confidential, got it?"

Anna glanced at Lenny, who nodded. She sipped some lemonade to give her time to formulate her words.

"Okay, cards on the table. We're stumped. The only thing that keeps cropping up in my head is Carys could have got a bee in her bonnet and paid someone to do it. Get rid of every man who's upset her. If you were her, who would you ask?"

"The Kings, but she hasn't done that. We'd have told her to fuck off anyway. She's a bullshitter, so, anything she said about those men, we'd think they were her usual stories."

"Has she been seeing anyone apart from Matthew, Nigel, Gordon, and Parole? She's here a lot, so you'd see who she hangs around with."

"She cops off with plenty, but they're the only ones I noticed went with her more than once or twice. I'd have said O'Reilly was your man, he got a bit possessive if he saw her chatting up another fella, but he can hardly cut off his own head, so that theory's gone down the shitter."

Anna turned to Lenny. "We really must ask her why she didn't mention Gordon going to her house." She remembered Wheels was listening and looked at him.

He held his hands up. "You carry on, I went a bit deaf there."

"Thank you."

"For what it's worth, I reckon you've got a bloke who's taken it upon himself to remove all the competition so she only has him to turn to."

"That's creepy," Anna said. "Cornering her almost."

"Yep. I see it a lot in here, love rivals, although I can't say I've noticed anyone other than O'Reilly looking at her in that way."

"What will you do? You and the Kings?"

"Sniff around. A few of them have already arrived. Once I realised Parole might be next on the list, I got hold of Trigger. He said to hold a meeting, find whoever's doing this. We won't step on your toes."

"Parole's said he'll put his ear to the ground, too, so thanks for that."

"Not a problem." Wheels stood. "We're only in on this because one of our own might be in the firing line. We wouldn't normally help the filth."

"Don't I know it." Anna smiled and got to her feet, picking up her lemonade. She popped the Maltesers in her jacket pocket and gave him her card. "There's my number. Can I have yours?"

Wheels grinned. "One of them." He keyed her number into his phone to drop-call her.

"We're not all bad, you know," Anna said. "We're still people at the end of the day, like you. Even coppers have feelings."

"Hmm. Now fuck off, I've got a meeting in here and I need to get rid of the stench of bacon."

Anna laughed and returned to the bar. She groaned and whispered to Lenny, "Check out your two o'clock, by the Guinness pump."

Lenny peered over. "Saves us a trip."

Carys clocked them and her shoulders slumped.

Why would she be upset we're here?

Anna walked up to her. "Can we have a quiet word outside?"

Carys picked up her cup of coffee. "Here is fine."

"It's about Gordon."

"What about him?"

"There's been some crossed wires."

"Such as?"

Anna explained that O'Reilly had used Gordon's name and that Gordon was the anonymous man she'd slept with on Friday night. "Why didn't you tell us he went to yours? That's a significant piece of information you left out."

Carys shrugged. "Didn't think you needed to know my private business."

"Of course we do. For all we knew, that man could have been the killer."

160

"And is he?"

"No."

"There you go, then."

Anna gritted her teeth. "He's a policeman, did you know that?"

"We didn't exchange life stories."

"Why did you tell us Nigel was your boyfriend when he wasn't?"

"He was for a while."

"But not now. Are you deliberately misleading us?"

Carys scoffed. "Oh, get over yourself. I was upset. I said the wrong thing. So what?"

"What other 'wrong' things have you said?"

Carys narrowed her eyes. "What are you getting at?"

"Various sources have said you lie a lot. How are we supposed to know what's the truth and what isn't?"

"Everyone tells fibs."

"They shouldn't when murder is involved. Is there anything else you may have 'forgotten' to tell us?"

"What about?"

"Whether any of your partners may have got jealous and decided to take it out on the others."

"What do you mean, 'others'?"

"Matthew was attacked yesterday, and the man who claimed to be called Gordon, a Mr O'Reilly, was murdered. His head is currently on a fence post."

Carys reared her head back in shock. "*What?*"

"So you can see why we need the truth. What haven't you told us?"

"I knew nothing about Matthew or that O'Reilly bloke. It's nothing to do with me."

Anna glared at her. "It had better not be."

Carys turned away and sipped her coffee.

Anna walked round to stand in front of her. "Oh, and I'd appreciate you not propositioning police officers on duty."

"I have no idea what you're talking about."

161

Anna came close to blurting something inappropriate, but bit her tongue. Carys was nothing but a liar, wasting their time. Anna stalked away from her and leaned on the bar farther down. Lenny joined her.

"She's a piece of work," he said. "Christ, and another one's just come in."

Anna turned. Parole strode past and winked at her, heading for the staffroom door. She sipped her lemonade, checking herself. Why had her stomach flipped over in *that* way?

CHAPTER TWENTY-SEVEN

Sally stood at the bar in the Plough, Peter next to her. She glanced around. Not many people, given it was a Saturday, although she supposed thirty or so wasn't a bad number of customers. A few men and one woman played darts, probably the pub team gearing up for tonight's match — due to start at eight, according to the poster on the door. With her son, Ben, away at his dad's for the weekend, Sally would likely be tucked up on the sofa under a blanket by then.

Her ex-husband, Richard, had turned into an arsehole who enjoyed winding her up at drop-off and pick-up times. Ben had said he questioned him whenever he was there, trying to find out what Sally got up to. Nothing much. Work, home, bed, repeat. Still, he was convinced she'd split up with him because of another man, not because he'd changed after they'd married and treated her like shit. The funny thing was, they'd been divorced for three years and not a fella in sight. Richard, however, felt he was free to have as many one-night stands as he liked. Of course he did.

Sally turned off those thoughts and swerved her focus to the staff behind the bar. One of them had gone to get the landlord, had returned, and hadn't said whether he was coming to speak to them. Instead, she'd carried on serving customers.

Catching her attention, Sally asked, "Is the landlord busy or something?"

"Oh, shit. I forgot to say. He said to go through that door there and speak to him in his office. Menopause brain, me."

Sally smiled. She didn't like the idea of entering that phase of her life. Her mum had suffered badly with early menopause and ended up having a hysterectomy at forty-one. Sally had years before she got there, but the horror stories her mother told her lingered in her mind.

"No worries," she said.

Peter nudged her and some of her Diet Coke spilled over the side of her glass.

"Oi," she said. "Did you have to?" She preferred working with Warren. Peter wasn't her cup of tea.

Peter grabbed a nearby bar towel and wiped her hand. "Sorry. I just meant to get you moving, that's all."

"Lovely, now my hand's going to smell." Sally took a deep breath. It didn't *really* matter, what he'd done, but it pissed her off regardless. One thing she hated was sticky mitts.

She drank half of her Coke, left the glass on the bar and walked towards the door the lady had gestured to. She pushed it open. A corridor stretched ahead. She marched down it, checking each door until she found one with 'office' on a silver plaque. She knocked and waited.

Peter lumbered towards her, his bald head shining beneath the spotlights. "A King's come in. Reckon they're on the same fact-finding mission as we are?"

"Not our business unless they cause us hassle." Sally frowned. "Why isn't he responding to my knock?" She tapped the door again.

"Come *in*, I said!"

"Blimey, he's arsey," Sally whispered. "I didn't hear him the first time." The barked command reminded her of Richard, and she walked inside, her teeth gritted, ready to do

164

battle if need be. "DCs Sally Wiggins and Peter Dove. Can we have a quick word about one of your customers?"

"If I know them, yes, although I might not reveal their secrets. Have a seat. Dump that shit there on the floor."

Sally and Peter removed the piles of paperwork from the chairs and sat.

The landlord, about sixty, pulled at his long, greying beard. "Who is it you're after?"

"Can I have your name first, please?" Sally asked. "For our records."

"Al Capone," he said.

Sally sighed internally. Why did she feel tested some days more than others? "Your real name."

"I'd have thought you'd have checked the licensee sign above the door before you came in. Some copper you are."

Sally smiled, although a mean retort sat on her tongue, one she wouldn't voice. "We can't all be perfect. So . . . ?"

"Harry Wells."

"Okay, Mr Wells. What can you tell us about a Cormac O'Reilly?"

"Oh, fuck me, the filth questioning me about one of their own. This can't be good."

Harry's evasion got on Sally's nerves, and she bit her bottom lip for a second so she didn't snap at him. He was wasting time by not giving straight answers.

"He's come up in an investigation." *Come up dead.* "People have said he's unpleasant towards women."

"He pinches a lot of arses, if that's what you mean. Can't say that's unpleasant, can you, son?" He grinned at Peter, laughed at his own gross joke, then coughed up a lung.

"It's assault," Peter said. "I don't condone that sort of thing."

"Well, *that* put me in my place, didn't it?" Harry chuckled. "Look, he's handsy, I'll give you that, but he's harmless. What's happened to the days when a pinch on the bum was

165

considered a compliment, eh? I mean, how else are men supposed to let birds know they fancy them?"

Sally didn't feel that needed an answer. "Regarding his
behaviour, do you know of anyone who has been upset by it?"

"Loads of that lot on Rowan. The scutty cows are jealous
he hasn't touched *them*. Always moaning about him, they are.
Mind you, there's a few blokes he's naffed off an' all, said they
could do with punching his lights out. I don't know what all
the fuss is about myself."

"Any specific names spring to mind?" Peter asked.

Harry smirked. "I've suddenly gone a bit thick up top.
Can't recall any, no."

Sally linked her fingers and squeezed out her frustration.
She may as well tell him about O'Reilly. It was probably all over
Rowan by now anyway. "Mr O'Reilly has been murdered. *Now*
do you recall anyone who may have wanted to harm him?"

Harry leaned back, a hand to his lips. "Ah, you've put me
in a tricky spot."

"Why?" Sally asked.

"If I divulge names, I'm likely to get walloped."

"The Kings, by any chance?" Peter queried.

Harry slid his eyes away. "I wouldn't like to say."

Sally sat forward. "Was there a price on his head?"

"Something like that."

Sally didn't think she'd get any more out of him, but
she had to try. "We're in the process of finding anyone who
O'Reilly inappropriately touched, to help them. Can you
remember who they might be?"

"Yep, but it's up to them to come forward. If they haven't
already, it means they want to keep it to themselves. I'm not
telling their stories for them."

Sally glanced at Peter, who got up.

"Thanks for speaking to us," he said.

Sally rose, forced a smile and left.

In the corridor, the office door closed, Sally whispered,
"We know Trigger and Wheels have been waiting for their

chance, so it's a given they're the men Harry's on about. Anna said the Kings are helping us. Why? To make it look like they didn't top Nigel and O'Reilly and attack Matthew?"

"I'm telling you, they would have slashed their faces first, and killed them later if they didn't behave."

Sally eyed him. "You seem pretty sure."

"Everyone knows that's their style."

Peter stalked off, and Sally followed him into the bar, her mind going over what he'd said; or, rather, *how* he'd said it. There had always been an iffy air about him, but she hadn't been able to put her finger on it. He wasn't the same as Warren. He was an open book, you knew where you stood with him. But Peter?

I'll be watching him from now on. Something's not right.

CHAPTER TWENTY-EIGHT

At four o'clock, Anna stood in front of the whiteboard and studied everyone's faces. The team looked weary after a couple of days out in the field.

"Right, you lot go home," she said. "We've got nothing to go on. Forensics and Herman still haven't made contact, and they'll be busy with the O'Reilly business anyway. As we spent the afternoon running round Marlford trying to find people who had a beef with O'Reilly and getting nowhere—"

"Except that the Kings were after him," Sally said and glanced at Peter.

What was that look for?

"Have I missed something?" Anna asked.

"Um, no," Sally said. "It's just that Harry at the Plough implied the Kings were after O'Reilly, that he had a price on his head. I was checking it with Peter, that's all."

"Peter?" Anna stared at him.

The DC shifted uncomfortably. He never did like the spotlight on him. "Yes, Harry said that, although he didn't outright *say* it, if you get me."

"That's why I said *implied*," Sally snapped.

What the hell's going on here? Anna wasn't one for secrets and private grievances. They brought about divides, and she wasn't having it. "Out with it, Sally."

Sally blushed. "Out with what?"

Anna tapped her foot. "Something's miffed you off. I want to hear it."

"It's nothing, I'm just tired."

Anna didn't believe her. She'd get it out of her later. "Then all the more reason for you to call it a day. I'm going to visit Hawthorn Farm and speak to Matthew's father. That pig death, the mother, it's bothering me."

"You're not going on your own," Lenny said and held his hand up to stop her retort. "I know you're capable and all that bollocks, but it's a fair way from other houses, a bit too remote. What is it you always say? We're not lone wolves like in the films and books."

Anna conceded his point. "Fair enough. I'll shut my computer down and be with you in a second. Everyone else, have Sunday off. By Monday we might get a DNA result on Nigel and word from Herman. There's no one else to speak to as far as I can see, we covered it all today."

She left them to gather their things, going into her office and closing the blinds so she could sit and think for a moment. She switched off her computer, sat back and closed her eyes. Thought about things logically.

One, it wasn't just Carys they had to watch. Matthew was also a common denominator here. He could harbour grudges against Nigel and O'Reilly, perhaps Gordon and Parole, too. All of those men could have, in his mind, stolen his wife away and prevented them getting back together.

Two, the attack on him might not have anything to do with Operation Jewel. He could have pissed someone off and didn't want to tell the police why.

Three, if pigs had eaten his mother, could they have also eaten Nigel and O'Reilly? But was she stretching here? Could that mild-mannered man *really* have done this?

She cleared her mind and breathed deeply, sinking into a meditative state.

A knock on the door pulled her out of it. DCI Placket popped his head in.

"I was taking a breather, sir."

Placket came in and closed the door. "Don't get up on my account." He sat in the chair opposite her desk. "I need a word."

"Something wrong?"

"No, you're all good. You know I trust you to run with the current line of inquiry. It's something else, although it could well be related."

She tensed. "Go on."

"I had a phone call yesterday."

Anna schooled her features so they didn't betray her. She didn't want to get Karen in the shit for gossiping. "Right."

"It was from an officer calling from a public phone."

He seemed to battle with whether to tell her. Maybe he'd also done that in his office, convincing himself he needed a second opinion, and now he'd changed his mind again.

"And?" she prompted.

"This goes no further."

"Of course not."

"It was Parvati Jahinda. She had a panic attack while out on a job by herself and didn't want to get hold of me by our usual channels — listening ears an' all that. She didn't know my direct number so had to phone the main desk to be put through."

"A panic attack? Is she okay now?" Anna asked.

"Yes, but she wasn't. Anyway, I needed to go and get her. She couldn't even drive back to the station until I'd calmed her down." He paused. "I found her standing on the ledge of the Gear Hub building. She'd regretted phoning me and ran up there to end it all."

Anna's heart lurched. "Bloody hell! What for?"

"She's going through something and her family aren't happy with it. The email I sent yesterday."

"Oh God, the sexual misconduct?" *Did I sound suitably surprised?*

"Unfortunately, yes. Now, she said her family would see it as a shameful thing. She explained their customs, how she might be cast out of her community because she brought the matter to my attention. They would have asked her to keep it a secret, to not make a fuss, and they would deal with it themselves. Parvati couldn't keep it to herself, didn't want the man in question to get away with doing it to someone else, so she pushed aside her family's needs and told me."

"Poor love."

"I know, a terrible quandary for her. Okay, so in light of me being appraised about what's going on, what Operation Jewel is, I've had to come forward to speak to you. She understands why, but, if you can see it from her point of view, what was already a big deal for her has escalated."

"I don't understand where you're going with this."

"Parvati had a short fling with Nigel Fogg. Eight months ago, to be exact."

"Oh."

"Hmm. He promised her the world, which is the only reason she went with him — seeing a man outside of marriage is also a black mark against her. Her family want an arranged marriage, but so far she's refused. A difficult situation all round. Anyway, he later made it clear she was just a fling, and she confided in her sister. She also told her about the man involved with the sexual misconduct investigation before she informed me. The next thing she knows, Nigel winds up dead."

"So she thought what?"

"That her father or brothers had something to do with it. Then I find out O'Reilly's been murdered — she doesn't know that yet as I told her yesterday to stay off work for a bit."

"Oh shit, *he's* the man she reported?" Again, Anna hoped she'd sounded shocked enough. "Unfortunately, that doesn't surprise me. We've heard some horror stories about him during the investigation."

"Really? Filthy bastard. So now she thinks her family has picked off two men she had dealings with. She said her community will close ranks. We won't get anything out of any of them unless we find a chink in the armour. She thinks she's found one but she needs my help."

"So if we're going with that theory, where does Matthew Brignell come into it? Did she see him as well?"

"No."

"I think this is a big coincidence, to be honest. From what we've learned, Operation Jewel centres around Carys and Matthew Brignell. She went with *all* of those men, plus Gordon White and Joshua Cribbins — Parole."

"*Gordon?* Good grief. If the latter two wind up dead, I'll be inclined to go with it being Carys as the one who links them, but we can't ignore the Parvati angle."

"You said this goes no further. How can I investigate it without my team knowing?"

"I'll deal with the Parvati side of it. Having one officer as a point of contact with them will be sufficient. I don't want to rock the boat. They'll take offence if your lot go in, it'll feel like an ambush and they'll clam up. I'm meeting Parvati in a few minutes and going to see someone she knows in the mosque. He's aware of everything that's going on when it comes to this sort of thing."

"What, like he's the man people go to when they want to commit murder? Do they need to run it by him?"

"Something like that. It's complicated. Parvati said they'll think they're doing the right thing by killing Nigel and O'Reilly, if they even did, because they're defending her honour. She's explained quite a bit to me, and I can see where they're coming from. Naturally, I can't outwardly agree with it because I've promised to uphold the law, but . . . She just wants to find out if it was them."

"And you think they're going to admit it to her — and you — when you're police officers? Highly unlikely, sir."

"I know, but she wants to try. She could have kept this quiet. It'll be frowned upon that she's told me of her suspicions. She might well find herself with no family after this. She's been very brave in coming forward."

Anna felt for the woman. "Did she plan to kill herself because of pressure from her community?"

"Yes. Her sister blabbed, so there's been a discussion about Parvati's 'behaviour'. Someone suggested that was her only way out."

"God, really?"

"I know. She felt she was stuck between a rock and a hard place. The only reason I've come here and told you all this is in case you and your team stumbled down this avenue."

"We haven't found out about everyone Nigel slept with yet. That's something for next week."

"Right. Going in there all guns blazing, questioning them, when Parvati's family may not have anything to do with it . . . Not a good look for us if it came out in the press. That's not the reason I want it kept quiet, though, absolutely not. My main priority is Parvati."

"I know that."

She really did, too. Placket was one in a million. He cared about everyone at the station, only wanted the best for them. Anna felt guilty now for even *thinking* he was the Kings' copper.

"I should have something for you by Monday. If it's looking like it's Parvati's family by then, you'll have to let your team in on it, but if it isn't you keep it to yourself."

Anna nodded. "That's doable."

"Where are you at now?"

"Me and Lenny were about to visit Hawthorn Farm." She mentioned Matthew's mother being eaten by pigs. "It's bugging me. Where's the rest of those bodies? We only have heads."

"I was the SIO on that one. Fascinating things, pigs. Matthew's father told me all about them." He informed her of their behaviours. "Who knew they'd get so arsey and eat the poor woman?"

Anna digested the information. "Maybe her son was inspired by the experience, about getting rid of bodies?"

"Do you think? If I remember rightly, he's a quiet chap. The father didn't strike me as a killer either."

"Most of them don't." Anna sighed.

"True." Placket stood. "So it could be Matthew. But what about the attack on him?"

"What about it? It's easy to nut a window frame, isn't it?"

Placket nodded. "But with no proof . . ."

"Exactly. It's just a case of plodding on until we find some."

Placket glanced at his watch. "I'd better go."

"Give Parvati my love."

"I will."

He left, and Anna pondered what he'd said. While the Parvati perspective would tie it all up in a neat bow, it didn't explain how Matthew Brignell was involved. The strong suspicion that it centred around Carys wouldn't go away, so she got up and collected her coat, determined to clear Parvati's family of any wrongdoing. That woman had enough to contend with as it was without another shitstorm raining all over her.

CHAPTER TWENTY-NINE

Anna drove past a lay-by and turned off onto the track that led to Hawthorn Farm, a wonky, handmade wooden sign pointing the way. The place stood in darkness apart from one square of light, presumably a downstairs room in the farmhouse. Everything else, the barns and such, presented as dark, shadowy hulks, crouching ominously in the night. It gave her the creeps, to be honest, but she stuffed down the smidgen of unease and blamed it on the fact that killer pigs could live on the property. She parked on a forecourt in front of the house and cut the engine.

She glanced at her partner. "Are you all right?" Lenny had been quiet on the journey over.

"I was going to ask you the same thing," he said. "Placket was with you for a fair old while."

"Oh, that was nothing. Just discussing the case."

"He seemed harassed when he left your office, as if he'd given you a roasting."

Anna laughed nervously. She hated keeping things from Lenny, he was her best friend as well as a colleague, but she wouldn't break Placket's trust in her. There had been many times she'd had to keep things from the team, so this was just another to add to the list.

"Maybe he was dreading going back to work," she said. "It is Saturday, after all. He could have had a nice night in front of the box lined up but had to go off and report to his seniors about Jewel."

"True."

Anna left the car and waited for Lenny. She switched on her torch. A black Mini sat to the left, one they'd already established belonged to Matthew. *He must be here.* Anna approached the front door. It looked more like a gate with vertical slats, the green paint stripped away in places from the weather, revealing the greyed grain. It even had a metal ring as a handle with a keyhole beneath.

"Not exactly secure," Lenny muttered.

"No." Anna knocked, then, receiving no response, moved to the nearest window and pointed her torch beam at it. "A mudroom leading onto a kitchen. Let's go and nose through the window with the light on." She trudged farther along and was met by open curtains and the view of an old-fashioned living room straight out of the eighties, all teak furniture and a three-bar fire.

Matthew sat on a flower-patterned sofa, his head back, asleep. Anna knocked on the glass and he snapped his eyes open, glancing their way. She aimed the beam at her face so he could see who she was. He got up and disappeared through a doorway.

The gate-door opened and he switched on the outdoor bulb, poking his head outside. "Can I help?"

"Hi, Matthew," Anna said, noting his clothing. Black train-ers, blue jeans, and a blue sweatshirt. "We came for a chat with your father. Is he around?"

"No, he's on holiday in Calais. I've been feeding the ani-mals while he's away, mucking them out an' that."

"What type of animals?"

"Chickens and pigs."

How do I broach this without it sounding like I'm accusing him of something? I don't want him to know he's a suspect. "Ah, that's why we wanted to speak to him. About the pigs and whether anyone's been hanging around here recently."

"No one's been here while I've been around. I was going to go home, actually. Why would you need to know?"

"During our investigation, we found out about your mother. Sorry for your loss. It occurred to us that, as the bodies haven't turned up, just the heads—"

"Bodies?" Matthew blurted. "Heads? Has someone else been killed?"

"Ah, yes. A Mr Cormac O'Reilly."

"That man who fancies Carys?"

"Yes." *So he's been listening in on conversations or asking about her?*

"Blimey." He raised a shaking hand to his forehead and massaged the lines in his brow.

"Did you know him well?"

"No. I knew *of* him, though. Bloody hell . . . That's not good, is it? So what's that got to do with my dad?"

"Nothing. We wanted to see if perhaps someone had come here to feed the pigs. Maybe someone's been giving them bodies for dinner."

"*What?*"

"Sorry to be so blunt about it. Have there been any new pigs introduced this week?"

He seemed startled that she knew that kind of information. She wouldn't have if Placket hadn't told her.

"Err, yes, Dad asked me to do it slowly, so I've got a few more to add to the main pen over the course of the week. Saves the other pigs getting too upset if I do it a couple at a time."

"That riles the pigs up, yes?"

"Yeah, but they've been eating as normal. Haven't been acting like they're full up or anything. I can't believe you think someone's put Nigel and that other fella in the pen."

177

"We have to follow all avenues. Have you noted any tyre tracks that shouldn't be there? Any footprints?"

"Nah."

"So you'd say no one other than you has been here, correct?"

"That's right."

"Okay, thanks for your time." Anna turned to go but spun back. "One more thing. Were you here last night?"

"Yes. I came to make sure everything was all right."

"What time was that?"

"I didn't check, but it was before seven. I went to bed early. I wasn't well, remember."

"Does your dad own a Transit?"

He frowned. "No."

"Do you?"

"No."

Sally had already looked into that, but Anna wanted to hear it from the horse's mouth. Well, she wanted to scare him really. If he was the killer, he'd know she was onto him and might leave off going after Gordon and Parole, *if* that was his intention.

"So you went to bed at your flat, yes?"

"Yes, at seven."

"You went nowhere near the services on Westgate?"

He lowered his hand and shoved it in his pocket.

Anna tensed in case he had a weapon.

"Why would I go there?" Matthew asked.

"Oh, I don't know. For a McDonald's?"

"Not me, no."

"Thanks." She strode back to the car, sensing Lenny following her. Behind the steering wheel, she stuck her seat belt on and then revved the engine, the headlights blasting at Matthew, who'd remained on the doorstep.

Lenny got in, buckled up and muttered, "Did you get the impression he was shitting himself or was it just me?"

"I wouldn't go that far, but he was certainly flustered, if only marginally. Not like this laid-back persona he's usually got. But we did wake him up, so he might be ratty or disorientated. I asked him those questions so, if it *is* him, I can remind him later that he lied."

"I gathered that."

"Like I said to Placket earlier, there's sod all we can do without evidence. For all we know, there could be blood and all sorts in with those pigs, yet we can't get a warrant as we don't have any reason to believe Matthew's guilty of anything. Just because his mother got eaten doesn't mean Nigel and O'Reilly were." She reversed onto the track. "This is the part of our job that really gets my back up. We're stuck."

"So you think it's him?"

"Don't you? The attack aside, we'd normally have him at the top of our list."

"Hmm. Bit weird to injure yourself, though, isn't it?"

"Not if it saves your arse." Anna drove down the track and onto the country road. "I wonder if he'll go in and muck those pigs out now before he goes home, get rid of whatever it is that goes in those pens. I don't know, mud?" She swerved into a lay-by and cut the engine.

Lenny sighed. "Aww, what are you up to?"

"Fancy a bit of trespassing?"

"I *knew* you were going to say that."

"Come on, we'll watch for a bit."

They got out and made their way through the trees, into a field, then approached a hedge that blocked it off from the farm buildings. She gazed past the track that led to the house. The living room and mudroom lights had gone off, but a wide shaft of brightness flooded a swath of concrete. A white Transit drove out of a barn, then stopped. Matthew got out, closed the double doors and climbed back in the van.

"That little liar," Lenny muttered.

"Quick, I need to move the car, else he'll see it if he goes towards Marlford."

They ran back to the lay-by and dived inside the vehicle. Anna sped away, going as far as the next track. She took a left, did a U-turn into a short pathway that led to a gate, then shot forward and parked on the verge at the junction, ready to follow Matthew, her headlights off.

"The Transit didn't have any decals on the side," Lenny said, "so he might have lied about him or his dad owning the van for whatever reason."

"The lie's enough for me. If he's got nothing to hide, why bullshit us?"

They sat for five minutes.

The van didn't come past.

"He must have gone the other way," Anna said. "I didn't catch a number plate either, did you?"

"It was too dark. The light was coming from behind the van, so I couldn't see the front."

"What do you reckon he's done, bought one cheap for cash and hasn't registered it? Stolen plates from an Audi because subconsciously it's a link to Nigel?"

"That's what I'd do if I was going round murdering people."

"Same."

Another five minutes crawled by. Anna phoned the station and asked them to keep an eye out for a white van jaunting around Marlford, specifically around Gordon White's and Parole's homes.

She stared into the distance, squinting.

What the hell?

"Can you see what I see?" She pointed.

Lenny looked that way. "Fire?"

"I bet he's lit the damn thing up." Anna got the engine going and drove in the general direction. "Keep an eye out for him on foot. Phone it in. Get uniforms out here."

Down a narrow lane, she slowed by a man and woman walking their dog. She opened the window. "Excuse me. Police. Did you see a white Transit come this way?"

"No, but I heard an engine before we came out," the man said. "We're in that cottage down there, but some bloke almost knocked us over, rushing past us."

"When was this?"

"About five minutes ago. He went into that field there. We'd only just been in there with the dog."

"What did he have on?"

"I couldn't really see in the dark," the woman said, "but he had a balaclava on. Frightened the life out of me."

"Thanks. Would you mind going home and locking yourselves in, please?"

"Bloody hell, what's going on?" the man asked.

"If you could do as I said." Anna raised the window and drove on. "Keep the station informed for me, will you, Lenny?"

He got on with that while Anna concentrated on the road, periodically glancing at the field on her right. Hedges prevented her from seeing much, but if a drone was sent up they might spot Matthew — if it was even him.

"Who am I kidding?" she muttered. "Who the hell else would it be?"

"Talking to yourself again?" Lenny smiled.

Ahead, the fire grew brighter and the flames taller. She came abreast of it. The van had been left in the mouth of a lane, all the doors closed, but the windows had busted from the intense heat. Flames licked out into the night. Anna reversed her car to a safe distance, then jumped out and jogged to the lane. In the corner of her eye, blue lights flashed on the road from Marlford, presumably a fire engine as they were quite high up. She gave the van a wide berth and circled it, in case Matthew was hiding nearby, even though the couple had said a man had rushed past them. She returned to her car and backed down the lane, parking in a passing spot so the fire engine could get by without any hassle. It barrelled along, and Anna followed it while Lenny gave a running commentary on the phone.

"I'll let them know what's gone on," she said and left the car again.

A fireman walked towards her, others behind him unravelling the hose. "What's the story?"

"Evening, Chris." She gave him a quick rundown. "We ought to go and see if we can catch up with him at the farm — if he's torched the van, he'll need his car. I don't suppose I should hold out much hope of getting evidence out of that Transit once your lot have put the fire out?"

"I wouldn't count on it, it seems too far gone, but you never know."

Anna waved goodbye and drove towards Hawthorn Farm. "Have uniforms been sent out?"

Lenny nodded. "They've been informed, put it that way. There's been a disturbance in Southgate, a load of pissheads in a fight, so they're held up there. Someone's been stabbed."

"Poor sod."

She sped up the farm track and swung onto the forecourt. The Mini had gone.

"Shit." She whacked the steering wheel and gunned it back out onto the road, narrowly missing a patrol car. She stopped and, window down, passed on who they were looking for to the driver. "And we've got no evidence that will allow us to go inside that house or the barns, so don't enter unless there's a threat to life or just cause. At the minute, all he's done in the eyes of the law is setting his Transit on fire."

"We'll stay here for a bit, see if he comes back," the officer said.

"If he does, I want to know about it. I'll get word to you if we catch up with him elsewhere."

Anna zoomed off towards Marlford, adrenaline pumping. She hadn't expected this to happen, so there went her idea of having dinner in her village pub, another lazy night without cooking. She'd been envisaging a lasagne and chips all day.

Lenny finished on the phone. "The drone's up, but there's no sighting of him."

"No, because he legged it to the farm and fucked off in that Mini," Anna said, veering onto Matthew's housing estate. She made it through the streets without having to stop for any pedestrians and parked outside his block of flats.

"No Mini," Lenny said.

In the foyer, Anna knocked on the door, Lenny beside her, ready to act if Matthew answered and got bolshy. With no response, she left Lenny still knocking and walked down the alley between blocks and tried the back gate. Locked. She peered through a knothole and made out the faint shapes of yesterday's washing still on the line, the basket with the trousers on the grass. Taking a deep breath, she vaulted the fence and prowled the garden in case Matthew hid in the dark. Her torchlight didn't pick him up, so, back in the car, she belted up and waited for Lenny.

He got in and stared at her. "You should have waited for me when you went in that garden."

"Yep, but I didn't. Stupid of me, sorry. Can you find Parole's number and warn him to keep an eye out? If we're going by who Carys went with in order, we need to get to Gordon first."

It took ten minutes to reach the house. Anna dived from the car and pelted up the path. She hammered on the door with the side of her fist, pleased to see a light shining through a crack in the curtains, although that didn't mean Gordon was okay.

He opened the door. "Where's the ruddy fire, woman?"

"In one of the fields by the Brignells' farm."

"Eh?"

"Doesn't matter. Are you all right?"

"Why wouldn't I be?"

"Can I come in?"

Gordon smiled. "Checking up on whether I did the cleaning, are you? Well, I did. Come and have a gander at this. I'm knackered but feel a lot better for doing it. Now I know why the wife went hammer and tongs at it when she was pissed off at me. It's quite cathartic."

Anna went inside and was assaulted by the various scents of cleaning products. She poked her head into the living room. The sight of hoover stripes on the grey carpet was satisfying. "Brilliant." She turned to Lenny, who'd come inside, smiled, then told Gordon what had been going on. "Is there someone you can stay with for a while? I'm worried Matthew Brignell's going to come after you."

"I'd like to see him try." Gordon puffed his chest out.

"I know you can take care of yourself, but are you a match for an axe or machete?"

"Fair point." Gordon stared at the ceiling, thinking. "Um, I'll have to go and kip at the Premier Inn. There's only the wife, and she's not going to want me staying at her flat."

Anna felt for him. No one to call his own anymore. "If you see a Mini, keep driving until you lose it. We don't need him knowing where you are." She ran a hand over her face. "Lenny, did you get a message to Parole?"

"Yep. He's in the Kite."

"Maybe we should warn Carys."

Gordon frowned. "You think she could be in danger?"

"I don't know, but I don't want to take the risk." Anna bit her lip.

"It might not even be him," Gordon said.

"I realise that, but why torch his van if he's got nothing to hide?"

"He could have some hooky gear," Gordon suggested.

"He could, but this is all a bit too weird for me," Anna said. "Better that we follow this line of inquiry rather than let it slide."

She let out a long breath.

Where have you gone, Matthew? And what the bloody hell are you doing?

CHAPTER THIRTY

Matthew had parked his Mini in a disused area behind a row of empty shops on Eastgate, too paranoid to drive it anymore. Unless someone went round there, it would be safe. It was Shanks's pony from now on. He waited down an alley, balaclava on, hands in his jeans pockets. Those coppers going to the farm had shit him up. Specifically that they'd worked out what he'd done with the bodies. How, though? He'd been so careful. Was it as Anna had said — they'd found out about Mum's death during the investigation? At what point had they joined the dots without anything else to go on?

The Transit. They know about that an' all.

The net seemed to be closing in, and he couldn't work out why. Had the van been caught on camera after all? Or had one of those nosy fuckers in O'Reilly's street seen him and phoned the police? He wouldn't put it past them. He'd taken the plumber decals off, but a white Transit was a white Transit, so the police could have wanted to have a look inside it regardless. If they had, they'd have seen it decked out in plastic sheeting. Yes, he'd cleaned all the blood off, but they'd have still asked why it even *needed* sheeting. What would he have said? How could he have explained himself?

You could have made out you put the new pigs in there when you picked them up. Why didn't I think of that before?

At the time, panic overtaking him, he'd had no choice but to torch it. All had been fine until he'd bumped into those people walking their dog. No one would have spotted him otherwise, as he'd made it back to the farm without seeing anyone else. He should have waited until it was dark, the middle of the night, then got rid of it.

Were officers waiting for him at his flat? He hadn't driven near there to check. They'd know he owned a Mini, so he could have been stopped on the way.

Calm down. If they thought it was you, they'd have arrested you.

Wouldn't they? Or didn't they have enough proof? Were they only guessing it was him because of his affiliation with Carys?

Not knowing did his head in.

He stamped his feet, trying to get some warmth into them. Tonight was as cold as anything, and he was out earlier than usual. He wouldn't be able to go home to switch his phone off at ten and leave it there either. He'd turned it off at Hawthorn and put it in the kitchen cupboard after Anna and Baldy had gone.

He imagined what they were doing now. If they'd twigged his plan, they'd likely have told Gordon and Parole to watch out. That's why he'd changed tack.

Jealousy boiled inside him. Even though he'd known they weren't suited, it still bugged him that she'd cheated on him. Treated him badly before that. He'd been nothing but good to her, discounting the fact he'd barely been at home some nights. He hadn't hit her, he'd given her money, and he'd bought her flowers and little gifts. Mum always said a wife needed to be spoiled. And he'd tried so hard to do that. Why hadn't that been enough for Carys?

Had she found out he was a freak? Was that why she'd turned to Nigel? Did she know his mother had done things to him — and that, shamefully, despite it being so wrong, he'd kind of liked it? Who could have told her, though? Dad wouldn't have. Or had Matthew talked in his sleep? He was known for that.

Footsteps approached, and he moved back to disguise himself behind some bushes that were mainly bare branches, autumn stripping their leafy clothes away. In the shadows, he quietened his breathing. The person he was after strutted past, and rage burned a hole in his gut, acid zipping up his throat to coat the back of his tongue. They didn't have a care in the world. That was the thing about people, he'd found. They didn't realise how quickly their lives could be snuffed out. They didn't realise when they woke up that today would be their last.

Was he guilty of being the same? Was today *his* last? Of freedom?

The thought unsettled him. In no way, shape, or form had he envisaged being caught for this. And that was another thing. How come the police suspected him when he'd been attacked? Had those forensic people in his garden worked out he'd done it to himself? Could they even do that?

The target had almost reached the end of the alley. He had the urge to chase after them, drag them to his car and take them to the farm. Do his thing. But he couldn't trust that the police weren't there, waiting for him. They'd certainly be attending the scene of the fire. That couple would have phoned it in.

Instead of following his gut, he mooched down the other end of the alley and walked into a residential street. Checked it for observers. There would be no waylaying outside tonight. No, he'd break into the house and wait.

He slipped gloves on and approached the property, a smile stretching out beneath his balaclava. This person was supposed to be his finale, so bringing it forward annoyed him. Still, as long as the job got done, it didn't really matter *when*, did it?

He scooted down the side of the house and entered the back garden. Glanced at the windows of the neighbouring homes. Nodded.

It'd go without a hitch, he'd make sure of it. The only problem was, who would take care of the pigs and chickens until Dad got home? And where would he go once this was all over? Because returning to his flat or Hawthorn was no longer an option, not if those detectives had worked out it was him.

Fuck it.

CHAPTER THIRTY-ONE

Anna wouldn't normally be fond of someone like Parole eyeing her up but, for God's sake, she found herself liking it. They sat at a secluded table, Parole opposite her, Lenny beside her, Wheels leaning on the booth divider. It reminded her of banisters. It gave the illusion of privacy with the struts close together, but anyone could hear their conversation. Thankfully, the booth was in the corner and no one was within earshot. Wheels hadn't wanted to have this discussion in his office; he'd said people were already gossiping because of visits from the police earlier. If it was done in the open, no one would think they were being questioned about the murders.

"So you definitely think it's him?" Wheels asked quietly.

"Yes and no," Anna said. "We have no proof."

"Doesn't matter," Parole chipped in. "Proof or not, it makes sense that it's him."

"Didn't you say he got attacked?" Wheels asked Anna.

Parole snorted. "Anyone could do that to themselves."

Wheels nodded. "What can we do?"

Anna thought about that. She shouldn't ask them for their help, not really, not in the way she wanted to. As in asking them to root Matthew out and bring him to her. "If you see him, let me know where he is."

"I'll do more than that." Parole sipped some Coke. "I mean, if I'm on his list, then I'll beat the shit out of him."

"Anna's not the type to go deaf," Wheels warned. "If you openly threaten to harm someone, she might do something about it."

Anna smiled. "I can go deaf if I have to, but I draw the line at being there when you catch up with him. If you go for him, I can't stand back and do nothing about it."

Parole grinned. "Who said I'd do it when you're around?"

Lenny sighed. "No disrespect, but this isn't getting us anywhere. Where would he go, d'you know?" He looked at Wheels, then Parole.

"No idea," Wheels said. "We're not exactly buddies, and he hasn't come up on our radar enough for us to follow him until now. He's got, what? His flat, his job, and that farm. Sounds to me like he's a terminal loner. No mates. No girlfriend. His dad's in Calais, you said."

"What about Carys?" Anna asked. "Would she harbour him because they were married? For old times' sake?"

"Fuck, no." Parole shook his head. "She can't stand him. She wouldn't piss on him if he was on fire."

"Thanks for that image." Anna drank some lemonade.

"All we can do is get some of the Kings out there looking." Wheels took his phone out. "Want me to get hold of Trigger? With your lot going after him, plus our lot, someone's got to catch up with him."

Anna nodded. "Okay, but no hurting him, I mean it. I could get in the shit if it comes out that I had a hand in him being attacked."

Wheels walked away, the phone to his ear.

"So, his old dear got eaten by pigs, did she?" Parole asked. "I did hear you right, didn't I?"

"Yes," Lenny said. "And he confirmed that he's introduced new pigs this week."

190

Parole frowned. "What's that got to do with anything?"

Anna explained. "So you can see why I'm worried. Pigs going wild because their snouts have been put out of joint is an ideal way to get rid of bodies. As those bodies haven't turned up, I did the maths. I could be wrong, but I've felt uneasy about him right from the start."

"Clever bastard." Parole opened a bag of cheese and onion crisps. "Want one?"

Anna's stomach grumbled. "No, ta. I'm going to order a sandwich or something. Do you want one, Lenny?"

He bobbed his head. "Yep, your turn to pay."

She smiled. "Good, because that means the bill is cheaper. Full meals are more expensive."

Lenny laughed. "Crafty cow."

Anna left the table and stood at the bar. She placed her order for two ham and tomato baguettes. The door creaked behind her, and she turned. Carys waltzed in, a big smile stretching her ruby lips. She sashayed up to the bar and caught sight of Anna. Her breezy demeanour switched to a frosty glare.

"Bloody hell, not you again," she muttered.

"You don't seem too cut up about Nigel's murder," Anna said. "Anyone would think you're glad, the way you walked in."

"People cope with grief differently. There's no rule book."

"Clearly."

Carys ignored the dig and asked for a vodka and Coke. She faced Anna. "Anyway, why are you here? Shouldn't you be out there, searching for who did it?"

"We are. It can take days, weeks, months. Investigations mean a lot of legwork. Look, I'm not being funny, but what is Matthew *really* like? Does he have a dark side?"

Carys laughed. "You what? Are you joking? He's a quiet moron, couldn't be dark if he tried."

"Did you know about his mother, what happened to her?"

191

"His dad told me. Matthew wouldn't talk about it. Anyway, it was in the papers. Did you have your head stuck up your arse at the time?"

"I did a stint working in Nottingham, it happened while I was away. Would you say the incident scarred him?"

"It would scar anyone, but I get what you're saying. Was his mum being eaten by pigs enough to twist his melons? If it did, I saw no evidence of it. Listen, I said it could be him who'd killed Nigel because of what happened, him finding us in bed, but I don't *really* think he's capable. He's such a wet lettuce."

"Have you ever seen him driving a white Transit?"

"Nope. Last I knew, he had a Kia."

The barmaid placed the baguettes on the bar.

"Thanks," Anna said. She waited for the woman to walk away. "Have you ever felt he posed a threat to you?"

"Me? Ha! Not likely. I'd cut his balls off if he came at me. Considering he only took a few clothes and walked out of the house crying that night, no. If he can't even get arsey about his wife shagging his best mate, then when can he?"

Confused, her emotions warring with her suspicion gene, Anna drummed her fingertips on the bar. "What I'm trying to get at is, did it ever seem like he was hiding his anger?"

"No."

"So in all honesty, you don't really think he's capable?"

"No. Although they do have axes at the farm. I assume that's what Nigel's head was chopped off with."

Anna pondered that. Again, with no proof that it could be Matthew she couldn't get a warrant to collect those axes. Frustration bubbled. "Okay, thanks for speaking to me again. You'll be careful, won't you? Just in case?"

"In case what? He's going off on a rampage because of me?" Carys gulped half of her drink. "I can see why it would look like that, with Nigel and that creepy copper being killed, but Matthew wasn't even that bothered I'd cheated on him, and he rolled over on the divorce. He didn't correct my solicitor, who filed for unreasonable behaviour on my say-so. He could have cited that I'd committed adultery, yet he didn't. Seriously, he hasn't got a backbone."

"Did you know that when you met him?"

"Yes, and it churned my stomach."

"Then why marry him?"

Carys smiled. "I like the finer things in life. I earn a packet but want more. His dad's getting on, and I thought he'd die and leave the farm to Matthew. I married him because I wanted half of the pie. When it became clear his father just *looked* half dead, I moved on."

Anna stared at her, aghast at such an honest answer. "You don't mince words."

"Well, you did ask."

Did Matthew know what she'd planned?

"Do you keep a diary?" Anna asked.

Carys narrowed her eyes. "Why do you want to know?"

"If you do, could Matthew have got hold of it? Would you have put that in there, about getting half of the farm?"

Carys paled. "Um . . . Should I be worried?"

"Why ask me that if you're so sure he's a wet lettuce?"

"Because finding out something like that could tip any-one over the edge." Carys finished her drink. "And I only wrote that in my diary a few months ago while I was ranting about everything going wrong, so if he's seen it . . ."

Anna's heart pounded. "Then he's been in your house?"

Carys shook her head. "This is daft. There's no way he could know."

"Is there anyone you can go and stay with until we find who did this?"

"Why, do you think I'm next?"

"I don't want to take the chance."

"But you said it could take weeks, months. I'm not stay-ing elsewhere for that long. It's okay, I have a house alarm."

"Be vigilant, all right?" Anna's conscience wouldn't let her leave it at that. "Can we go and check your house now?"

"What? I've only just got here. I'm not traipsing all the way back there." She fished in her handbag and took a bunch of keys out. "Here. Bring them back when you're done."

If she was the killer, she wouldn't want us in her house . . .

Anna took them. "I need to eat first, though."

Carys nodded, ordered another drink and effectively ended the conversation when she flashed a predatory smile at some poor bastard leaning on the wall by the gents' toilets.

Anna walked back to the table. Parole had gone, so she sat and handed Lenny his baguette, telling him about the conversation she'd had.

"Do you think I'm reaching? Overreacting by wanting to check her house?" she asked.

"No, just covering all bases."

Anna nodded to herself, jolting at the sight of Peter coming in. He strode straight to the bar, to Wheels, and spoke in his ear. It reminded Anna to message Sally, so she took her phone out.

Anna: *What's your issue with Peter? I realised you didn't want to say anything in front of him earlier.*

Sally: *He's always been odd, but today things felt weird.*

Anna: *In what way?*

Sally: *When it came to discussing the Kings.*

Anna: *Are you saying what I think you're saying?*

Sally: *I don't know. It all sounds so silly now.*

Anna: *We'll keep tabs, all right?*

Sally: *Okay.*

194

And it didn't sound silly, especially when Peter caught Anna staring over and his cheeks flared bright red.

Now why would he blush if he wasn't doing anything wrong?

CHAPTER THIRTY-TWO

They had prowled Carys's house and found nothing. Anna dropped Lenny home so he could spend the rest of his evening swiping right on the dating app. She returned to the station to check something that had been bothering her, needing to do it alone as she'd already peopled too much today. She'd roped a uniform in to do the necessary digging, and Matthew's father had indeed gone to Calais and was currently enjoying an all-inclusive. If Matthew was their man, he'd clearly chosen this week so he could get rid of the bodies undetected.

That told her something, or maybe some *things*. He valued his dad's opinion and didn't want to disappoint him. *Disappoint is an understatement*. Or he was so secretive he wanted to keep his kills to himself. Or he didn't want his father to come under fire from the police if it came out that the bodies had been "disappeared" at the farm. *Or* his father knew what he was up to, and Matthew had sent him on holiday so he wasn't directly involved.

She delved into the holidaying man. Vernon had been married before. His first wife, Wilma Brignell, née Olwin, had gone missing aged twenty-three. Vernon had been forty. He'd reported it, and the usual investigation had commenced.

Sadly, she hadn't turned up, and became another statistic. Notes on the file indicated she hadn't been happy with her marriage — friends and family had attested to that — and she'd struggled with being a wife, feeling her freedom had been taken away. Though her nearest and dearest didn't have a bad word to say about Vernon. Her mother had assumed she'd "done away with herself". Apparently, Wilma was "prone to exaggeration" and "enjoyed histrionics".

Looking at this as an outsider, Anna had no trouble reading between the lines. Wilma had suffered with her mental health and, all those years ago, help for that kind of thing wasn't particularly forthcoming. She would have been told to pull her socks up and march on, which may have left her floundering with nowhere to turn. Perhaps, with no one there to hold her hand, she *had* chosen to end it all.

The farm had been scoured. No signs of foul play. Vernon's statement came across as heartfelt, a husband worried for his wife, wishing he'd listened to her more instead of burying himself in farm business. All in all, a sad affair.

But what if he'd been lying?

Anna pulled up Matthew's mother's case files. Evelyn had been younger than Vernon by twenty years — the man clearly liked spring chickens. According to statements, Evelyn had been a strong woman who'd had a vivid sense of what she'd wanted. Ambitious, "reaching for the stars *and* all the planets", her father had said. One friend had mentioned that Evelyn didn't suffer fools gladly, was a tad abrasive, and brought her son up in a strict environment. She'd smacked him on occasion while with this friend.

She had died when Matthew was eighteen. A difficult thing for anyone only just walking into the adult world, the strings of childhood still stubbornly attached. Age didn't make you a man, and he may have struggled with losing his mother despite her being a tyrant.

Vernon, now in his early nineties, was certainly "getting on", as Carys had said. He hadn't married again.

Anna read through the reports. Placket had signed Evelyn's case off as death by misadventure, as had the coroner. With only teeth and a jawbone left, the Brignells had chosen to pace the halls of grief by themselves, support offered but none taken.

She scanned earlier in the report, where Wilma was mentioned. Placket clearly hadn't thought anything suspicious about the first wife's disappearance, otherwise he'd have noted it. It seemed the general consensus was that Vernon was an incredibly unlucky man when it came to his wives. The universe just didn't like some people, Anna had seen that first-hand, plight after plight raining down on them with no respite. Could these incidents be put down to that? *Was* that what had happened here? Or was Vernon responsible for Wilma vanishing and Evelyn's death?

She poked into his background. Nothing other than filing the missing person report and phoning in the pig attack. A law-abiding citizen, not even a parking ticket. Still, something nagged at Anna regarding Matthew. Could a man who had such dark things in his past really be so laid-back? Or had the tragedies forced him to lock the horrors up in order to survive? Had his mother's strictness instilled a sense of "behave and be quiet"? Had that spilled over into his adult life?

We need to go to his work, see what his colleagues have to say about him. If he's legged it, he won't turn up there on Monday.

The Transit, though. She couldn't ignore that. Had she not seen him getting into it and later found it engulfed in flames, she might have been inclined to put her suspicions down to her brain doing overtime, too many threads tangling together.

She powered down her computer. A cold cup of Earl Grey tea in hand, she left her office to use the microwave. She added the information to the whiteboard and studied everything. The attack aside, everything pointed to Matthew. Now, if they could find something concrete so they could search the farm and his flat, that would be grand.

"Still at it?"

She turned. Placket stood in the incident room doorway, his face wreathed in tiredness.

"How did it go?" she asked.

He came in and shut the door. "Parvati feels the person we spoke to isn't hiding anything. He appeared shocked that we asked whether anyone he knew had committed the murders."

"Do you believe him, given what we know?"

"I did. He had that look about him that spoke of true surprise and confusion. If her family did this, he had no knowledge of it."

What he said brought to mind Placket's assessment of Evelyn's case. He'd believed Vernon, too. Anna was fully aware of how people could pull the wool over their eyes during an investigation, but was Placket guilty of believing what he wanted to in both instances?

"Can I pick your brains?" she asked.

"Of course." He sat at Peter's desk and linked his hands over his belly.

Anna sat at Sally's and sipped some tea. "Okay, I know it was a long time ago so you might not remember, but during Evelyn Brignell's investigation did you wonder about the coincidence that *both* of Vernon's wives had left his life?"

"I certainly did. I went through his first wife's case with a fine-tooth comb and found nothing. Remind me of her name?"

"Wilma."

"That's right, yes. From what I could gather, people thought she had a screw loose." He caught Anna's wince. "Hmm. Things were different back then. None of that politically correct stuff going on. Rather than take her mental health concerns seriously as we would today, they were swept under the carpet. I think she either walked away and went to live somewhere under a different name, or she took her own life."

199

"Vernon waited years before he remarried," Anna pondered. "Obviously, he couldn't marry until the required amount of time had gone by for Wilma to be declared legally dead. So my thinking is, was he seeing someone on the side and needed Wilma out of the way? Or had he truly loved her and couldn't face starting afresh too soon? Or . . . had he purposely refrained from starting another relationship so it didn't look suspicious?"

"So you're saying he could have done away with Wilma."

"It isn't unheard of, that sort of thing."

"And this is related to Operation Jewel because . . . ?"

She went on to describe what had happened during their visit to the farm. "I'm beginning to wonder if Matthew's more damaged than we thought. A strict mother, a household where secrets boiled under the surface. A child, growing up isolated on a farm, turning into an insular man who has his own mental health issues." She sighed. "I don't know, maybe I'm reading into this more than I should."

"Any news on where he is now?"

"No sighting of him or his Mini. We also went to Carys's house. I was paranoid he'd go after her next."

"And you found nothing, I take it."

"No one there, not even in the garden. Lenny checked that and the loft."

"And Gordon?"

"He was going to the Premier Inn. Let me make sure he's there." Anna messaged him and received a response straight away. "He's gushing about how powerful the shower is."

Placket smiled. "Maybe the break there will do him good, like having a little holiday."

Anna nodded. "I know about his situation. He told us."

"Right. I won't discuss that. I said I wouldn't." Placket slapped the desk to end that part of the conversation. "So, if Matthew isn't the killer, he's still wanted for questioning about that van, so at least there's that. You *did* check his father's in Calais, didn't you?"

Anna crossed her ankles. "Yes, because I wondered, what with Evelyn being eaten, whether Matthew had bumped his dad off the same way. I went so far as to find out who Vernon had booked the holiday with and whether he'd arrived. I got a uniform onto it."

"And there's nowhere Matthew could have gone? No family members, friends?"

"No, it's just him and his dad left, and Carys wouldn't give him the time of day." She passed on that the woman had basically outed herself as a gold-digger.

"Blimey. She doesn't sound pleasant."

"No." Anna stood. "There's nothing I can do now but wait for word that our lot have spotted Matthew. Two of them are at the farm, and another two are sitting outside his flat. How long is it feasible to keep them there, though, when all we've really got him on is arson? They'll need to be relieved at some point."

"Losing four officers to observation can't be helped, not when it's a murder inquiry. I'll deal with any fallout on that score and arrange cover for shift change. Although, it's busy downstairs, what with the mass brawl in town, so there will be grumbles from above that we've got officers on surveillance. The person who was stabbed died."

"What was it over, do you know?"

"Football."

"Ah." Anna had never understood the footy mentality. It was just a ball of air being kicked around. "Okay, to recap: You don't feel the investigation leads towards Parvati — fine by me, as I have Matthew in the frame. We can now bring him in for torching the Transit and question him on why he lied and destroyed the vehicle. Hopefully, that will lead us towards getting him to slip up with regards to Nigel and O'Reilly. What will your public stance be on that, by the way? What I mean is, will you be telling the media that O'Reilly was an upstanding member of the force, or play it low-key? It feels a bit icky to give him a commendation-type press eulogy when he did what he did."

"I'm going with an officer being brought down in the line of duty." Placket stood. "Parvati suggested that, despite what he did to her."

"She's a kind woman. Too kind. In her shoes, I'd have wanted everyone to know exactly who he was; but, like you said, she has her family and community to consider. Can I ask, how is she now? It's been playing on my mind."

"She's going for counselling. Wants to remain at work so she doesn't have time to dwell on things. She'll be back Monday."

"Has anyone else come forward regarding sexual harassment? Or are you going to tell me to mind my own business?"

"Mind your own business." He smiled. "It's their story to tell, not mine."

"You're a good bloke." She recalled thinking he might be the Kings' mole, and a flush of guilt swamped her. "Can I bug you with one more thing?"

He shrugged. "Yep. It's not like I'd love to go home and have my dinner or anything . . ."

"Sorry, I'll be quick. What would you do if you *slightly* suspected a police officer worked for the Kings?"

"We know someone does, just not who. There's an in-the-background investigation into that, but keep that under your hat. The super wants it kept quiet, for obvious reasons. Why do you ask?"

She told him about Sally and how she'd behaved with Peter.

Placket frowned. "Have *you* ever felt Peter has stepped over the line?"

"No. He can look shifty at times, but I thought that was just how he behaved. Now Sally's said what she has . . . Plus he walked into the Kite earlier and beelined straight to Wheels. He went bright red when he saw me."

"Interesting. I'll let the team dealing with that know. They might opt to watch him."

"I feel such a plank, though."

"In what way?"

"He's been on my team for five years and I've never suspected him of *anything*."

"It happens. Bent coppers are good at what they do. I know he used to be a King, he told me, assured me he'd left before they'd gone to the dark side, just before he'd enrolled as a police officer. The team *did* look into his background and found nothing iffy, but maybe surveillance is in order now. I heard they've all got tattoos now. Of a crown. Such a shame we can't ask officers to strip so we can see who has one. If Peter does, that means he didn't leave the Kings after all."

"I hope Sally's wrong."

Placket grimaced. "But she never is, is she . . . ?"

Anna couldn't disagree with that.

* * *

She parked outside her cottage and walked to the pub in her village. The Jubilee, named after the lake in Marlford, was a community hub in Upton-cum-Studley and currently hosted the Saturday night quiz. She weaved through the tables, where people sat glazed in thought pondering the answer to the latest question. At the bar, she quietly ordered a vodka to go with her lemonade, plus a lasagne and chips. She chose a seat in the far corner, at a small round table scarred from years of use. Losing herself in the quiz while eating, although she wasn't officially playing, took her mind off the case and gave her a chance to relax.

Maureen and Albert Frost won. They reminded her of her parents, who lived too far away for her to visit regularly, although she rang them once a week, on a Sunday evening. They'd opted to live out their retirement in Cornwall, and in a way Anna was glad distance separated them. While she loved them to pieces, she preferred that they didn't know how much danger she was in at work sometimes. She kept her life updates on the breezy side, skirting over any cases she led, and steered the conversation towards what *they* were getting up to.

Albert got up to collect the winnings — a meal for two in the Jubilee and as many drinks as they could get down their necks over the course of a week. Maureen clapped to herself, smiling at people who congratulated them, although Anna detected a hint of malice coming from Toby Potter, their biggest rival.

Anna smiled, finished her drink, then wandered home. The crisp night air blew the cobwebs away, gusting through her mind to clear it of the fog that built up every working day. In her living room, she flopped on the sofa, a sense of calm sweeping over her. Here, she was safe from the pick, pick, pick of life outside her front door. Here, she didn't have to think of anyone but herself. And, unlike other officers, as soon as she walked inside her sanctuary she didn't let the cases bother her. She'd mastered compartmentalising. Carrying the burden of an investigation during her free time wasn't good for her well-being.

She closed her eyes, drifting on the sea of alcohol in her veins. She'd ended up having three vodkas, all told. And a packet of cheese and onion crisps, which had immediately got her thinking about Parole.

She should compartmentalise *him*, too. He was younger than her, so why did he flirt? She didn't consider herself anything to look at, so his interest confused her. No, she needed to distance herself.

Going in his direction could only mean trouble.

CHAPTER THIRTY-THREE

At the sound of an engine, Matthew had looked out of the living room window of Carys's house. The tent had gone from the garden, as had the stake and obviously Nigel's head. Only a blue-and-white cordon, snapped down the middle, flapped from the gatepost. Carys must have been too lazy to remove it, or maybe she liked the attention it brought, a reminder that she'd been the star of Bishop's Lock for a short while. When Anna and Baldy had got out of the car, he'd bolted into the kitchen, unlocked the back door using the key already in the hole, then stepped outside. He'd locked up and pelted down behind the shed, one he'd put up when he'd lived there, and wedged himself behind the tree trunk there.

Had they, like him, noted that the alarm hadn't gone off when they'd entered the property? Carys was such a stupid cow for not setting it before she'd gone out.

Time had seeped by, and he'd contemplated going back inside, but the car hadn't started up again. One of the officers had come into the garden, flashing their torch about. He'd held his breath, worried they'd check behind the tree, but no beam had picked him out amid the darkness.

Finally, the rumble of the engine, and he'd crept out and walked to the wooden gate and peered down the side alley through a knothole. The car had gone, so he'd entered the house and waited.

Now, at eleven thirty, yet another engine. In Carys's bedroom, the scene of that awful, adulterous crime, he nosed outside, keeping away from the glass so he wasn't spotted. Carys got out of a taxi, and for a moment Matthew worried she'd brought a bloke home, as someone still sat in the back of the cab. She staggered down the path alone, though, and he relaxed. She must have shared the ride. He listened for her key in the lock. The door closing. The chain being put on. The alarm being set.

Had she changed the code since he'd left? An idle thought, because it didn't matter to him whether she had or hadn't. He'd have run down the alley by the time any nosy neighbours came to their windows to see whose alarm was going off.

He pulled the wool of his balaclava away from his face to get some air to his skin. Carys had left the heating on, money-waster that she was, and he was sweating. She sang, her voice floating upwards, and he allowed himself a moment to pretend. That they were still together. Happy. Kids asleep in the other bedrooms. Life steady and predictable.

Her footsteps on the stairs tugged him from his world of make-believe. He moved to stand behind the bedroom door. She always slept with it open. Stupid, because if the house caught fire she'd be either dead from smoke inhalation or toast from the flames. But she'd closed the door on that night he'd caught them together, and he suspected she'd done it so he'd had to open it fully in order to discover what they were up to. The big reveal.

Cruel cow.

He pressed his back to the wall, his heart thudding painfully, chest tight. The soft pad of her walking along the landing increased his nerves, and he clenched his gloved hands into fists. He inched his head across so he could watch her

206

around the edge of the door. She wandered in and undressed in front of the window, the curtains open. He thought of who lived opposite and gritted his teeth. Was she trying to catch the man's attention? He was married, for God's sake, and he didn't seem like a Peeping Tom.

Her silhouette no longer called to him. He didn't get excited. She'd ruined any feelings he had for her in that regard. Ruined him for all other women, too, not that any of them paid him attention. He blended in, that was his trouble, became wallpaper no one took any notice of. Was it any wonder after being brought up by his mother? To be loud meant getting her unwanted attention. Then again, even when he'd been quiet she'd come to his room anyway. There had been no escape from that or the slap of her hand.

Carys got into bed naked, and his face warmed at her *doing* something to herself beneath the covers. She'd always been sex mad, and he'd loved that because he hadn't thought he'd ever *have* sex until he'd met her. Turned out she'd only wanted him for the farm, all that land. It would make a pretty penny when it was sold. He didn't want the damn place, it housed too many memories. He'd never have known why she'd married him if he hadn't eavesdropped on her talking to Debbie over the garden fence that time. Summer, it had been, the windows open, and he'd lain in the bath.

* * *

The Remember Room

"God, I thought Matt's dad would have died long before now," Carys said, sighing.

His muscles clenched at that. Shock at her words brought on goose-bumps, and he lowered his arms beneath the water.

A gasp. "Bloody hell, Carys, don't say things like that."

"Why not? He's a creep, anyway. Did I tell you about that time he pinched my bum?"

207

"No!"

"Well, he did, the pervert. I told him if he ever touched me again, I'd knock him out. He's into younger women. He's way older than his wives were."

"Wives?"

"Hmm, he was married to some other woman before Evelyn, my mum said. Matthew's never spoken about it, so I don't think he knows. I mean, what kind of family doesn't talk about the past? Too weird if you ask me."

"How odd, his dad never saying anything to him. Do you think Evelyn knew?"

"Probably. The first wife went missing. Sorry, but with what happened to Evelyn I wouldn't be surprised if the other wife got eaten an' all."

"Bloody hell. The police would have arrested him if they thought he did it, and they didn't, so . . . Maybe you shouldn't talk about this. I feel bad just knowing. Poor Matthew."

"There's no 'poor Matthew' about it. He's getting right on my nerves. I know I married him for half the farm, but Vernon's still alive and kicking when I was led to believe he was on his last legs. He's old-old, for Pete's sake. I don't think I can see this through to the end."

"I can't believe you married Matthew for money."

"Why not? Loads of people do it. Totally easy to fake loving someone."

"Don't you feel bad?"

"What for? Securing my future?"

"I don't get it. I can't imagine using Terry like that."

"Hmm, that's because you properly love him. I don't feel anything for Matt. He's not even my type."

Matthew pretended the tears on his face were condensation from the steam in the bathroom. Quietly, so as not to slosh the water, he got out and dried himself, catching bits and bobs of what else the women said. How Carys had to "think of England" while in bed with him and "the things I do for money" and "his dick's about as long as my finger". Shame roiled inside him, and he glanced down at his penis, something he rarely did. He hated looking at it because, when he did, all he saw were Mum's fingers wrapped around it.

Emasculated, he snapped his attention to the razor on the side of the sink. Thought about taking the blade out and slicing his wrists. He'd imagined doing that so many times in his life, and the only reason he was still here was because of Dad. He couldn't put him through that.

* * *

How strange, that he couldn't put his dad through his son dying, yet he could put him through finding out he'd killed people, if it came to that. Which it would if he didn't get away from Marlford soon. The police were on to him now, there was no denying it.

Suggesting Dad took a holiday had at first been met with a firm, hard "no", but in the end he'd capitulated, agreeing that he'd spent his whole adult life working Hawthorn and he could do with a rest.

Sometimes, Matthew reckoned Dad loved the farm more than him.

Carys moaned. He waited for the burn of anger to come. It lingered, just beyond his reach. She snuggled onto her side. The old gripes resurfaced, ones he regularly tormented himself with. He should have known someone like her wouldn't genuinely pick a man like him, yet for a while he'd fooled himself into thinking he'd been rewarded for all those years of suffering with his mother. That he'd won the big prize. Got luckier than Nigel for once.

Slowly, he stepped from behind the door. Approached her where she lay facing the window, his old space beside her empty. Numerous other men had slept there since he'd walked out. She let them out early in the morning — if they were privileged enough to stay over. Many of them snuck out straight after the act, though. He'd watched them from the Mini.

Had she been looking for another rich bastard all this time? Had she tried to snag Nigel because he'd been loaded? *Why* did she want more? She was rich herself — or rich in

Matthew's eyes anyway. She didn't have to worry about paying the mortgage. She didn't have to tot up the bill as she went around the supermarket.

Greedy, that's what she was.

And then the anger came, roaring, violent, filling him up, erasing any common sense. He lunged for the bed, landing on her. She let out a squeak of surprise, and he clamped a gloved hand over her lips. Turned her on her back and straddled her waist. She fought, kicking and scratching at anything she could get her nails into, failing to hurt him because of his clothes and the balaclava. He pinned her arms by her sides with his knees.

She stopped fighting abruptly and stared up at him.

He relaxed his hand over her mouth. Needing to hear . . . hear what? Sorry? I didn't mean it?

"It's you, isn't it?" she said, the words muffled beneath his palm.

She'd likely pissed so many men off, "you" could be any one of them. But it was *him*, he knew that.

"I can smell it's you," she said, all cocky. "I bet you've got pig shit or something on your shoes."

His blood ran cold. He'd panicked so much after Anna and Baldy had come to Hawthorn that he hadn't been thinking straight. He'd hadn't changed into his kill clothes and boots because he couldn't go home. Luckily, he kept a kit in the Mini, a small bag with a few items in it. The balaclava, the knife, the gloves, cable ties. But by keeping his current trainers on he'd have brought proof of the farm here.

He took the flick-knife from his pocket and flashed the blade out. Sliced across her neck. Wished he'd had the axe so he could cut her head clean off, take it away with him and present it to the world as proof of her deception. The blood appeared black in the darkness, soaking into the white pillow. She gurgled and jerked beneath him, and, as the life drained out of them, her eyes caught the light from the lamp post coming through the window. He knew then what he had to do. Not only couldn't he chop her head off and display it anywhere, he couldn't leave this house as it was. In her cockiness, she'd alerted him to a mistake, and it would end so differently now.

Terry and Debbie next door. Would they get out of their home in time? The semi-detached houses had alleys down the outer sides in order to get into the back gardens, but the fire might damage the middle walls. Get through them somehow.

He got off the bed and went onto the landing. Used the knife to prod the button to turn the smoke alarm off. He couldn't risk it blaring after he'd set the bedroom on fire and before he'd got one going in the living room and kitchen.

Downstairs, he disabled that alarm, too, then rooted in the kitchen drawer for the box of matches, always kept there for when they'd had a barbecue. It pained him that some things had stayed the same. When he'd prowled around after Anna and Baldy's visit, he'd spotted so many familiar things.

He returned upstairs. Closed the bedroom curtains in case what's-his-face over the road was up and happened to glance across. He struck a match and crouched to place it on the carpet behind the door. The flame spread quickly, and he lit another match and tossed it towards the bed. It went out before it hit the quilt, so he had to use another. Slower this time, he placed it down, and was amazed by how fast the covers caught.

He left, closing the door, and dropped matches every so often on the landing and stairs on his way down. He *had* to get rid of all traces of Hawthorn, couldn't risk one speck being discovered. Living room ablaze, he put lit matches on the hall-way carpet while fire devoured the stairs beside him and thick smoke tickled his throat, his eyes watering. The kitchen was another matter. Lino covered the floor, and the only thing he could think of to set alight were the curtains at the back door and the adjacent window. He did that, then went into the garden. The fire alarm was screeching. He locked up behind him and scooted down the side alley, checked the street from the shadows, and imagined himself as a black shape, unrecognisable. Flickering light played on the grass out front where the flames must have scoffed the living room curtains.

Bishop's Lock, so still save for that alarm, would keep his presence a secret only for a few more seconds. He snuck down the garden path, opened the gate and then, about to turn and leg it down the alley, paused at a shout.

"Oi, what the fuck do you think *you're* doing?"

Terry.

Matthew shot down the alley and kept running through the estate, keeping to the dark patches. He legged it across a playing field and nipped round the back of the abandoned shops. Got into his Mini. Caught his breath.

With nowhere to go and no one to shield him, he'd have to sleep here. He'd chance it, go and find Parole, then Gordon.

But what the hell was he going to do when the sun came up and exposed him?

CHAPTER THIRTY-FOUR

Pulled from bed by the phone call to attend the scene at Carys's house, Anna stood bundled in her puffa jacket on the path in front of the garden. She hadn't bothered calling Lenny in and was relying on PCs to do the door-to-door enquiries. The fire had been put out, and by one o'clock in the morning she was speaking to Terry and Debbie, both in their dressing gowns and slippers.

"Did you hear anything during the evening?" she asked.

"Not after Carys went out or before you and that other copper went in. I saw you," Terry said. "But I heard Carys come back and checked outside. She'd got a taxi. Someone else was in the back."

Anna made a mental note of that. "What taxi firm was it?"

"ABC."

"When did you gather something was going on?"

"I was just going up to bed. Deb had gone up way before me, hadn't you, love? Anyway, Carys's alarm went mental, and I saw lights flickering on the hedges outside, orange, and went to the front door to see what was up. Sounds stupid now, but I thought it was the kind of flashing light they use for roadworks, know the sort I mean?"

Anna nodded.

"I opened the door and saw this bloke — I say bloke because of the build, but I s'pose it could have been a woman. I asked what they were playing at, something like that. They stopped near Carys's front gate for a second, then ran down the alley. I came outside and saw the flames through the windows, got Deb up and rang for the fire brigade. Do I dare ask if Carys is all right?"

They're going to find out soon enough. "Unfortunately, a body has been found. It may not be hers, though, so I'd appreciate you keeping it quiet until I've spoken to her parents. Could it have been Carys who ran away?"

"Nah, they were too big."

Debbie shivered. "I know she was a lying bugger, but I wouldn't wish this on her."

"No one in their right mind would." Terry hugged her to his side.

"When will we be allowed back home?" Debbie asked.

Fire officers had gone into their property not five minutes ago.

"They'll only let you in if it's safe," Anna said. "I suspect you'll be advised to stay somewhere else for the rest of the night to ensure it's been put out properly. Sparks and embers . . . they're not going to want to risk them reigniting. Do you have somewhere to go?"

Debbie nodded. "My mum's."

Anna recalled something Carys had said in the Kite. About the sort of childhood she'd had. "Debbie, did Carys ever tell you anything about when she was a kid?"

"Only that her mum and dad are posh and she never felt as if she belonged. Like she was an accessory, just something they owned. That's why I think she has all that casual sex. She's looking for someone to love her properly. Odd that she had that with Matthew but threw it away. She mentioned her parents wanted her to be perfect, which was a strain. I did wonder if that was a load of lies, too, but she sounded genuine."

"Thanks."

Terry turned towards the officers coming out of their house. As Anna had predicted, they wanted the couple to stay elsewhere. She said goodbye to them and caught sight of another fire officer leaving Carys's. He took his helmet and breathing gear off, then jerked his head for her to follow him. She joined him at the mouth of the alley.

"Arson," he said. "Several fires started throughout the house. Whoever it was wanted to make sure the resident burned."

Matthew. It was easy to see why he'd want her dead, but the fact that he'd taken two years to wreak his revenge still bugged her.

"Or maybe they wanted to burn any evidence of a crime," the officer went on. "That body, which is a tad crispy . . ." He paused at her glare. "Sorry, I forget some people can't talk about it the way we do. Anyway, what I'm saying is she hasn't burned all the way through. We see a lot of this type of thing and, going by experience, there'll be flesh under the top layer of char. What was clear to see, despite that, is her neck doesn't look right. It isn't a smooth column, for want of a better description."

"If you think it was sliced, just say so."

"Okay, I reckon it was sliced. I heard about that head being left in her garden. Maybe the killer was going to chop hers off but got disturbed?"

"I doubt that. If you felt you had to get out quickly, you wouldn't hang around for the amount of time it would take to set several small fires, would you?"

"True. Ah, well. I'd best get on." He strode off.

She crossed the road to catch up with the PCs, who'd congregated on the corner. "Got anything?"

One shook his head. "No one saw a thing, but some did hear Carys come home. They looked out and saw she'd been

215

in a taxi. An old woman stayed at her window until it had driven away."

Anna glanced across at a Neighbourhood Watch plaque on a lamp post. "Vigilant people, then."

An officer chuffed a laugh. "Can you blame them, living on Eastgate?"

"I suppose. Did any of them manage to see who was in the taxi when she got out?"

"Dark shape, that's all I got from the oldie."

"Okay, if you've spoken to everyone then I'll be off. I need to get to the station to get the next of kin's address."

She crossed the road again and went down the cordoned-off alley, her protective shoe covers rustling with each step. The killer had run down here, and she wanted to see where they'd have gone. Behind the gardens, another street with an alley either side of the semi-detached homes, the same as in Bishop's Lock. She walked over there, and, behind *those* houses, the same thing. He'd have easily escaped without being spotted at that time of night. While officers had been sent out almost as soon as the call from Terry had come in, Matthew — or whoever it was — would have been in the wind.

She returned to the station and found Carys's next of kin, her mother and father, who lived in Westgate. She took a PC with her to speak to them, warning them that a body had been found but reiterated that they didn't know for sure it was their daughter, just that it was looking likely. She sat with the distraught parents for an hour. Carys had come from posh stock; the house was perfect, two corgis asleep in front of a switched-off fire in the fancy living room. Neither Mum nor Dad could think of anyone who'd want to harm their "perfect" daughter. According to them, Carys lived a pure life and was sweetness itself.

"What are your thoughts on her ex-husband, Matthew?"

"Oh, jolly nice chap, I thought," the dad, Boris, said. "Such a shame he left her like that."

"Like what?" Anna asked.

"Well, he decided he didn't want a wife after all, said he preferred the farm in the evenings rather than going home to our princess."

So they don't know she slept with Nigel?

Anna chatted with them for a while longer, and it became clear the parents were clueless as to who their daughter really was. She wouldn't burst their bubble. That would happen in court once the killer had been found.

She left them to their quiet, stoic grief and phoned ABC from the car.

A gruff-voiced man answered. "ABC Taxis."

"Hello, I'm DI Anna James. Is it possible for you to tell me who was dropped off after a Carys Brignell in Bishop's Lock around eleven or so?"

"Like I'd give out that information over the phone. You could be anyone."

Anna sighed. "Is your office open?"

"Well, yeah, else I wouldn't have answered the ruddy phone, would I?"

"I'll come down, then. See you in a bit."

She drove into Southgate and parked outside ABC, a narrow shop wedged between a phone place and a Tesco Express. She tried the door, which was locked, so knocked on the glass. A broad, bearded man, sitting behind a desk, glanced her way. She held up her ID, and he lumbered over to let her in.

"Don't you need a warrant for the kind of info you're after?" he said.

Anna stepped inside. "I realise you can't give out names and addresses willy-nilly, but it's to do with a murder investigation. We don't think the passenger had anything to do with the death, but I need to speak to them in case they're a witness. I could do with having a word with the driver as well."

"Bloody hell. All right, then." He ambled over to the desk and clicked the mouse. "They were dropped off in Northgate. Sixteen Wimbledon Avenue."

"Thank you."

"Phil's out the back on a break. I'll get him."

He came back, a skinny man with pockmarked skin and a receding hairline behind him. Sadly, the cabbie hadn't seen anything untoward, but he mentioned Carys rowing with the man in the back.

"A woman's got the right to change her mind," he said. "I told the prick that when I took him home. Soon changed his way of thinking, I did."

Anna thanked them for their time and drove to Northgate, conscious she was flouting her own rule of not going anywhere alone, especially in the dead of night. She rang the bell and waited. A light snapped on, likely on the landing, and a young blond man of about thirty answered in a pair of tight briefs, his hairy chest bare.

Anna raised her ID. "Can I have a word?"

"What about? I haven't done anything."

"I didn't say you had. What's your name, please?"

"Barry Shields."

"Okay, you shared a taxi home last night?"

"Yeah, so?"

"I need to know if you saw anything when the other passenger got out at Bishop's Lock."

"Carys? Don't talk to me about her. Fucking tease."

"Trouble in paradise?"

"I didn't get anywhere *near* paradise. I was meant to be going home with her, and on the way she changed her mind."

"Why was that?"

"She asked what I did for a living. I told her, then she said she wasn't in the mood."

"And what is it you do?"

"I work in a factory."

He doesn't earn enough money for her. "Did you happen to see anything suspicious in Bishop's Lock?"

"Nope, unless you count some old granny standing in her window, staring at us as we pulled up."

218

"Was Carys drunk?"

"She'd had a fair few, yeah. Why do you want to know?"

Because I hope she had a skinful and didn't feel the pain as the killer sliced her neck open. "No reason." Anna smiled. "Thanks for speaking to me, and sorry to get you out of bed."

She drove to the station to file her report, then went home. Climbing into bed at about five, she groaned at only being able to get two hours of sleep. She'd have to work on Sunday after all.

One of the pitfalls of being a copper.

CHAPTER THIRTY-FIVE

Parole drove his car around Marlford, Trigger in the passenger seat. Other Kings were out and about in search of the Mini — Wheels had got the number plate and colour from Peter. While it was good to have a pig on the books, the copper's help was limited. He could warn them if the police were going to be around when the Kings conducted business, things like that, but he couldn't — or wouldn't — take the risk of using the database to look things up. Something about needing to use his login, which was unique to him. Trigger had suggested Peter use someone else's, but Peter had said no one shared their passwords. Plus, if Peter went back to work tonight to gather more intel after he'd already been sent home by Anna, it would look suss.

So, with the limited information they had, the Kings stalked the streets.

"What if it isn't him?" Trigger asked. "What if we find him, duff him up, and it turns out he didn't do it?"

"If Anna suspects him, then I doubt she'd be wrong."

"How do *you* bloody know? It's not like you're pally-pally with her."

"Just a sense I got from her."

Trigger glanced across. "You fancy her, don't you?"

"Hard not to."

"She's attractive, I'll give you that."

"It's her personality I like." Parole turned into yet another residential street. "There's something about her. Chemistry."

"Christ, here we go. You're going to go off on one of your lectures about connections, aren't you?"

"People *do* connect, though, some more than others." Parole glanced at Trigger's expression. "What, you've never felt chemistry before?"

"Yeah, after a fashion, but I'm more bothered that you want to get involved with a copper — one who won't ever help us in the ways we'd need her to. It's dangerous, going for someone like that. I heard she's straight as a die. Mind you, saying that, she can't be if she's agreed to us helping her. Maybe she's so desperate to find this fella so he doesn't kill anyone else, she's willing to use us."

In an ideal world, Parole would like to think she was desperate for *him* not to be killed, but he wasn't stupid. She'd made it clear she wasn't interested — on the outside. But he reckoned she fancied him back, he'd seen it in her eyes and the way she'd responded to his flirting. She liked the attention, and he wanted to delve beneath the surface and find out who she really was. Lone wolves like her intrigued him.

And he enjoyed playing the long game.

Trigger sighed. "Look, he's probably holed up somewhere, fast asleep. We've been out all night. Fuck this, I need some kip."

Parole dropped him home and drove around for another two hours, until seven o'clock. Admitting defeat, he parked by the lake and entered his apartment building. Ken Marshall, the security fella, was hanging his jacket on the coat tree behind the desk. He must have just arrived to relieve the night-time guard.

"Morning," Parole said, expecting one of the usual conversations where Ken tried to get all friendly. He wasn't a bad bloke, just annoying.

221

"Morning. All-nighter?"

And he's off . . . Parole smiled. "Something like that."

"I'm that naffed off." Ken frowned.

"What about?"

"Ian wasn't here when I arrived."

The other guard. "Oh right."

"Thing is, his car's still out the front."

"Maybe he's in the loo. Got caught short."

"Nah, I've looked."

Parole turned to stare out of the glass double doors at the car park. Ian's blue Ford had condensation on the windows from the cold air overnight. He walked outside and checked the vehicle over. Nothing seemed off. He used his coat sleeve to wipe a porthole in the driver's window.

No one inside.

He strode into the building. "I'm going out the back to see if he's having a ciggie."

Ken wiggled the mouse to bring the computer to life. "I'll check CCTV."

Parole walked to the rear fire door. It wasn't on the latch, as it would be if someone had gone out and needed to come back in. He pushed down the security bar and shoved the door open. A motion-sensor light flashed on. A courtyard housed the wheelie bins inside wooden huts, a row of them going down the left-hand side. Iron tables and chairs dotted the large patio, and three hot tubs sat to the right beneath an overhanging roof, their lids secured.

With no Ian in sight, Parole went over to look inside each hut and every bin. Nothing. He removed the lid of the first tub. Again, nothing, and the same with number two. At three, he undid the clips. He was annoyed at having to waste time doing this when he needed a shower and his bed, but he couldn't cast aside the uneasy feeling in his gut, not when Matthew was likely after his arse. He moved the lid aside — and stared. A shape in the water. A body, facedown, brown hair swaying as he kicked the side of the tub to elicit some response, jolting the body.

His guard uniform gave away his identity. Ian.

Not one to leave a job half done, Parole turned Ian over, hoping there was a chance of resuscitation. He dragged the body out of the water and dumped him on the patio, then got on with the CPR he'd learned on a course in prison. Ian was long gone, though. Still, Parole had tried.

He took his phone from his pocket, and was about to ring Anna when Ken came barrelling outside.

"Fuck me, come and have a gander at this—" Ken gawped at Ian. "Oh shit. Oh God. What the bloody hell?"

Parole followed a retching Ken back inside and eyed the monitor. Ken had several browser windows open, the top one paused on a person standing in the lobby. A balaclava covered his face, and he held a knife by his side. In the overhead lights, he appeared menacing. Parole snorted. Matthew wasn't anyone he'd have considered menacing, but looking at him now, and knowing what he was capable of, he changed his mind.

"Play it so I can see what he does," Parole said.

Ken hustled by and took control of the mouse. He hit play, and Balaclava advanced towards the desk. Ian came round it to stand in front of him, a hand up to stop him going any farther. Balaclava stepped back, raised the knife and waved it. Ian lifted his other hand, as if to say he didn't want any trouble. Balaclava gestured to behind Ian, and they disappeared out of shot. Ken switched to another browser. It showed them leaving via the fire exit. The door swung slowly towards closed, but remained ajar. Again, Ken picked another browser. Ian undid the clips on the third hot tub and swung the lid off. Behind him, Balaclava flicked the blade back into the handle and put it in his pocket.

Then pushed Ian into the water and held his head under.

"I can't hack this," Ken said. "Jesus Christ."

"Stop it, then. I don't need to see it either. Go back to the one with the fire exit on it. Press fast-forward so we can see him coming back in."

Ken did that, then hit play. Balaclava entered, closed the door and ran to the lift. The glowing green number above matched Parole's floor. Seven.

"Shit." He got the information from his phone and wrote down Anna's name and number on a nearby pad. "Ring this woman."

Ken peered at the pad. "Oh, that bird who came here."

"Yep. I'll go upstairs."

Phone in his pocket, Parole took the lift, quickly jabbing at the button for his floor. He took his gun out of the holster strapped to his chest, aware that if he used it he'd have to explain to the police how he'd got it. Hopefully, just the sight of it would be enough of a threat and Balaclava would behave. The doors slid open, and he braced himself for the man to be standing there, waiting. The landing appeared empty, dark. He stuck his foot next to one of the doors to keep them open and poked half of his head out.

Balaclava's figure stood at the huge arched window that faced the back of the building.

Parole stepped out and raised the gun and the security lights flicked on. That explained why Balaclava hadn't turned when Parole had come out of the lift. It would have triggered the lights, exposed him, given Parole the advantage.

"What are you playing at?" Parole asked, his reflection in the window staring back at him. "It's Matthew, isn't it?"

"How do you know my name?" Matthew sounded panicked.

"It's obvious who killed Nigel and that copper."

"And Carys."

A shot of adrenaline ripped through Parole. Although he'd suspected she'd be killed at some point, the news still alarmed him. "When did you do *that*?"

"A few hours ago. Slit her throat and set her house on fire." Matthew laughed, but it sounded unsteady, unhinged, as if he couldn't believe he'd done that. "Bet you didn't expect that, did you?"

"I did, actually. Stands to reason you'd go after her an' all. So I'm next, eh?"

"I thought so until I saw that gun."

ı "It's not so easy to attack someone when they're armed, is it?"

"I need to leave. Go."

"I'd be wary of using your car if I were you. The police and the Kings are looking for it."

"It'll take them ages to spot it. I left it somewhere safe." Matthew shifted from foot to foot. "Did she love you more than me?"

"Who, Carys?" *So that's what this is about?* "Nope, we didn't have that kind of relationship. I dumped her because she's an out-and-out liar."

Matthew bowed his head. "Yeah, she does that a lot."

"The police are on their way."

"Just my luck. Life always shits on me. Carys didn't love me enough, neither did my dad, and my mum loved me too much."

"Going down the pity-party route, eh?"

Matthew raised his head. Took a few steps back.

He ran at the double-glazed window. Bounced off it, landing hard on the floor. He got up and tried again with the same result so scrabbled to his feet, growling in frustration, then lifted a heavy brass ornament of a naked woman from one of the occasional tables positioned between each apartment door. Parole remained where he was. What did he care if the bloke managed to throw himself through the glass? One less bastard walking the earth.

Matthew lobbed the figurine, which also bounced off the window, then picked it up again, went up to the glass and bashed at it. The pane finally cracked, then splintered and gave way, and a hole the size of an orange formed. Matthew whacked the edges to create a large space, a body-sized space.

The commotion brought Parole's next-door neighbour, a wealthy King called Jane, out onto the landing. She glanced at Parole, who flicked his head to the side for her to go back indoors.

"Suicide, is it?" Jane asked. "I take it you're forcing him to jump."

Parole shook his head. "Nope. He's doing that all by himself."

Matthew ignored them and got up to stand on the sill. He stared down.

"You'll only feel fear for a second or two while you drop," Parole said. "Prison isn't suited to the likes of you."

Jane laughed. "He'd get shafted in more ways than one." She went inside and closed her door.

Matthew jumped.

Parole shrugged, then let himself inside his apartment and collected his laptop. The camera above his door recorded everything, and he didn't have time to erase the footage. He returned to Jane's door, knocked, and when she answered, handed her the laptop. "Look after that for me, will you?"

She smiled. "Good job no one else along here has a camera, else you'd be for it. What are you going to do, make out yours is a dummy?"

"Yep."

"I assume he's the bloke everyone's been looking for."

"Hmm."

"I couldn't help in the search. My kid's here for the weekend."

"But she's twenty."

"And? I don't see her that often, so any time she's here I don't work." She returned inside and her door snicked shut.

Parole got in the lift to face the music downstairs. In the foyer, he caught sight of Anna talking to Lenny, and she glanced his way.

He winked.

She blushed.

CHAPTER THIRTY-SIX

Anna, her face still burning from speaking to Parole after that wink, stood out the back in full protective gear next to Lenny. Tents had been erected, the photos had been taken, and Herman had done his initial visuals of both bodies. They'd already visited the tent where the dead security guard, Ian Calder, lay on his back on the patio beside one of the hot tubs. SOCOs did their thing, silent collectors of evidence. Ken had showed them the video footage, and Anna had asked to see what had happened when Parole had rolled up. It matched what Parole and Ken had told her. As for what had gone on upstairs, Matthew jumping from that window, she wasn't so sure.

How did she feel about Parole possibly having a hand in Matthew taking his own life, or at the very least not stopping him? Aggrieved. He'd said it had all happened so quickly, but Anna didn't buy that the window had smashed as soon as Matthew had struck it. Double glazing didn't just smash like that.

She preferred people to pay the price for their wrongdoing, and in her eyes Matthew had got away scot-free. Parole's little tale about how it had gone down didn't sit right, and the fact that he'd said the camera above his door didn't work, it was a dummy — well, that was a load of crap, wasn't it? *Two rashers of bacon*, he'd called them. It had worked then. She'd questioned him about having a laptop that the footage would be streamed to, but he'd denied owning one, said his phone was all the computer he needed.

Once again, with no proof to the contrary, she couldn't do anything about it.

Jane, Parole's neighbour, had confirmed what he'd said. She'd apparently witnessed the whole thing. Had he threatened her to agree to tell a story that matched his? Offered her hush money? Anna wouldn't be surprised.

In the second tent, she stared down at the body. The clothes matched what Matthew had been wearing when they'd spoken to him at the farm the night he'd torched the van. Forensics had got back to her on that. Despite the van being burned, they'd detected plastic sheeting, which had fused to the insides. Tests on that were ongoing, but it looked increasingly likely that Matthew had used the van to transport Nigel and O'Reilly. They'd noted the VIN and located the previous owner, a Rowan resident, who'd sold the Transit to a man matching Matthew's description on Wednesday afternoon around five. He hadn't had the chance to send in the change-of-owner documents yet.

Blood coated the patio slab beneath Matthew's head; it must have cracked like an egg upon impact. His arms, one up by his face, the other straight to the side, gave the illusion that he'd fallen asleep, his eyes closed inside the circles of the balaclava. His legs, though, told another story. Both lay at unnatural angles, one foot bent backwards beneath his lower calf, so the shin and ankle bones must have snapped.

"Could you survive a seven-storey fall?" Anna asked.

"Only about five per cent manage that," Herman said. "There's this man who fell and lived, but he broke nineteen bones, had collapsed lungs, his shoulder blades had been shattered, and he'd torn his liver. He was in a coma for a while." He waved a hand at the body. "This chap here may look intact, but I assure you, when I X-ray him and open him up, inside will be a very different story."

"Is it all right for you to take that balaclava off now? I need to confirm his identity before we contact his father and get him to come home."

"This is like one of those *Scooby-Doo* moments you love so much," Lenny said. "The gang standing round to reveal who the killer is."

"Who are you, a bald Fred?"

He laughed. "Bog off."

"I suppose I'm Shaggy," Herman grumbled.

Anna smiled. "I'd love to claim I'm Daphne but I'm more like Velma. Anyway, we *know* who it is, so it isn't going to be as dramatic."

Wilma came to mind. With the big reveal showing this man to be Matthew, plus the CCTV, they had probable cause to send SOCO to the farm and his flat. He'd clearly come here to kill, the footage had confirmed that.

Herman removed the balaclava.

"I've been waiting for a lead so we could go to Hawthorn," Anna said, "but I'd rather Matthew wasn't dead when we went over there."

"At least we have a reason for what he did, of sorts," Lenny said.

Anna recalled what Parole had said. "What, that he was upset because Carys might have loved the other men more than him? That his dad didn't love him enough, his mother too much?"

"It's something."

Herman checked Matthew's pockets and brought out a flick-knife. "There's blood on the handle. Likely belonging to Carys." He passed it to a SOCO to place in an evidence bag.

Anna sighed. It was all a bit of a damp squib, this. She'd envisaged taking Matthew in, interviewing him for hours on end, getting to the crux of his thought processes. Instead, she was left with his lame excuse and no real *reason* for why he'd done this. Yes, he'd been cruelly hurt, but other people who walked in on their partner cheating didn't go round murdering, earning themselves the title of spree killer. Some would say his death was justice, that he didn't have the right to live when he'd taken other people's lives. She'd have to get over the fact she wouldn't have the satisfaction of seeing him in the dock.

I might not have anyway. He could have pleaded guilty. No trial.

Anna left the tent and sought Steven Timpson out. He stood by the row of wheelie bin huts, studying the ground. At her approach, he looked up.

"Lost in thought?" she asked.

"I was mourning my Sunday roast. It's not the same when you have to heat it up hours after it's been cooked. I won't be home in time to eat it when it's dished up."

Anna had planned to have hers at the Jubilee. She'd planned many things for today: reading all morning, going for a walk around Upton-cum-Studley after lunch, feeding apples to the two horses that lived in one of the surrounding fields. Instead, she was dealing with death.

"I don't think we quite realised how much of our actual lives would be interrupted doing our jobs," she said.

"No. Still, we should be thankful we've got the chance to even *eat* a roast, unlike these two. I feel for Mr Calder's family."

Anna had sent uniforms to do the death knock. Knowing it was Matthew under that balaclava, she'd accepted she'd have too much to do today. A stop to visit the man's next of kin would have eaten up too much time. She was sad that she had to factor that in, but that was life. A series of decisions that went against your heart on occasion, your head overruling your emotions.

Steven stared at the sky. Let out a breath that inflated his mask. "Best crack on."

"Hmm. How do you want to play this?"

"What do you mean?"

"I need you to organise teams to go to Matthew's flat and Hawthorn Farm."

He sighed again. "I'll piss a lot of people off, bringing them in on their day off, but it can't be helped."

"Sorry."

"Don't be. I'll sort that now."

Anna removed her protectives at the fire exit door, signed the attendance log and entered the lobby. Parole sat behind the reception desk, giving his full statement to a PC. Ken perched on a sofa near the double doors, doing the same. She gave Parole a quick glance, and their eyes locked. Face heating, she rushed outside to her car, flustered and annoyed with herself for letting him affect her like this. Thank God she'd never have to see him again.

While waiting for Lenny, she phoned the station to arrange for Vernon to be informed of his son's death by the French police. With any luck, he'd be back in England in a few hours. At least she could interview *someone*, then.

CHAPTER THIRTY-SEVEN

Anna and Lenny had been at the farm for hours, and her stomach grumbled. SOCO had found what they assumed was Matthew's kill clothes and boots at his flat. Blood had the excellent habit of seeping into the stitching, invisible to the naked eye, so she kept her hopes up. Surfaces had been swabbed, and testing might pick up minuscule blood splashes that had dried and then flaked off his clothes when he'd returned home. His Mini was still missing in action.

That didn't matter, though. A steel table in a barn, covered in plastic sheeting, had evidence of blood on it. The floor, also covered in plastic, a square cut out over a drain grate, spoke loudly of wrongdoing. With the van also having plastic in it, albeit melted now and fused to the interior, her suspicions had been confirmed. He *had* transported the deceased. On a wheeled trolley table, an axe, a roll of black bags and a bottle of disinfectant, another of bleach. A filing cabinet with a kettle and mug on it. So he'd had a cuppa after cutting those heads off? A little break from all that hard work? Christ.

Carys's For Sale sign leaned against the wall, and plumber's decals lay on the floor. There was no doubt it had been Matthew now, although she was annoyed she couldn't ask him what the significance was as to why he'd put the heads where he had.

A farmer from Upton-cum-Studley had been called in to help feed the animals, but he'd gone now. Anna had found three pigs snuffling in a small shed-like building, likely the remaining ones still to be introduced to the main pen in the larger barn. Three pigs, three kills, three more bodies to be eaten. Had he burned Carys because he couldn't come back here? The planning that had gone into this angered Anna. Matthew may have appeared to be a meek and mild man, but his mind had been a dark and nasty place.

Chickens clucked from the side of the farmhouse, pecking at the ground for seeds inside their wire enclosure. Without the police here, this place was an idyllic farm, although it hid many secrets. If she closed her eyes, she could pretend none of this was happening. Except it was, and she couldn't take another second of it.

"Shall we nip off for some lunch?" she asked Lenny. "Vernon's not due back for a couple of hours, and everything's in hand here."

Lenny nodded. "Glad you said that. I'm starving."

They went to the pub halfway between Marlford and her village. The Guard's Arms, modern on the inside, a cottage feel to the outside, catered to people who could afford the more expensive meals or those passing through who needed a break from driving. Or a wee, she thought, which prompted her to use the ladies' while Lenny browsed the menu.

She returned and sat. Lenny was a picture of displeasure.

"What's up?" she asked.

"Have you seen the bloody prices? It's my turn to pay, and it's nothing like what those baguettes cost."

Anna picked up a menu. "Oh. They've gone up since I was last here. I'll pay for mine, you pay for yours, then you get the next one."

"Cheers."

They ordered via the QR code on the napkin holder. That trend had spread everywhere, and only the Jubilee and the Kite still provided the old-style table service around here. Still, it suited her, because she wasn't fond of having to speak to people when she didn't have to.

She glanced around and her breath caught.

Peter sat in a corner with Parole.

"What's the matter?" Lenny asked.

Anna squirmed inside at having to decide on whether to let him in on Sally's suspicions. Lenny was her best friend, she trusted him, and maybe he'd have something to add regarding Peter.

"Okay, this is to be kept on the quiet, all right?"

Lenny nodded. Anna told him what had gone on. He appeared shocked, as if he hadn't encountered the shifty looks Peter sometimes gave.

"What do you think?" she wanted to know.

"I wouldn't have him down as straddling the line, but then you'd have to be good at playing the bent-copper role if you were working for the Kings on the side."

"He went straight up to Wheels when we were in the Kite, didn't you notice? Peter wasn't working, he doesn't usually drink there, so *why* would he need to speak to him?" Anna checked over Lenny's shoulder. "And don't look, but why would he need to be sitting in the corner now, talking to Parole? *On his day off.*"

Lenny itched to turn round, it was obvious, but he remained staring at Anna. "Shit. What do we do?"

"I'll have to inform Placket, and between us we'll keep an eye on him."

"Will you let Warren in on it?"

"No, he's good mates with Peter. They play squash together and all sorts."

"You don't think Warren's involved, do you?"

"I don't even know if Peter is, but it's all a bit weird, if you ask me."

"Maybe Peter was working in his time off and asked Wheels to help us with Jewel."

"And his reason for being with Parole now is . . . ?"

"The same thing?"

"Seriously?"

Lenny grimaced. "I hate the idea of him going behind our backs, being in with *them*. They might have *some* decent bones in their bodies, we saw that with Wheels and Parole wanting to find Matthew for us, but deep down they're all scum."

Anna winced. Any idea she'd had, however small, of seeing where things went between her and Parole had been doused forever. Not that she'd entertained it. Much. Well, maybe a tiny bit, a brief what-if scenario.

"We'll watch him in future," she said. "I bet we notice small things we didn't before, now we suspect he's flirting with losing his career. Keep your eye out for a crown tattoo. They've all had them done recently."

Their meals arrived, cutting off their conversation. Anna ate her roast, and it lived up to her imagination, the crackling on the pork perfect. For pudding, they had treacle sponge and custard, and when she got up, ignoring Peter and Parole as if she hadn't seen them, waddled out of the Guard's Arms and got in the car, she wanted to go to sleep.

But a murder investigation didn't allow for it, and, with a few hours still left in the day and Matthew's father to speak to, there was nothing for it but to press on.

* * *

In the farmhouse kitchen, Vernon wiped his eyes. He looked all of his ninety-odd years and more. No doubt the news of his son's death had given his wrinkles a more ravaged appearance. His slack lips wobbled as he digested what Anna had told him. She was recording the conversation.

"I can't believe what you're telling me. To find out he's dead was bad enough, but this? Murder? He hasn't got it in him. Are you sure?"

"He's on CCTV," Anna said gently. "While we know for certain he killed the security guard, considering the setup in your barn we have reason to believe he also killed Nigel Fogg and Cormac O'Reilly. As for Carys . . . Forensics will undoubtedly pick something up at her house, despite it being set on fire. Did you know about the Transit?"

"No, he must have bought it as soon as I went away. What on earth must have been going through his head?" Vernon asked.

"That's where my next questions come in." Anna took a deep breath. "With murder investigations, we look into the victims' and suspects' pasts to determine what links them and why the murders were committed. We also look at family members. Your past has two harrowing events, and I wondered whether either of them, or both, could have affected Matthew's mental health. His reason for killing was a fear that Carys loved the other men she'd been seeing more than him. How do you think that ties in with his life before he killed?"

"I don't know."

"He told a witness that you didn't love him enough, like Carys, and his mother loved him too much. Can you shed some light on that?"

Vernon closed his eyes. He opened them, and tears fell. "I was always so busy on the farm. It was my life, all I was bothered about. Working stopped me thinking."

"About what?"

"Things. I didn't . . . I didn't see what was going on right under my nose."

"Which was?"

"His mother, she . . . he said she . . . she fiddled with him."

Anna didn't like feeling sorry for Matthew, but how could she not? Or at least the lad he'd been. "She sexually abused him?"

"Yes."

"Then she died?"

"Yes."

"Was her death an accident?"

Vernon's sigh raised the white hair over his forehead. "Now he's dead, I can tell you. Matt pushed her. She was standing on the pen fence, and he shoved her. She fell in, and the pigs, they tore into her. There was no way we could stop it else they'd have gone for us, too."

"So you lied to the police at the time. To protect him? Or did you kill her and you're blaming it on your son?"

"It wasn't me. I lied to make up for what I didn't know. What she'd been doing to him. I wanted to show him I was there for him, no matter what."

"It seems that incident gave him the idea to get rid of other bodies the same way. Forensics have found blood splashes on the inside of the pen fence, perhaps where he threw the bodies in or because of the pigs biting them, ripping them to pieces."

"Oh God, what have I done?"

Anna sensed things were about to change. "What do you mean by that?"

"If it wasn't for the Wilma thing, none of this would have happened."

Anna feigned ignorance. "The Wilma thing?"

"My first wife." He stared at her with watery blue eyes. "I killed her."

* * *

Vernon, suited up in protectives along with Anna and Lenny, had taken them to a potato field. In the far corner, he pointed to a tall tree. "She's there. That wasn't the first place I put her, though."

Anna raised her eyebrows at him. "Where was she to begin with?"

"I hid her in the bunker under the kitchen floor to start. There's a trapdoor, you can't see it unless you're looking for it. It blends in with the floorboards, see, so, when the coppers came after I reported her missing, they didn't notice it. The kitchen table stands over it. After the police had been and said she must have walked out on me, I took her into the back garden and buried her. Only Evelyn found her years later, didn't she, when she dug up the ground to plant her stupid bloody flowers. I was away that day, off to Scotland to buy a new tractor, and when I got back she confronted me. So we moved her here, out of the way."

"We?"

"Me and Evelyn. I should never have married her, she was a headstrong sort, never did as she was told, even when I lost my temper with her. She took it as an opportunity to hold something over me, to threaten to tell on me if I ever stepped out of line. Said if I didn't do whatever she wanted, it might be convenient if I had an accident with the harvester one day, then she could sell the farm and take all the money."

Similar to Carys. Creepy parallel.

"What was life like for Matthew as a child?"

"Oh, she was a cow to him, that woman. She hit him a lot, sent him to his room, and . . . and did what she did. I didn't know about that last bit, I promise you that, but as for the rest . . . What else was I supposed to do but let her get on with it? I faced either going to prison or suffering some 'accident', and I couldn't leave Matthew solely to her. Maybe he thought I didn't love him enough because I let it go on, and he'd be right. I was more bothered about myself than him."

A shout went up. Anna left Vernon with Lenny and walked over to a SOCO who stood beside disturbed earth. On closer inspection, it wasn't disturbed but put in a pile.

"Looks like the same stuff that's in the pig pen," he said.

"Matthew probably dumped it here after he'd put the bodies in there, an attempt to get rid of evidence." It gave her the willies that he'd chosen a spot so close to where Wilma's remains lay.

She sighed and cast her gaze towards the farm buildings. Had he carried the mud in bags all the way here? This field was a fair way from the pig barn.

"There's a wheelbarrow in with the pigs," the SOCO said. "I bet he used that."

Anna turned towards Vernon. Lenny held him upright, as though the man was on the verge of collapse. Maybe all the years of hiding such a big secret had caught up with him. Vernon's sobs echoed in the air, and, if there was such a thing as life after death, Anna hoped Wilma heard them. It was the least she deserved after what she'd been through — sorrow and regret, at last, from the man who'd killed her.

CHAPTER THIRTY-EIGHT

On Tuesday after work, Anna sat in the Hoof with her colleagues. She watched Peter surreptitiously. Two men in casual clothing also observed. She'd met them yesterday on the quiet. She'd had a chat with Placket, who felt there was enough suspicion to warrant surveillance. Lenny was aware, but Sally and Warren were kept out of the loop. Sally, although damn good at her job, didn't have much of a poker face, and she sometimes got flustered. With Warren being good friends with Peter, it was best he wasn't involved.

To anyone watching, this was a lead detective and her people out for a drink after wrapping up a case, although there was still so much to do in the background. Paperwork, all that. To Anna, it was a sad moment when her team might well be changed forever if Peter slipped up and got caught doing something he shouldn't. She hoped it was a coincidence, those chats with Wheels and Parole. Placket had ordered her to question Peter about it, and he'd responded as Lenny had suggested, that he'd wanted the Kings' help with finding Matthew. His chat with Parole had revealed that Carys and Matthew had died, so he'd claimed to have finished his pint and left.

She hadn't told him she and Lenny had been there. He'd had his back to them, but she reckoned Parole had clocked her. Should she also question *him*? No, he wouldn't tell her who the police mole was, he'd said as much already.

But could she do what Placket had suggested and get close to Parole, enough so he'd spill the beans? An undercover role, so to speak. She wasn't comfortable with that, not knowing how Parole sent butterflies spinning in her belly, and what if he kissed her? Wanted more than she could give? Was she prepared to have sex with him in order to bring Peter down? To give herself over in that way, all in the name of her job?

It disturbed her to find that the answer was yes. Although she had a sneaky suspicion that it was only so she could blame her work for it instead of her emotions sending her down that path. A little shady of her, she could admit that, having her cake and eating it. Wanting the cake in the first place. It had strains of Carys about it.

Peter's phone bleeped, and he held it up to look at it. Anna froze. The tips of what might be a crown tattoo peeped from beneath his shirt cuff on his inner wrist. How *stupid* to have put one there! Sally's eyes slanted towards him, but Peter must have seen from the corner of his eye, as he stood so she couldn't view the screen. His cheeks flushed, and he cleared his throat.

"Just need a bit of fresh air," he said and walked out.

The observing men walked out, too.

Anna stared at Sally, silently asking: *Did you see anything?* Sally shook her head to say either "no" or "can't talk here". Warren looked from her to Anna.

"What's going on?" he asked.

"Nothing," Anna lied.

Lenny picked up on the fib in Anna's tone and rose. "Another round? Help me carry them, Warren."

Crisis averted, and Lenny having created the perfect moment for Anna to question Sally, she sipped her lemonade and asked, "What did you see?"

"There was only a snippet of the message on the screen. It was from TM — Trigger Mike? — and it said, 'I'm outside'. I couldn't make out what else there was because he stood up."

"Thanks."

"Two men followed him out."

"I saw," Anna said.

"Kings?" Sally stared over at the door, then back to Anna.

"I haven't got a clue." Anna hated keeping this from her, but she had to follow Placket's orders. "Anyway, enough about him. What's Ben been up to?"

Sally lit up at the mention of her son, and dived in to tell Anna all about his latest antics. By the time Lenny and Warren came back, the Peter issue had been swept away, although it lingered in Anna's mind. She'd prayed Peter was on the level, but unfortunately it wasn't looking likely, was it?

CHAPTER THIRTY-NINE

Nervous, Peter sat in Trigger's car outside the Hoof on the other side of the road. Two men in suits smoked in the designated garden area, sitting at one of the wooden tables. He'd worried he was being followed at first until they'd sparked up. God, working for the Kings was doing a number on his nerves lately. Earlier, he'd messaged Trigger for a meet so he could announce he was backing out. He hadn't expected him to turn up so soon, to even know he'd gone to the Hoof, but here they were.

"What's the problem?" Trigger asked.

"I need out."

Trigger snort-laughed. "You what?"

"I can't do this anymore. Playing the two sides. I think I'm being watched." He gestured to the smoking men. He *didn't* think they were watching him now, but he'd use that as an excuse.

"Then take a break. Six months. If someone's tailing you, they'll see fuck all and get bored."

"But I'm sitting in your *car*."

"Then say I contacted you with some information."

"Like what?"

"That Smithy has drugs in his warehouse, which he does."

Smithy, a former King, had distanced himself from the gang, but kept a low profile after Trigger had threatened him with death if he stepped on their toes or grassed on them.

"Okay, I'll go back in and tell my boss now, but how do I explain you having my number?"

"Tell them the Kings have ways and means, which we do. It isn't difficult to find your number. You hand out enough business cards."

"True. But I mean it, I can't do anything for you lot for a good while. Something feels off." Sally's comment came to mind, and Anna querying her about it. Then Anna had seen him speaking to Wheels in the Kite.

"Sod off, then," Trigger said. "Delete all of our numbers, just in case."

Peter got out of the car, preparing his lie to Anna. He crossed the street, deliberately not making eye contact with the men, and entered the Hoof, wishing he'd never wanted to be in the Kings as a kid. Once you were in, you were in for life, and if you walked away you paid the price, like Smithy would. At least he'd only face a drugs charge. He wouldn't be dead for daring to want a life outside of the gang.

Yet. He won't be dead yet. Trigger will get someone in prison to kill him.

Peter swallowed. What the fuck had he done?

He strode back to the table, puffing himself up with false confidence.

Anna seemed to accept his explanation without batting an eye, but he'd seen that face before, the one she pulled when what came out of her mouth didn't match what she thought. With six months off from the Kings, he had ample chance to show anyone watching that he wasn't in with them. The problem was, Trigger would expect him to do something outrageous when he went back into the fold, another initiation, to prove he was still loyal. With half a year's reprieve to stew over what that would be, Peter dragged his happy face on and chatted to his colleagues while Anna called it in about Smithy. Sally kept staring at him funny, and he didn't like it.

Something was going on.

Shit.

CHAPTER FORTY

After the Hoof, Anna took Lenny home and then went to the Jubilee. She ordered dinner — fish and chips — and pondered Peter's likely tale. She concluded that he'd clocked the men who'd followed him and had come up with a cock-and-bull story to cover for why he'd gone outside to speak to Trigger. That Trigger had given up one of his own men, albeit a chap who'd left the Kings, didn't ring true.

Bingo was due to start in half an hour, so she bought a strip of five games and prepared herself to wind down. She'd already phoned Placket to tell him she was sure Peter had a crown tattoo. Still, whatever was going on with Peter would be dealt with in the future. This evening was her time, and she looked forward to having the coming weekend off, seeing as she'd worked the last one.

Maureen and Albert Frost twittered among themselves at a nearby table, glancing across at old Toby Potter and laughing. But bingo wasn't like the quizzes they usually won, it was a game of chance, and they might end up with egg on their faces. Toby glared back, shaking his head, and high spots of colour invaded his cheeks. They had a past, those three, although Anna didn't know what it was and didn't much want to.

The first game got underway and, between crossing off her numbers, Anna watched how the trio interacted. Though they sat at opposite sides of the room, it didn't stop them sending rude gestures to one another or flinging filthy looks. Glad she didn't get involved enough with people to let them drain her, Anna concentrated on listening for the numbers.

"Bingo," Toby shouted, and stood, waving his ticket.

"Bloody fix," Albert muttered.

Later, she walked home, locked the front door and sighed with pleasure at being by herself. She allowed her introvert side to run free at last, having a nice long bath and thinking of the phone call she'd had with Mum and Dad on Sunday night. They'd lived in Marlford when Wilma had been married to Vernon, and Mum remembered everything about when she'd gone missing.

Anna caught herself. No, home was separate from work. It had to stay that way.

She rested her head back and closed her eyes, the warm water a cocoon.

Plenty of time to think about her job tomorrow.

THE END

THE JOFFE BOOKS STORY

We began in 2014 when Jasper agreed to publish his mum's much-rejected romance novel and it became a bestseller.

Since then we've grown into the largest independent publisher in the UK. We're extremely proud to publish some of the very best writers in the world, including Joy Ellis, Faith Martin, Caro Ramsay, Helen Forrester, Simon Brett and Robert Goddard. Everyone at Joffe Books loves reading and we never forget that it all begins with the magic of an author telling a story.

We are proud to publish talented first-time authors, as well as established writers whose books we love introducing to a new generation of readers.

We won Trade Publisher of the Year at the Independent Publishing Awards in 2023. We have been shortlisted for Independent Publisher of the Year at the British Book Awards for the last four years, and were shortlisted for the Diversity and Inclusivity Award at the 2022 Independent Publishing Awards. In 2023 we were shortlisted for Publisher of the Year at the RNA Industry Awards.

We built this company with your help, and we love to hear from you, so please email us about absolutely anything bookish at: feedback@joffebooks.com.

If you want to receive free books every Friday and hear about all our new releases, join our mailing list: www.joffebooks.com/contact

And when you tell your friends about us, just remember: it's pronounced Joffe as in coffee or toffee!